William Battrum

Battrum's Guide and Directory to Helensburgh

and neighbourhood

William Battrum

Battrum's Guide and Directory to Helensburgh
and neighbourhood

ISBN/EAN: 9783337369866

Printed in Europe, USA, Canada, Australia, Japan

Cover: Foto ©Andreas Hilbeck / pixelio.de

More available books at **www.hansebooks.com**

MACNEUR & BRYDEN'S

(LATE W. BATTRUM'S)

GUIDE AND DIRECTORY

TO

HELENSBURGH AND NEIGHBOURHOOD.

SEVENTH EDITION.

HELENSBURGH:

MACNEUR & BRYDEN,

50 & 52 East Princes Street, and 19 West Clyde Street.

1875.

PREFACE.

In issuing the seventh edition of the Helensburgh Directory, the publishers, remembering the kind appreciation it received when published by the late Mr Battrum, trust that it will meet with a similar reception.

Although imperfect in many respects, considerable care has been expended in its compiling. It is now larger than any previous issue, and the publishers doubt not it will be found useful as a book of reference in this daily increasing district.

The map this year has been improved, showing the new feus, houses, and streets that have been made; and, altogether, every effort has been made to render the Directory worthy of the town and neighbourhood.

September 1875.

NAMES OF THE NEW POLICE COMMISSIONERS.

Thomas Steven, *Chief Mag.*
J. W. M'Culloch, *Jun. Mag.*
John Stuart, *Jun. Mag.*
Finlay Campbell.
Alexander Breingan.
Andrew Provan.

William Bryson.
John Cramb.
Donald Murray.
John Dingwall.
R. S. M'Farlane.
Martin M'Kay.

Town-Clerk—Geo. Maclachlan.   Treasurer—R. D. Orr.

CONTENTS OF GUIDE.

ILLUSTRATIONS.

HELENSBURGH GUIDE.

THE earliest notice of a public kind concerning Helensburgh appears in an extinct newspaper, called the *Glasgow Journal*, under date 11th January, 1776, in the form of an advertisement, and runs thus:—

" NOTICE.—To be fued immediately, for building upon, at a very reasonable rate, a considerable piece of ground upon the shore of Malig, opposite Greenock. The land lies on both sides of the road leading from Dumbarton to the Kirk of Row. The ground will be regularly laid out for houses and gardens, to be built according to a plan, &c. There is a freestone quarry on the ground.

"For the accommodation of the feuars, the proprietor is to enclose a large field for grazing their milk cows, &c.

" *N. B.*—Bonnet-makers, stocking, linen, and woollen weavers, will meet with proper encouragement. There is a large boat building at the place for ferrying men and horses with chaises."

The idea of founding a town on these shores suggested itself to the great-grandfather of the present Sir James Colquhoun of Luss, who purchased the land of Malig or Milrigs from Sir John Shaw of Greenock, and in furtherance of this design, laid it out in prospective streets, and advertised it to the public. The town itself, as appears from the advertisement, was nameless for some years. A very old form of the name of the barony was Muleig, with which the local pronunciation accords, and the infant town was recognised under that patronymic, or the more unmeaning one of the New Town, till the course of events brought a change. Probably its name was a matter of considerable family discussion, till at last some ingenious friend solved the difficulty by happily suggesting it should be called after the lady of its new owner, "Helensburgh." A more noble and permanent memorial of that distinguished lady could hardly have been devised than this happy suggestion gave birth to.

Notwithstanding the tempting advertisement above quoted it seems to have made slow progress for many a year. In 1794, we find from an old rental-book, that there were only about seventeen houses built on the lands, and the gross feu-duty paid to the superior amounted to only £8 16s. 8d. Of the few houses then built, only one or two now stand.*

Helensburgh was created a free burgh of barony by royal charter, dated 28th July, 1802. Under this charter, the government of the burgh is committed to a provost, two bailies, and four councillors, and weekly markets and four

* The following seem to have been the first adventurous feuars, and the rates of feu-duty paid by them. What a contrast it affords betwixt the value of land half a century since and its price now! We have heard it said, that the whole shore ground from the pier to the east boundary of the town was offered at a perpetual rent of £1 to the ancestor of one of the Malig feuars, and refused as too serious a speculation.

William Stewart,†	£0	6	8	John M'Aulay,	£0	13	4
Donald M'Kinlay,	0	13	4	Malcolm Taylor,	1	0	0
Andrew M'Lachlan,	0	6	8	David Reoch,	0	6	8
Robert Watson,	0	6	8	Robert Colquhoun,	1	0	0
James Walker,	0	13	4	Agnes Ferguson,	0	13	4
Donald Smith,	0	6	8	Archd. M'Auslane,	0	14	0
John M'Naughten,	0	8	0	John Govan,	0	6	8
William Bruce,	0	6	8	Patrick Gray,	0	8	0
				John M'Auslane, 6s. 8d.			

† William Stewart's feu seems to have been without the boundary of the burgh as existed in 1802.

annual fairs are appointed. In a community of seventeen householders, one naturally thinks that considerable ingenuity must have been exercised at times to find a staff of seven such officials to govern the other ten, and we consequently find among the old records repeated instances of householders fined for failure to accept the honour conferred on them by their townsmen. As in some degree throwing a measure of light on the past history of this burgh, we give a few extracts from the older official records. There is not much amusement to be gleaned from them, but they may afford insight into the inner life of an infant town, and thus prove of some interest to the curious in such matters:—

EXTRACTS FROM RECORDS OF THE TOWN COUNCIL OF HELENSBURGH.

By-Laws.

HELENSBURGH, 11*th Nov.*, 1807.

Markets and Fairs.—The Magistrates and Town Council convened, " agreed that the annual markets of Helensburgh should be published in the newspapers and handbills ; and likewise inserted in the almanack, and also the following articles concerning the same—viz., all cattle coming and entering the market for sale, shall pay the following dues:—For each cow or horse a penny ; sixpence for each score of sheep ; a sixpence for each sow ; and if sold to pay the above same rates when returning from the market. And we likewise further agree, that the two town officers are authorised to uplift the same at their proper stations, and to be paid only off the funds for so doing."

Attendance at Church, Officers and their Halberts.

HELENSBURGH, 6*th Jan.*, 1808.

We, the Magistrates, having convened this day, we therefore ordain that the two town officers shall attend church in their uniform with the Magistrates. Only with the exception that the town halberts are not daily required, but upon certain occasions to be ordered by the Magistrates.

John Campbell's disobedience in relation to the above By-Law.

(Literatim.)

HELENSBURGH, 10*th March*, 1808.

. . . . And likewise the Magistrates having ordered their two officers upon Saturday the 16th of February, to attend divine service at the Row Church, upon Sunday the 17th of February ; but upon John Campbell's disobeying our orders thereanent, it is agreed by the Council, that the said John Campbell be decerned in the fine of one pound sterling for misbehaving in such a manner, and likewise liable to pay the above fine for every Sabbath and fast day lawfully ordained he absents himself without a lawful excuse.

Court days—Absence of Magistrates.

At Helensburgh, the third day of July eighteen hundred and nine years,—Convened the Magistrates and Town Conncil of Helensburgh, and have taken into our consideration the following articles:—1st, We have mutually agreed that our first court will be held upon Tuesday the 10th current, at the New Theatre, and five o'clock in the afternoon, and regularly, afterwards, the first Tuesday of every month ; 2d, We have likewise agreed that, after the Provost is regularly warned by the Officer to any of the courts and not attends, that he will be liable to a fine of ten shillings sterling, unless a regular notice be given to the Council beforehand as impossible to attend ; the Bailie, as above, a fine of five shillings, and councillors half-a-crown.

(Signed)   HENRY BELL.
JOHN MOODY.
WILLIAM MICHAEL.

HELENSBURGH, 16th March, 1810.

(A long minute, in which it is ordained that an assessment of one penny per pound of the valued yearly rent be exacted annually from each proprietor, till the town is by this means supplied with water.)

Non-attendance of Burgesses at Public Meetings.

11th September, 1811.—It is moved and unanimously voted that, when intimation was given to the feuars by the bell, through the streets of the Burgh, to attend any meeting of the Magistrates and Council, any magistrate, councillor, or feuar, who shall fail to attend, shall forfeit and pay the sum of two shillings and sixpence sterling of a fine for each failure, without a reasonable excuse, to be levied by legal measures if not paid.

Declinature of Office by a Bailie.

9th December, 1812.—A meeting of the feuars called by the bell.— Bailie Jardine stated to the meeting, that Mr. John Gray, the other bailie named at last election, had been called on to signify his acceptance of the office, when he refused to do so ; and as he had hitherto failed to attend any of the meetings, he considered it proper to call the meeting to consider what should be done in this matter, &c.

The meeting considering the propriety of keeping up the Magis-
tracy, declared that Mr Gray had forfeited his office of Bailie and the
fine annexed to his refusal, and they therefore proceeded to elect a new
Bailie in his stead, &c.

Members of the Council to sit in one seat in the Church.

The meeting, by a majority, fix that all the Bailies and Councillors
who shall go to the Row Church, shall at all times sit in the seat
appropriated for them, and failing any of them so sitting in church,
he shall forfeit a shilling for each offence, to be levied by the treasurer
for behoof of the common good of the burgh.

Court Terms.

The meeting consider it is sufficient to have a court once every
quarter, and therefore, they fix that in time coming, a court shall be
held on the first Saturday of every quarter; reserving, however,
to call occasional courts, if necessity requires, oftener.

John M'Auslane and John Napier fined for declining office.

11th September, 1813.—Mr John M'Auslane paid five shillings for
declining to be a Councillor, after election; and Mr Thomas Napier
paid ten shillings for declining the office of Bailie, after election.
These two fines paid to the treasurer.

Gratuity to Officer.

12th September, 1815.—It was moved and agreed to, that each
feuar shall annually pay one shilling to the officer; and that, in
respect of that allowance, the officer to be elected shall be obliged to
do all the business relating pertaining to the town, warn to, and
attend all meetings, &c. The said sum to be levied by the officer
himself,—the officer to be continued during pleasure.

Fines for declining Office.

11th September, 1823.—James Colquhoun paid ten shillings, as a
fine for refusing to accept the office of a Bailie. Anlay Lennox paid
ten shillings also for declining the same office. Robert Leuchars and
William Lennox each paid five shillings for declining to accept the
office of Councillors.

Customs for Fairs let for Five Shillings.

6th November, 1821.—The customs for the fairs were let for five
shillings to Robert M'Neil, highest bidder.

List of the Provosts of the Burgh of Helensburgh from 1807 *to* 1868.

1807-9. Henry Bell.	1839. James Bain.
1811-28. Jacob Dixon.	1840-9. Richard Kidston.
1828-34. James Smith, of Jordan-	1850-3. Peter Walker.
hill.	1853. James Smith, of Jor-
1834. James Bain.	danhill.
1835. John M'Farlane.	1854-7. William Brown.
1836. Richard Kidston.	1857-63. William Drysdale.
1837-9. James Breingan.	1863. Alexander Breingan.

But more prosperous days were dawning on Helensburgh. With the introduction of steam navigation, it began rapidly to increase in size and population. As the residence of Henry Bell, and scene of many of his labours, it is intimately linked with the history of steam traffic. In 1812, the little *Comet*, built by Wood and Company, of Port-Glasgow, was stationed on the Clyde by Henry Bell, and made her first trip to Helensburgh safely, notwithstanding the dismal prophecies and doubts even of its well-wishers, at a speed of about five miles an hour against a head wind. Fame and fortune ought to have flowed to its enterprising proprietor. Fame did flow to him; fortune only in the shape of an ugly stone obelisk. From the date of steam communication with Glasgow, Helensburgh grew rapidly in importance. It presented an easily accessible and pleasant summer retreat for Glasgow merchants and their families, and a pleasant residence for those retired from business. The lands were admirably adapted for feuing, lying in a gentle slope upwards from the Firth of Clyde ; and in the old feuing plan wide streets were laid off at right angles with each other. With the exception of the front street, where most of the shops were kept, the houses were built detached, and surrounded by lawn and shrubbery, and considerable emulation prevailed regarding the neatness of the houses and the cultivation of the gardens. This uniform plan it is to be regretted, was afterwards departed from, and in consequence some of the best feuing lots were compara- tively spoiled for want of proper access.

In 1846 a Police Act was obtained, under which the affairs of the town are now managed. The governing offi- cials were increased in number, and the powers conferred on them enlarged, so as to enable them to carry out modern ideas of improvement and order. Almost simultaneously with this Police Act, gas was introduced into the burgh. The streets formerly were badly kept and ill-drained, and not lighted at all. They are now, after nearly twenty years' indefatigable effort on the part of the corporation, nearly all in good condition, and though not so well lighted by any means as they ought to be, and might be, they are better than most of country towns.

One great drawback to the prosperity of the place for many years was the want of a good harbour. The original plan of the town included a harbour. A provision of £1500 was made by Government towards its formation, on condi- tion of an equal sum being raised in the locality; but as the sum on the subscription list, though it reached £1100, never attained to £1500, the matter was allowed to drop. This was before the era of steam navigation, and long before col- lecting money in aid of any useful object was reduced to a science. The pier, originally a stone dyke, for landing and embarking passengers from steamers, by small boats, was lengthened and increased by degrees. It was under the management of a committee of subscribers till 1834, when a piece of ground to the south-east of the pier was, through the enterprise and liberality of Provost Smith, purchased from a Mr Henry Taylor for the Helensburgh Town Coun- cil. In order to turn this acquisition to account, Provost

Smith and the Committee of Management of the Pier first resolved to erect a bazaar, or market-place, on it; but this plan was superseded by Sir James Colquhoun making a grant to the Council of all the vacant ground eastward to the granary, on condition of the whole being kept clear for future improvement of the pier and accommodation of passengers. As the original subscribers to the pier had no right of property in it, they transferred their management to the Town Council, in hope of an improved and enlarged harbour being erected. This has never been obtained; but a tolerable pier now supersedes the old stone dyke at which steamboat passengers used to land; the want of a harbour is, however, now less likely to be felt since direct railway communication with Glasgow has been opened up. Since the opening of the railway in 1857, a great impulse has been given to building in the neighbourhood, and the size of the place has almost doubled, as well as the value of property increased. The population in 1851 was, according to the census then taken, 2895; in 1861, it was 4769, and and has since that time rapidly increased. Probably now it reaches to 6000. During the past two or three years the progress of building has, notwithstanding a continual demand for houses, very much decreased. Various causes have contributed to this, but chiefly amongst them were, we think, the want of regular water supply, and the limited number of walks and drives in the neighbourhood available to invalids. These operated very seriously in the way of speculators, at least, erecting houses for sale, and were a continual source of grumbling and discontent; but a water supply has now been introduced by the Town Council, under the provisions of the General Police Act. On the Mains-Hill, above the town, a large reservoir has been constructed for storage of various springs and small streams, and from whence it is distributed through the town. In March, 1868, the works were formally opened by the lady of Provost Breingan, and since then there has been an ample supply. Of the permanence of the supply, it is, perhaps, yet premature to speak, but in point of quality, it bids fair to equal that of any town, and it is to be hoped the measure will prove what it is undoubtedly designed to be—a permanent blessing to the community.

Under the old charter, the bounds of the burgh extended from the Glenan Burn to the old Luss road at Drumfork on the east, and about as far northward as the present line of King Street. The marches of the barony passes on the south—in fact, formed the northern boundary; but the precise line is now somewhat difficult of definition, partly from the fact of the boundary stones having been removed; and the discontinuance of the old custom of perambulating the marches. This was observed annually by the magistrates and council in official character, accompanied by a crowd of boys, who, at each march-stone, hedge, or dike, received such an allowance of corporal chastisement, administered by the town-officers, as was deemed necessary to impress the recollection of the boundary line on the memory of the rising generation. The practice was said to have been most efficacious in securing a clear and decided recollection of the old landmarks. In obtaining the Act of Parliament, these old boundaries were very wisely extended. It now reaches from the East Toll, on the one side, to Ardencaple wood on the other, a distance of nearly a mile, and runs back from the sea rather more than a quarter of a mile,— thus covering a very considerable area. The general aspect of Helensburgh from the water in front is that of a long, straggling white town, with a screen of hill and wood be-

yond. Owing to the gradual slope of the ground, a great
portion of the town is not visible from the water, those of
the upper and lower parts of the town, with a few of the
principal buildings, alone standing out prominently to view.
The two best points for obtaining a favourable view are
from the rising ground on the Dumbarton road, near Lyleston, and the point below Roseneath Castle. From the first
of these the scene that opens to the eye on a clear day is
like one of fairyland. Each house and building in Helensburgh stands out clearly defined on a gently rising upland,
and in their midst the tall spires of the churches pointing
heavenward, glisten in the sunlight. On the west, hemming
in the town, is the leafy barrier of Ardencaple woods, and
beyond the long promontory of Row stretches seemingly
across the deep blue waters of the loch, in whose depths are
mirrored the white sails of the boats and surrounding hills.
Still beyond rise like an impassable barrier, the bold ridges
of "Argyle's Bowling Green," ever varying in their trans-
formations as cloud or sunshine, or soft vapoury mist, rests
on their furrowed brows and hoary peaks. The eye never
wearies of the scene; for, though scarcely twice does it present the same aspect, that aspect is always beautiful, and
the beautiful in nature and art alike stir the diviner nature
within us without satiating desire or wearying the feasting
eye. Day by day, and hour by hour, as you gaze on it, a
fuller, fresher sense of its glorious beauty showers upon you,
filling the heart with an inexpressible poetry of beauty, that
dwells in the memory for ever. A better point of view for
a painter or a sketcher, however, is Roseneath. There an
almost equally good view of the town is obtainable, and the
range of scenery behind and on either side is more limited.
The range of hills stretching across from Drumfork to Glen-

fruin, beautifully wooded in part, and softened down by distance into harmony with the rest of the scene, with the lazy clouds lingering about the highest points, as if loath to leave the scene, form an appropriate background to the picture ; while the long, irregular sweep of the bay in the foreground, nowhere else so well seen, gives a fitting unity to the whole view,—a view, the remembrance of which will not pass away readily, but will, in future years

> " Enter unawares upon the mind,
> With all its beauteous imagery. "

The general plan of Helensburgh, as we have already said, is a good one, and, if fully carried out, cannot fail to render it, so far as available means are concerned, both an attractive and healthy place of residence. It is built, as we have mentioned on ground rising with an easy ascent from the sea; and for fully a mile back this gradual elevation continues. It possesses, therefore, great facilities for thorough drainage, and for the maintenance of every necessary sanitary regulation. The town is laid off in rectangular squares, each of these containing about two acres of ground. There are abundance of wide open streets, securing a larger space of breathing ground than is found in most modern towns; and there is little danger of overcrowding the buildings, for, except in the two principal streets, Clyde and Princes Streets, the number of houses on each acre is restricted to at most four, and in many cases to two. The houses, save in these two streets, are chiefly in the cottage order, offering every variety of design and size of construction, though of late years taste has run more in erection of mansions of a large and handsome appearance, equal if not superior in many cases to the best country seats. To each house is attached a considerable piece of garden ground. These gardens are generally tastefully laid off in flowers and shrubbery; and as a degree of emulation prevails in the cultivation of flowers, this leads to the exhibition of considerable neatness in the aspect of these gardens; and in the summer mornings the atmosphere is at times so laden with sweet perfumes, arising like incense from them, that you almost realise what dwelling in a land of spices means. Owing to its southern exposure, and comparative immunity from cold winds and sharp frosts, flowers attain great beauty and perfection, and many varieties of plants, found elsewhere thriving only under shelter, grow freely here in the open air.

Attractive as it is, it might have been made much more so with the means at command of the corporation and inhabitants. The prevailing error which seems to rule at Scotch watering-places has done something to mar the beauty and destroy the attractiveness of Helensburgh as a popular resort. The idea all along has been to conform it in appearance as much as possible to a commercial town, which it never will be. All bits of attractive scenery have been carefully removed; the streets have been levelled with most judicious care; the streams bridged over and covered out of sight, and the square and park are utterly divested of any ornament whatever. Well macadamised road, and plenty of it, is no doubt a great boon—indeed, so is plenty of roadway, whether well or ill kept; but the great fact so thoroughly kept in view in Continental and English watering-places, that the prosperity of the place depends more on its attractiveness than on its purely useful features, has been very much ignored here. The idea in practice has been,—rout the visitor or inhabitant out of every cover; keep him to acres of bare street; give him no shelter, no pleasant wooded haunt; let the noonday sun bask and beat on him; provide him

with a park instead of a shade ; let there be no cooling fountain refreshing to the sense anywhere; and if, overpowered
by heat and dust, and anxiously longing for a plunge in the
clear inviting waters of the bay, the visitors should seek this
solace, keep him back from it by denying him every facility
for such a pleasure. This is precisely the result of the
erroneous Scotch theory regarding the character of a watering-place. With such an acreage of broad street, which can
at best be but indifferently kept, what was to prevent part
of it being planted with rows of tall trees, with sufficient
seats near them, which would have formed a pleasant summer
haunt to invalids and loungers; beneath whose shade
children could play in safety, and the pent-up stranger,
avoiding the glare and the heat of the dusty road, have obtained refreshing shelter and recreation? What was to
prevent the erection of a few fountains here and there in
public places, where the thirsty might drink, and at least the
dull monotony of road and square be enlivened and made
picturesque?* What was to prevent the adorning of the
public park with some kind of shade, which would tempt
stragglers, loiterers, and readers into its precincts? What
was to prevent the providing of bathing accommodation,
such as abounds at almost every other sea-coast village of any
note? What is to prevent all this being done now? Nothing
but a wholly mistaken idea of what a watering-place should
be, and of what is necessary to secure its permanent popu-
larity, by securing the comfort and adding to the out-door
recreations and pleasures of those who frequent it. These
are matters, however, which are beginning to impress them-

---

* This want is now being removed by the erection of public wells
in various places supplied by the Mains-Hill water.

selves more fully on the minds of those interested in our burgh, and which we hope, ere many years have passed, to see accomplished, and Helensburgh the first in attractiveness, as it is first in situation, of all Scottish watering-places.

Of late years the rapidly-increasing population has effected a change in the character of the property in the front street —most of the old buildings have been taken down, and re- placed by handsome modern erections fitted up for shops. Of these there are almost every variety, some of them equal to those in the first towns in the kingdom, and in which an abundant supply of every article essential to comfort and luxury can be procured. There are no buildings of any antiquity to interest the visitors. The almost only public buildings are the churches and banks. The first in order amongst the churches is

THE ESTABLISHED CHURCH.

It stands pleasantly situated close by the sea-shore, and is one of the first objects which greets the visitor's eye approach- ing the town by the water. It is a neat substantial build- ing, but its front view is completely obscured by an enormous granary, rising in the bloom of its native ugliness, directly opposite. The church was built in 1847, at an expense of about £2700, and was then intended as a chapel of ease to the parish church at Row. It was afterwards considerably enlarged and is now seated for 800. In July 1862, by a decree of the Court of Teinds, it was erected into a parish church, and Helensburgh attached as a parish *quoad sacra.* The boundaries of the parish extend on the east to Cardross parish, on the west to Ardencaple, and on the north to the northern boundaries of the farms of Kirkmichael, Stuck, Mallig, Glenan, Easterton and Woodend. The expense of the endowment was defrayed principally by the munificent bequest of the late James Hutcheson, Esq., long a member of the congregation, amounting to £2500, to which Sir James Colquhoun generously added £300, and the remainder was made up by grant from the General Assembly's Endowment Fund.

The Rev. John Lindsay, the present pastor, was ordained to the charge in 1847.

There is a flourishing school under the superintendance of Mr. John Fraser, in connection with the church.

WEST ESTABLISHED CHURCH.

A new station in connection with the Established Church was opened about a year ago in William Street. The congregation met for sometime in a large room used for photographic purposes by Mr. William Young. There has now been erected in that street a neat iron chapel, capable of holding about 300 people, in which the congregation meet. The Rev. John Baird has filled the charge since its commencement.

THE WEST FREE CHURCH,

A very handsome building with a graceful spire, in Colquhoun Square, erected from plans furnished by D. Hay, Esq., of Liverpool, 1852. Formerly a square plain erection stood here, built in 1827 by the Original Seceders of whom the Rev. John Anderson was minister. The Rev. John Anderson and his congregation, shortly prior to the Disruption, joined the Establishment, and at the Disruption left it. They secured the church building, and for many years it was the only Free Church in Helensburgh. Mr. Anderson, distinguished both as a preacher and author continued minister of this church till 1863, when, in consequence of failing health, a colleague, the Rev. Alex. Anderson of Markinch, was appointed to the charge, and since the death of the Rev. John Anderson in 1867, has continued sole minister of the church, which is a large and increasing one.

There are schools in connexion with the church under the superintendence of Mr. Sutherland.

PARK FREE CHURCH.

The accommodation for the adherents of the Free Church being found much too limited, a new congregation was formed in 1862, and this church erected. It is also in the Gothic style of architecture. The plans were prepared by John Honeyman, Esq., Glasgow, and the mason work exe-cuted by Mr. James M'Kinnon of Helensburgh. In many respects it is the finest building of the kind in Helensburgh, both as regards beauty of structure and comfort. The Rev. Mr. Carslaw is pastor.

THE UNITED PRESBYTERIAN CHURCH.

This Christian denomination in 1842 opened a preaching station here, in the Town Hall, and in 1845 erected a place of worship in King Street, now used as a public hall, which was seated for about 450. The Rev. Alexander MacEwan, now of Claremont Church, Glasgow, was ordained minister of it in 1845, and continued in the charge till 1856, when the present pastor, the Rev. David Duff, was ordained. The place of worship being found too small, the one now occupied by them was built and opened in 1861. It occu-pies a very prominent position on the rising ground, and forms one of the most attractive features to the landscape.

It was built by Mr. James M'Kinnon after plans furnished by William Spence, Esq., architect, Glasgow, and cost upwards of £5000.

· THE CONGREGATIONAL CHAPEL.

This body erected the first place of worship in Helensburgh. A square building, popularly known as the "Tabernacle," was erected by them, nearly on the site of the present chapel, in 1802, and remained for probably twenty years the only chapel in the place. The first minister of the congregation was the Rev. Mr. Syme, succeeded in 1809 by the Rev. John Edwards, afterwards by the Rev. Mr. Boag, and in 1824 the Rev. John Arthur, was ordained to the charge. In 1858, the Rev. James Troup, since resigned, was chosen colleague with Mr. Arthur. Mr. Troup afterwards removed to Lerwick, and the Rev. Mr. Arthur, having from advanced years, retired, the Rev. Wm. Milne was ordained in 1866. The original chapel was abandoned in 1850, and the present one, a neat building but for an apparently disproportioned height of roof, erected nearly on its site, in James Street. The first Sabbath schools in the district were commenced in connexion with this church.

ST. MICHAEL AND ALL ANGELS' EPISCOPAL CHURCH.

The Episcopal congregation was founded in Helensburgh in 1814. In 1842, a church was built and dedicated to the Holy Trinity. It was a small, plain edifice and was originally intended to accommodate the Episcopalians of Dumbarton as well as Helensburgh; but there is now an Episcopal church at the former place. In 1851, a school-

B

house was built in connexion with it, and in 1857, a parson-age. The erection of these was owing chiefly to the exertions of the then Incumbent, the Rev. John Bell, who took a very active part in promoting the means of education in the district.

The present Incumbent, the Rev. J. Stuart Syme, suc-ceeded to the charge in 1862, and Trinity Church having become too small for the wants of the congregation, it was in 1866 pulled down, and the present handsome structure of St. Michael and All Angels erected on its site. This new church is in the early French style and internally very striking in its design. It was formally opened and conse-crated on 7th May, 1868. The architect is R. Anderson, Esq., Edinburgh, and the builder, Mr. James M'Kinnon, Helensburgh.

BAPTIST MEETING HOUSE.

There is also a Baptist meeting-house in King Street, where a church, formerly under the pastoral care of the late Mr. Robert Dickie, meets. This congregation has existed for many years.

ROMAN CATHOLIC CHAPEL.

This religious persuasion has also a chapel in Maitland Street. As yet, there is no stated priest in charge. It is supplied from Dumbarton and Glasgow by various priests.

BANKS.

It speaks well for the economical habits of the population, that the first bank in Helensburgh was a savings bank. It was promoted, about 1827, by Mr. James Smith of Jordanhill, the late Mr. Richard Kidston, and others, and managed gratuitously and successfully for many years by Mr. Peter M'Callum, draper. About 1841, a branch of the Western Bank of Scotland was opened,—first under the management of Mr. Alexander Campbell of Roseneath, then of Mr. John Robson, and afterwards of Mr. Robert D. Orr, who continued in it till the suspension of that establishment. In 1857, the Clydesdale Banking Company opened the premises held by the Western Bank, with the enterprising agent of the closed establishment, Mr. Orr, as their manager, and shortly afterwards they built the handsome offices now possessed by them in James Street.

In 1856, the Union Bank of Scotland opened a branch under the management of their present agent, Mr William Drysdale, long the esteemed provost of the burgh; and in 1861 they opened their present elegant and commodious establishment in Colquhoun Square.

In 1867, the Bank of Scotland opened a branch in Clyde Street, under the management of Provost Breingan.

There is but one other public building, the Town Hall, where the corporation meets, and the courts are held; but it presents no claim to architectural exterior or internal convenience. It has been long a standing joke, till, "As ugly as the Town Hall," has almost turned into a proverb. It was originally a theatre; appears to have been built early in the present century, and in the palmy days of the drama, was well supported and liberally patronised by the surrounding country gentry. But the stage has long been darkened; the curtain has fallen for ever. A wall has been run up dividing the proscenium from the remaining part of the house. The whilome pit and boxes now form the body of the Court Hall, where the audience listen to the practical effusions of town-councillors instead of the eloquence of Shakespeare; and the gallery is devoted to rats and spare lumber. Behind the scenes were lately retailed grocery goods; now, telegraphic messages are despatched thence to the ends of the earth; while the ground floor, sacred of old to descending and ascending ghosts, and the tomb of Thespian brigands and murderers, is transformed into police cells. Truly a change has passed over all! It is gratifying, however, to learn that there is a speedy prospect of a new Town Hall being erected on an eligible site, and which will supply a growing want for a place of meeting and other purposes connected with the Burgh.

The Baths, now Queen's Hotel, a large square castellated building, occupies an imposing site fronting the sea at the east end of the burgh. It is of importance as one of the landmarks of the late Henry Bell's labours here.

The educational wants of the community have not been neglected, any more than their religious wants. There are institutions and academies adapted to every class of society, and some of them of the highest character.

Amongst other objects worth a visit to Helensburgh, is the Cemetery. Helensburgh being only a *quoad sacra* parish of recent date, no provision was made in connexion with the church for a burying-ground, and till recently the only place of interment was at Row, a distance of rather more than two miles. But as, independently of the distance, the parish burying-ground was inconveniently small and disgracefully kept, and such a memorial of apathy and indifference of the heritors and kirk-session, it was resolved, some ten years since, to erect a cemetery at the east extremity of Helensburgh. The ground has been tastefully laid off and enclosed; a superintendent's house has been built within it, and such rules and regulations adopted, as will secure its future maintenance and good preservation. A considerable part of the ground is devoted to raising nursery plants and flowers, which form an interesting feature to visitors; and the thorough order and neatness in which the whole is kept, reflect the highest credit on the superintendent. Already one end of the ground is occupied by many very handsome tombstones, some of them the work of Mossman, and placed with regard to position and order. The locality of the cemetery is good, and the soil of a light, gravelly nature, and drained to a great depth. The only drawback is the inconvenient approach to it. A continuation of the present line of King Street would lead directly to it; but this street not being fully opened eastward, the access is by the Dumbarton Road, as far as Drumfork toll, and then up the old Luss road. The distance is thus nearly doubled. A little effort would secure an excellent approach, and we hope that such an effort will soon be made.

The fine southern exposure, more than once alluded to, and the shelter which it enjoys from east winds, not only make Helensburgh a desirable summer residence, but pleasant winter quarters. To invalids, it is often recommended by medical men of the highest authority, in preference to any place in the west of Scotland. Although not possessing many of the attractions of its distinguished English rivals, still there is no modern Scottish town that can nearly approach to it.

There is no trade of any importance carried on in Helensburgh; it is almost entirely dependent on its visitors for prosperity and increase. This migratory population not only creates a demand for every kind of necessary, but is the means of supplying the wants of a class of the population whose time is divided between boating and fishing. A number of the adult population are engaged in herring and deep-sea fishing for a considerable portion of the year; and another part derives a livelihood by attendance on the demands of pleasure and fishing parties during summer, following other callings in winter. There is commonly a good supply of whiting, cod, flounders, and other sea-fish, on the coast, and any of the experienced boatmen can readily conduct a pic-nic or piscatorial party to some favourite spot, where, at least, a modicum of success is obtainable. On a quiet summer's afternoon, the whole bay and loch seem studded with such small craft, in groups of half-a-dozen or more, at every haunt where fish are traditionally or actually found. Whether the success is at all commensurate with the numbers of sport-seekers, we cannot find any reliable means of determining, as anglers' statements of their prowess are proverbially to be received *cum grana salis.* There is also during the early months of the year, some sea-trout fishing to be obtained by trolling in the loch, with sand-eel or partail.

There are several pleasant strolls and carriage drives in the immediate vicinity of Helensburgh. The three principal roads lead—eastward, towards Dumbarton; west, to Gareloch; and north, to Luss. The scenery on each of these is varied in character, and they possess respectively points of interest different from each other. The west road leads wholly along the banks of the loch, and brings the tourist within view of many bits of admirable water scenery. It is full of windings, and the various little bays of the loch, and their background studded with villas, rising amongst

the trees in terraces, and crowned with the hills, like Swiss
villages, are favourite haunts of sketchers and painters in
summer holidays. The east, on the other hand, after leaving Helensburgh, passes through a fine agricultural country.
There are few houses, save farm homesteads, along the way;
but the farms are in the highest state of good management,
and the land generally well cultivated. The scenery is irregular; tracts of rising land, stretching away back to the
hills, belts of wood above these, and the bare hill tops, on
the one hand; and cornland sloping down to the river, strips
of meadow along the river bank, the Clyde, and its opposite
shores, on the other hand, make up the picture. The road
to the north presents rather a steep ascent for the first mile
or two; but after this is conquered, and the tourist fairly
reaches the region of the heather, he will not regret his past
labours. Turning round, you command a view of almost
the whole Frith of Clyde, with parts of its lochs, and its
numerous villages and towns; and beyond these rise the
blue hills of Arran, sharply outlined against the sky. A
few steps further on in front, bring you in view of Lochlomond, in silvery repose, with its lovely islands and wooded
heights, on the farther side of which the mountains of Stir-
lingshire and Perthshire fill up the background. In addition
to these short walks, there are various other places of interest
in the neighbourhood worthy of a visit from the stranger,
and which deserve more than a passing notice. Some of
them are little known, save to the enthusiastic botanist or
pedestrian. Others, memorable in history and tradition, we
purpose at fuller length to notice; and our reward will be
sufficient if we induce those who have hitherto found a difficulty in filling up a leisure hour, to explore these spots, and
find interest and instruction in them.

THE HIGHLANDMAN'S ROAD.*

To amatory young gentlemen and ladies this walk presents many attractions—even its drawbacks to ordinary
pedestrians in the way of stiles and old dikes to be climbed,
and dry passages to be selected, are attractive, as affording
many charming opportunities of displaying gallantry and
provoking discussion between the parties. Besides, it is
comparatively little frequented, and the almost only in-
truders on a delightful *tete-a-tete* are the roe-deer and rabbit,
and they of course, communicate no secrets. It is a walk
you may have almost all to yourself, and this exactly suits
the temperament of the class alluded to, who are generally
selfish enough to desire exclusive possession of the path.
Nevertheless, it affords a pleasant stroll to any pedestrian
who is above such a base consideration as spotless boots,
and is willing to undergo a little fatigue for a large recom-
pense of pleasure. Why it has been called the Highlandman's Road is not very easily determined, as it leads to no

---

* We are aware that the title of this sketch is somewhat a misnomer.
It has been adopted rather in compliance with the popular phrase-
ology, which has dubbed the road in question, "The Highlandman's
Road," than in strict fact. The Highlandman's Road, correctly
speaking, led by a different route. When there was no road from
Arrochar coastwise, by Lochlong and Gareloch, the public thorough-
fare passed along the mountain brows, passing Craganbreck, Tambui,
(on the height above Finart,) continuing along near the ridge from
over Faslane by Ardencaple hill, and skirting along the sides of the
hills till it reached Dumbarton. This was an ancient highway from
the Highlands to the Lowlands, It was when returning home this
route that the clan Gregor were attacked by the clan Colquhoun, in
the sixteenth century, and the battle of Glenfruin, afterwards alluded
to, was fought. To any reader desirous of experimentally ascertain-
ing what we have indicated, it will yield what is eagerly sought in
more expensive and doubtful forms—a variety of new sensations;
only it must be tried with kilt and philabeg, as appropriate attire.

precise locality to which Highlanders could be supposed to
have any good inducement to travel. The most plausible
supposition is, that, as all highland roads were anciently
constructed in as nearly a direct line as possible, and with a
delightful disregard to all minor inconveniences of bog,
brier, and stream, this one, from these circumstances, has
fairly earned the designation. Passing through Woodend
farm, at the west end of Helensburgh—where if you have
any difficulty in striking the right path, information may
be probably obtained by any respectable wayfarer—the pedestrian finds a cart-road leading right up the hill for some
distance and then losing itself in a distinct footpath. To
this he keeps, as he best can, pursuing his course through a
rather difficult country, broken and irregular in surface, for
about a quarter of a mile further up the hill, and pretty
close to the boundary of Ardencaple estates. Pausing and
turning round when he has fairly reached the summit of the
first elevation, he obtains a beautiful view of Helensburgh,
and the lands of Camiseskan, from a point which introduces
many features quite new and different from any he has
previously seen. Indeed, there is no point in the neighbourhood from which, in such beautiful panoramic detail,
the eye can embrace the whole buildings, gardens, and
streets of the village as the foreground, and stretching out
beyond the fair pasture lands, woods, and hills of Cardross
parish. If a botanist, the visitor will find here many beautiful specimens of mosses, ferns, and the common flora of
our fields and woods, and may spend half a day in supplying his tin case with varieties not easily obtained elsewhere. In the spring months specimens of the lilac gentian,
blue cuckoo flower, sweet woodruff, blue hyacinth, buttercup,
heartsease, and primrose, are abundant; from the mossy

ground, later in the year, the orchis family; and from the alder and birch-grown banks of the little streams flowing across the path. the wild rose, hawthorn, and sloe, breathe a sweet perfume on the summer air. At certain seasons, the old pasture here is a favourite morning resort of mushroom collectors, amateur and professional; these eatables being found in considerable quantities near the old farmhouse. A mushroom party, in early summer morn, has certain pleasant accompaniments of fresh and fragrant nature and woodland melodies no other can furnish. Here, on the right hand in a romantic little hazel dell, are the sources of the Glennan Burn—now considerably diminished in volume from what it used to be, by surface drainage and other causes unknown to us. In this dell, the sides of which are somewhat precipitous and difficult of descent sheltered from the winds, and, fringed in the yellow broom, and almost isolated by the bounding stream, is a beautiful patch of smooth greensword known as the Fairies' Ring—always green and always sheltered from the storm—a little gem in a fair setting. Had you here wandered a century since, under the calm light of a glorious summer moon, bathing in its silver radiance the whole landscape, and had courage to examine its mysteries, what vision might have been enjoyed of the secrets of the fairy-folk, and what wondrous music of fairyland you might have heard! Alas! we have been born too late to enjoy these pleasures of a past and believing age: we can only envy those who have shared them. In this spot the good folk in our great-grandmothers' days enjoyed many a night of revel, and held high carnival on Beltane and Hallowe'en. Belated shepherds and benighted travellers have often listened to their weird-like music, stealing in measured unearthly strains down the glen; and more than one rash spectator has witnessed a fairy festival on that green. But Jock Bateson, more than half a century since, saw the last of them here. Indeed, Jock has the credit or dishonour, whichever you will, of having banished them from this favourite spot. Coming across the hill one harvest night from the Chapel of Glen Fruin, and naturally anxious to avoid any beaten path or stray traveller, by reason of a small suspicious keg which he bore, strapped to his shoulders, Jock, after wading through a mile or two of heather, struck down by the Old Mains farm, right above there, and into the channel of the burn. Resting the keg against a rock for a little, to recruit his strength, and fortify himself for the remainder of the road, Jock was startled by the sound of music, borne on the night breeze, mingled with the laughter and the echoes of tiny voices, proceeding from a spot not far distant. His first impulse was to leave his precious burden and run for it; but second thoughts are best, and after a short perplexing study of the question, Jock felt himself impelled by some ungovernable desire to ascertain who the musicians were. Again slinging the keg on his shoulders, with no small trepidation he crept cautiously along the banks of the streamlet, careful of every broken bough and loose stone in his way, and peering through the branches of the hazel as he went. Reaching this little dell, at a sudden angle, he found himself behind a large boulder, a witness of a scene bewildering and novel. In the beams of the bright autumn moon, resting in full radiance on the green ring, were scores of tiny men and women, some engaged in a fantastic dance, others, seated on the grass and on the branches of the broom and hazel, were playing a shrill unearthly melody, from pipes of reed and corn. Round and round in giddying circles the dancers flew, and tumbled over each other in uncouth gambols amid shouts of laughter. Suddenly the music ceased, and a grim visaged little fellow, with a tall, peaked cap on his head, amid temporary silence, stepped forth to the spot where Jock stood, tremblingly feasting his bewildering eyes, and said "Welcome, Jock Bateson." Amazed at hearing his own name uttered in such tones, Jock, who was no coward, would willingly have retreated, but in an instant he was surrounded by a score of small people, who dragged him forth into the centre of the ring, and presented him to one taller and more important-looking than the rest, and who seemed to be leader of the band, from the deference which was shown to him. "Sit down, Jock Bateson," said their chief, "and let us know what you have got in your cask." Jock obeyed the order to sit, and muttered something about the cask containing a drop of "small still brew." This information apparently being inadequate to convey the knowledge wanted, it was taken possession of forthwith and broached. A foxglove cup was filled with its contents and handed to Jock, who drank it off, to their united healths, with a mental observation that "the gude folks' measure was unco sma'." In succession the whole group quaffed from the same miniature goblet, amidst much laughing and gesticulation; and the keg, its owner feared, was sadly diminishing. The consequences of this imprudence, however, soon became apparent in the scene of excitement which followed. All order and rule was lost, and amid a confusion indescribable, Jock was led through a series of dances by a succession of partners, to a music unparalleled in the annals of fairyland till cockcrow, when suddenly Jock heard a rushing sound through the air, and was conscious of nothing more till the burning sun of the following morn, beating on his face, awakened him—sick and

bruised—to a dim recollection of his whereabouts. Casting
his eyes about, he saw his keg lying among the grass with
its plug drawn, and its contents escaped; and, at a little
distance, his cap and oak stick he remembered carrying over-
night. Gathering himself together, with pain racking all
his limbs, he made the best of his way home. It was some
months later before he fairly recovered and told the story of
his meeting with the fairies. Some few believed it, and
many disbelieved it; but unbelief was a little shaken by the
after history of Jock. He sunk into a drunken idler, spend-
ing his days in the gratification of the basest habit man is a
victim to, and unnerved for any steady application to his
work, was reduced to abject poverty. His death was attended by some peculiar symptoms—so unusual, that an
Edinburgh physician, who happened to be in the neighbourhood at the time, thought proper to carry off Jock's brain
with him for the benefit of medical science, and to the serious
future injury of Jock, who, it seemed, did not rest quiet in
his grave afterwards. For many years subsequently he was
reported, upon the best authority, to wander up and down the
burn, at full moon, howling and jibbering after his lost brains.

After ascending about half a mile above the source of
this stream, the foot-track diverges into a cart-road, which
stretches along the hill-side towards Row. A long, deep
belt of fir plantation clothes the hill on the right-hand side,
but towards the Frith the view is open. From this road,
which the visitor has a beautiful uninterrupted view of
Ardencaple Castle and policies—once the possession of The
M'Aulay, a formidable chieftain, and invested with considerable authority, if the old rhyme be correct—

" Aulay, M'Aulay, Laird of Cairndow,
Bailie of Dumbarton, and Provost of the Row."

The road winds along the side of the hill for about half a mile, till it reaches the Torr farm, a neat, comfortable house, in modern style, invisible from beneath, but well known in the surrounding district from the agricultural science and zeal of its tenant. Here the pedestrian may either strike down past the farm to the loch-side, or pursue his stroll farther westwards. The road continues to wind among the villas scattered on the hill-side, towards Row, passing gardens, orchards, shrubberies, and many picturesque little cottages, clothed with woodbine and roses, till further progress is debarred by Ardenconnal policies, and a descent to the highway becomes necessary at last, whence the return home may be effected pleasantly by the sea-shore.

THE OLD ROAD.

Among the nooks and corners worth exploring is the old turnpike road to Luss, now disused and neglected, save as it suits the convenience of the farmer through whose lands it may pass. It was once partly a main line of communication between the Lowlands and the fastnesses of Perth, Stirling, and Inverness shires, extensively used in connection with the ferries to the opposite shores of Greenock and Port-Glasgow. It was made at the expense of the Duke of Argyll grandfather to the present Duke, and in Helensburgh charter is termed "the Duke's road." His Grace is said to have been much displeased at the direction given to it by those interested, his desire being that it should have taken the direction of General Wade's road, that preceeded it. That road, after passing Daligan farmhouse, took the direction of little Drumfad, passed Culshot, crossed the greenburn above the mill-dam, passed above Glennan farmhouse to the east bank above Glennan Burn, kept nearly along the burn till it crossed it to the west side, just `at the back of Mr. A. Oswald's villa, and passed through his grounds, in a direct line to the shore. Not many years since, an arched bridge of this road remained entire between Daligan and Little Drumfad. The Old Road, as we now know it, leads from the east boundary of the town through the farm of Kirkmichael. Near this at one time, stood the remains of a chapel dedicated to St. Michael, with certain monastic buildings. The chapel was in existence about the commencement of last century, and, from old parish records, seems to have been used as a place of worship. It is difficult now to trace its exact site ; the stones of which it was built have been oppropriated for boundary dikes and farm offices, and other base uses, to the regret of antiquary and archæologists. Passing the farm steading, the road winds up hill over alternating ridge and hollow, between broom-clad banks, where the blue bell, meadow-sweet, primrose, and wild rose luxuriate in rich mosaic of colour, and shed their fragrance on the summer air. And it will be strange if you do not pass, in some sheltered nook, a camp or two of wandering Arabs, the gray tent erected in the lee of an old dyke or bank, with the cart tilted against a tree, and the donkey grazing placidly at the hedge roots, and encounter a group of impudent children rushing, in their tattered picturesqueness towards you, imploring "backshish." This road has from time immemorial, been a favourite haunt for these dwellers in tents. The little heaps of blackened stones and bits of charred wood dotting the roadsides, and mingled with scraps of tin and horn, show abundant vesteges of former encampments, and may in some future age be exhumed by antiquarians, and theorised over as relics of some ancient race—workers of metal and bone. Who knows what volumes may be written to prove their existence, habits and customs! Farther up the hill, the road is lined by a belt of wood, a famous place in former days and probably famous still, for nutting excursions in the autumn. Chumps of hazel abound among the more valuable forest trees, and yield, or used to yield, many a stock of nuts to the boys in Helensburgh against Hallowe'en. But the hazel does more than this ; for it also affords desirable shelter in the winter storms, and against the biting winds of spring to the cattle lying out on the hill and about its roots a picking of fresh grass can be found when the outlying fields are bare and withered. The view, as you reach the opening into the wood, is very extensive to the east and west commanding a long range of scenery on both sides of the Clyde.

Farther on, the road apparently intersects the remains of an ancient camp. A good deal of discussion has arisen whether these are traces of a Roman encampment or belong to more recent dates. No thorough investigation of the matter has ever been made. It certainly is not far from the line of the wall of Antoninus ; and as near Callendoon, about two miles distant, pieces of ancient armour, apparently of Roman origin, have been found, it is quite possible this may have been an outlying station.

After leaving the wood the road enters the moor, and is difficult to follow sometimes. The whole aspect of the scene changes. From the corn field and hay meadow you enter at once into a region of moor and peat. You seem to cross the threshold of civilisation, and are transported into a region which bears no impress of the hand of man, and undisturbed by any noisy device or busy handiwork, spreads its fresh beauties before you in all the attraction of nature. Passing through the moor for about a mile, the road diverges again, and joins the new Luss road, whence the route northwards may be prosecuted, or the pedestrian can return thus homewards.

TO ROW.

Learned Gaelic commentators have long ago found out that the original name of this district was "Rhue," or, Point of Land; and failing any more plausible theory, we are willing to admit the corruption of the text. Parishes were anciently often named from the localities selected for the kirk. This appears to have been the case here.* The name

---

* It appears from ecclesiastical records that the kirk of Row was at first an ease, or subordinate, place of worship for local accommodation, served by the minister of Roseneath. An act of General Assembly, of date 27th August 1639, empowered the Presbytery to take measures for settling both parishes of Roseneath and Cardross, with *Ease*. When the Presbytery began their proceedings, on 4th Feb., 1640, the "kirk upon the Row of Connel" existed, and M'Aulay of Ardencaple required the ease to be there. At another meeting, held the same month, Mr. George Lindsay, minister of Roseneath, offered security to maintain a helper; but Mr. Robert Walton, minister of Cardross, rather than that any part of his parish should be united to Roseneath, made a large offer for building a church and maintaining a helper in Glenfruin. There ensued a long and keen conflict between contending parties. The minister of Roseneath instead of being disburdened of the part of his charge east of Gareloch, was charged with having to preach every second Sabbath at the kirk of Row. At length (3d July 1643) the Lords Commissioners for the plantation of Kirks decreed the disjunction so long contended for. As much of Roseneath lying to the east of Kirkmichael was annexed to Cardross as was disjoined from Cardross to be annexed to the kirk of Row. The part of Cardross taken to make up the new parish embraced the Bannachras, Glenfruin, and lands about Gareloch-head. The compensation received by Cardross, from Roseneath, lay between Kirkmichael and the present church. Till then, that church stood on Cardross Point, at the influx of the Leven with Clyde. Row continued to be without a settled ministry till the presbytery, on 27th September 1648, appointed the admission of Mr. Archibald MacLeane, of Kingarth, as its first minister.

C

of the locality was Row, or Rhue of Connel, applicable to
the remarkable neck, or promontory, in the Gareloch, which
then approached much nearer Roseneath than now.   The
insignificance of this title, however, affords no fair criterion
by which to judge of the locality, any more than the name
of a man affords of his qualities.   Speaking of that part of
the parish properly known as Row, and inclusive of its neck

Row.

of land, there are few more beautiful or more romantic
places on the surface of the earth—few of the homes or haunts
of men so favoured with the attractions of all that is lovely
in nature.   The road thence from Helensburgh is the most
popular of all strolls in the neighbourhood, and well de-

serves the preference bestowed upon it. On a summer evening it is crowded with pedestrians, and on few days of the
year, and at few hours, will you not meet with walkers of
all classes. The road, once narrow, but lately considerably
improved leads along the margin of the Gareloch to the
village of Row, a distance of about two miles from Helensburgh. Immediately on passing Helensburgh, Ardencaple Castle and policies appear on the right hand side
of the road. The castle is a building of some antiquity, and
of some local historical interest. It stands on a rising knoll,
defended by an array of stately trees, by whose leafy branches
it is almost wholly concealed during summer. A cool shady
avenue, where lofty trees abound, leads up to it, but there
is nothing very imposing or architectually interesting in
the building itself. The more ancient part of it has been
added to at various times, without due regard to the original design ; and were it not for the clustering ivy, which
has

> "Clasped the gray walls with hairy-fibred arms,
> And sucked the joinings of the stones and rocks,
> A knot, beneath, of snakes, aloft, a grove,"

reaching, in some places to the very eaves, it would be rather
a dull unsightly mass of rough stones and mortar. The interior, contrary to anticipation, almost corresponds with the
exterior in containing little or nothing of interest to the
visitor. It lends nothing, but borrows much of its interest
and picturesqueness from the situation it occupies, and the
noble woods by which it is surrounded. Anciently Ardencaple belonged to the Faslane branch of the Lennox family,
In the fourteenth century, it became the residence of The
M'Aulay, a chief of some importance, and who, with his
predecessors, occupy a somewhat conspicuous, though not

enviable position in the freebooting annals of the country. For about a couple of centuries this family possessed a very considerable influence, not only locally, but in the stormy annals of the Scottish nation.   Their power, however, declined with the seventeenth century ;   and about the middle of the eighteenth, they had parted with the last of their possession here.   Ardencaple fell into the hands of a branch

Ardencaple Castle.

of the Argyll family; was for years possessed by the Duchess-Dowager of Argyll, and was, about five years since, purchased, along with the estates by Sir James Colquhoun of Luss, by whom the lands are now offered to feu, and the ground has been broken by the erection of a princely mansion here by William Kidston, Esq., J.P. Others will probably soon follow. A finer position for sea-coast villas than the range of fields adjacent to the shore presents, can scarcely be well conceived. The amenity of the castle and its immediate policies would not be injured, nor their seclusion encroached upon to any perceptable extent were this strip of land laid out in houses and gardens. The policies are now guarded against all public intrusion by watchers, dogs and placards. The bosky dells and sylvan beauties, once accessible to the tourist need not be described, for *caveat viator* is inscribed at every pass, and echoed in English and Gaelic, by the surly tongue of a gamekeeper and gillie to any stranger who has the hardihood to enter the road leading through it.

A little beyond the castle, the road separates a point of land, known as Cairndow and "Neddy's Point," from the policies. This point is understood to be still in possession of the Argyll family. Here, from time immemorial, a ferry to the opposite castle of Roseneath has existed, and of very recent date an obnoxious toll-bar has been erected, the advantages of which are not nearly so apparent as those of the ferry. The Cairndow Point embraces about half an acre of land rising to a considerable height above the level of the loch, and clad in some twenty straggling beech trees, whose shade in summer affords an agreeable lounge for travellers. Barring the toll-bar there are no houses now on the Point, though traces of foundations of one or two may still be discerned among the grassy inequalities of the surface. One or two cottages existed here within the memory of the present generation, the principal of these occupied by the Neddy, whose surviving name has since distinguished the locality. He was ferryman and fisherman to the Duke, and seems to have been somewhat of an original, if the traditions pre-

served of him deserves credit. His wife, a little English
woman, used to help him daily to launch his boat, and waited
on the beach for his arrival home at evening, invariably
saluting him, ere he stepped ashore, with "Welcome home,
Neddy, fish or no fish." The rocks about this point afford
shelter during summer to a succession of gangs of tinkers—
those nomads of civilisation who live in utter heathenism
and barbarism, despite all reformatory institutions and religious or philanthropic efforts. Nothing reaches their case
but the order of the policeman to move on; they know no
higher authority, and no purer law than that which can be
enforced by the baton, and society seems to consider them a
class privileged to live and die in the most debased ignorance
and idleness. The women and children beg all day; and by
night, around their glimmering fires, the families huddle together and divide the spoil, and fight and swear over the
liquor which their cunning or their importunity has procured.

From this point to Row Quay, Cairndow Bay, or Ardencaple Bay as it is sometimes termed, forms a beautiful cres-
cent-like sweep of about half a mile. It is said to bear a
very marked miniature resemblance of the Bay of Naples.
The ground ascends gradually from the water edge to a considerable height, and the white and gray villas, rising above
each other, look forth from the overhanging woods down
upon the loch beneath. Many of these villas have been
erected at great expense, and are furnished and decorated with
the most refined taste. On a calm summer day, when the
woods are in full foliage, abounding in varied tint and
shadow, and almost screening the houses from view, and
imaged in softer tone on the bosom of the waters, there is
scarcely a more beautiful bit of scenery over which one can

linger and admire than at this point. At the further extremity of the bay is Row Quay, and beyond it sweeps
another semicircle, forming the Row Bay—not so beautiful
as the first, yet possessing many attractions. In its centre
stands the village and parish church of Row—the village
consisting of a small cluster of houses, only partially seen
from the road, with Ardenconnal House, perched amid lofty
trees, like a protecting fortress occupying a commanding
situation on the heights behind. Adjacent to the village is
the parish church, erected about twelve years since—a very
handsome building, and decorated with several beautifully
stained-glass windows, the gift, we believe, of Robert Napier,
Esq., and others. A sad drawback, however, to the architectural beauty of the church is the utter ruin and neglect
of the churchyard—imperfectly fenced, and with tombstones
lying in every condition of dilapidation and disorder. Row
parish, as already noticed, was disjoined from the parishes of
Roseneath and Cardross about the year 1643. The part of it
which extends from Shandon to the east boundary of Helensburgh, belonged to Roseneath. From Shandon to Garelochhead, and the Strath of Glenfruin, belonged to Cardross; and
from Gareloch-head to the boundary of the parish of Arrochar,
is mentioned in the report of the Commissioners appointed
for the Valuation of Teinds, in 1630, as lying in the parish
of Inshalloch,* an old parish, which is now unknown even

---

* Inshalloch, says an antiquarian friend, is a name disguised by one
of those freaks of orthography common in old documents. It is Inch-
Cailliach, the name of the island of Lochlomond, adjacent to Balmaha,
where it is believed the churchyard and remains of the church may
yet be traced. The church was transferred to Buchanan, which had
formerly a chapel subordinate to Luss. All the lands belonging to
Luss on the east side of the lake were annexed to this ancient parish
to form the modern parish of Buchanan; while a large portion of the
parish of Inch-Cailliach, on the west side was annexed to Luss. The

by name in the district, and seems to have merged into the
parish of Cardross. The district now comprehended as the
parish of Row, though not a parish till 1646, possessed
several places of worship. One at Faslane, where the Lennox
family had a castle, and a considerable part of which yet
stands; another at Glenfruin, to which considerable church
lands were attached, but the only remnant of which is the
stone baptismal font, built into a modern cottage—the
schoolmaster's house; and another at Kirkmichael, in
Helensburgh, of which no vestige now remains, but religious
service is said to have been performed in it in the early part
of last century by an indulged Episcopal minister.

At the time the parish was formed, the most populous
portion of it was the now almost lonely glen of the Fruin,
where it was at first intended the parish church should be
placed; but the tenantry succeeded in getting it erected
where it now is by giving land for the church, church-yard,
and glebe. The first minister was chosen in consequence of
his ability to preach in Gaelic; but that tongue has long
ceased to be used in preaching or conversation in the district. The last minister who used it was Mr. Allan, who,
along with his son as successor, were ministers of the
parish for about a century previous to 1812. The present
beautiful church appears to be the third that has been
erected since the formation of the parish. More than half of

territories included Caldannach, Prestelloch and Conglen, and as
they would thus include the narrow strip of Luss, Craig-cn-shee—
which separated Row from Arrochar—they must have extended westward to Lochlong. Whatever of Inch-Cailliach may have been included in Row must have been annexed beforehand to Roseneath or
Cardross, since the others were dismembered in the construction of
Row. Buchanan was disjoined from Luss in 1621, twenty-two years
previously, and the old parish of Inch-Cailliach broken up.

its cost was subscribed by few of the parishioners on Gare-lochside, as an inducement to the heritors to build it. Its immediate predecessor had been built in 1862, and remained unseated for a year after it was occupied, the parishioners bringing stools and chairs or other conveniences with them on the Sundays, according to taste or resources. The present esteemed minister, the Rev. John Laurie Fogo, has laboured acceptably and efficiently since 1832.

Row parish, in 1830, attained considerable ecclesiastical importance in consequence of a religious movement, known as the " Row heresy," originating here. This movement excited deep attention throughout Scotland and England at the time. It agitated the Presbytery, and ultimately the General Assembly took up the matter, and it resulted in the exclusion of the then minister of the parish from his charge —a man who still survives the stormy discussions of the time, respected for his talents, faithfulness, and unblemished character.

Beyond the church, a long peninsula, called the Point, stretches out into the loch, encircling the village with an arm. On the neck of Row Point stands a beautiful Italian villa, built some years since by Daniel Walkinshaw, Esq., and which forms a most appropriate ornament to the land-scape, redeeming the otherwise bare point of its former bleak and unpromising aspect. A clump of fir plantation clothes the remainder of the point, lying above tide mark; and from thence, at ebb-water, a long narrow strip of gravelly channel reaches almost across the loch, leaving but a narrow passage betwixt and the opposite ferry of Rose-neath, in which the pent waters at ebb and flood boil and toss about at times with great fury. Standing on this nar-row isthmus, one cannot fail to note the contrast the waters

on each side present. With a breeze blowing freshly down
the loch, or upwards, the tide on the one hand is fretting
and angrily lashing against the opposing barrier, the waves
raking down, with each returning grasp, the loose sand and
pebbles, only to dash them back again on the shore. On
the other hand, not a breath disturbs the placid surface; the
leaves of the ebbed sea-gresses and tangle float listlessly on
the surface, and the medusa stretches out its hundred fibrous
threads in quest of its minute prey, and the water-spider
skims to and fro on its glittering pathway. How narrow
and how frail the boundary between the bitter, bleak shore
of wordly trial and adversity, and the calm rest of peaceful
life! To what slight interposition, which, men meaninglessly
term chance, are we often preserved from the storm, and our
bark rides safely in tranquil and untroubled waters! And
as one stands on this point and watches the fishing crafts on
the lake beyond, he cannot fail to feel a measure of sympathy
and interest in the humble lives of those who earn a livelihood from the treacherous deep; the poetry and peril of
which have formed an exhaustless theme of past and present
literature. The fisherman's boat itself, under the eloquent
pen of Mr. Ruskin, becomes a very poem. How graphic
and how true the description involuntarily rising before us
as we write—"All ashine with the sea she plunges and dips
into the deep green purity of the mounded waves more joy-
fully than a deer lies down among the grass of spring, the
soft white cloud of foam opening momentarily at the bows,
or fading and flying high into the breeze where the sea-gulls
toss and shriek; the joy and beauty of it all the while so
mingled with the sense of unfathomable danger, and the
human effort and sorrow going on from age to age—waves
rolling for ever, and winds moaning for ever, and faithful

hearts trusting and sickening for ever, and brave lives dashed away about the rattling beach like weeds for ever ; and still at the helm of every lonely boat, through starless night and hopeless dawn, His hand who spread the fisher's net over the dust of the Sidonian palaces, and gave into the fisher's hand the keys of the kingdom of heaven."

THE SMUGGLER'S, OR THE WHISTLER'S GLEN.

This beautiful and romantic glen is situated about half a mile to the north of the village of Row. It was anciently called Aldonalt, that is, the burn of Donalt, or Dualt. The lands that lay to the right were called Letru-alt. There was

Letru-alt-a-Mhailinn (Litrualt of the Mill,) immediately on
the right and further along Mid Letrualt and west Letrualt. The principal approach to it is through the grounds of
Ardenconnal or Aldonwick ; but there are several bypaths
which are preferable if the pedestrian does not object to
overcome a few obstacles such as hedges, dykes, and ditches.
The glen is about a mile in extent, reaches up from the
Gareloch northwards. At its termination there is said to be
a bottomless linn, where, according to the tales of ancient
days, many dark and bloody deeds were perpetrated. Certainly the rugged, rocky, picturesque character of the glen
is such to corroborate the most startling traditions associated with it. The south part of the glen is thickly wooded
with birch, fir, and hazel trees, and the craggy rocks are
overrun with brambles, ivy, and brushwood, presenting an
almost impenetrable jungle, while at the depth of twenty or
thirty feet the burn, a wilful little stream, flows slugglishly
along, or tumbles over some projecting rock in mimic falls.
The glen has of late years been made much more accessible
then formerly, a path having been formed on each side,
and rustic bridges thrown across the ravine at short intervals. In one part of the water, as if about to leave the little
glen, suddenly disappears under the ground and is distinctly
heard murmering below the surface, but again, in obedience
to an inexorable destiny, after a few hundred yards, re-
appears and continues its wandering course, till it finally
assumes the form of a considerable burn, which flows unin-
turruptedly into the Gareloch. The view from many points
of the glen is beautiful, and must attract the most careless
eye. Ascending the glen till you reach the outskirts of the
wood, there bursts upon you an almost unrivalled scene of
beauty : the clear and silvery Gareloch, bearing on its bosom

the bark of many an honest fisherman, now appearing a mere speck, or the noble vessel with its living freight, ploughing its way through its peaceful waters; the opposite shore stretching out into the Frith of Clyde, forming the peninsula of Rose-neath. Almost at the extremity, and partially hid by noble trees, stands the place of Roseneath, the seat of the Duke of Argyll ; and at a short distance westward, near the shore, is the Clachan, with its picturesque school house, and troops of merry children. Towering in the background are the rugged and heath-clad hills which border Lochs Long and Goil, while away to the west, and almost lost in the distance, the craggy mountains of Argyllshire ; and a little to the south, disappearing in the clouds, rise the shattered and thunder-splitten peaks of Arran. In former days this glen, as its name implies, was a favourite and secure retreat for smug-glers, and not a few drops of " mountain-dew " have been car-ried from it unscathed by government influence.

This glen is worthy the attention of the botanist, and would amply repay his toil; he might spend days in sup-plying himself with many rare and beautiful plants, espe-cially of the fern tribe, and mosses of every variety and rain-bow-coloured hues.

Tradition records that many years ago, beside the black linn, and always when the moon was at its full, the figure of a woman in gray might be seen by night on a stone, crouched down with clasped hands and murmuring in a low soft wail to the bubbling stream. Her lover was said to have been slain by some rival in the lady's affections, and his body subsequently discovered at the spot. We never met with any one who saw the apparition, and do not vouch it as a positive fact.

This glen is sometimes known as the Whistler's Glen; by

this name it is recognised in the "Heart of Midlothian." The author has connected it, despite a little anachronism, with the son of Jeanie Deans's sister. He, while an infant, had been sold by the person to whom he was entrusted, to a wandering tribe of gipsies, and by them given up to Donacha Dhu, the chief of a party of freebooters, who appears to have made the glen a place of retreat, and here the young lad was brought up in a state little removed from the savage, and only known by the name of "The Whistler." The reader of the Heart of Midlothian will remember that his mother, while on a visit to her sister Jeanie, then Mrs. Butler, nearly lost her life while wandering through the glen. She was attacked by a party of Donacha Dhu's followers, among whom was her son, though quite unknown to her at the time, and was only rescued by the free use of her purse, and the appearance of some of her sister's friends. The poor Whistler's end was a very melancholy one; he was taken prisoner while attempting to set fire to a house; but making his escape, he succeeded in hiding himself in this glen, till having mortally offended Donacha Dhu, he was sold by him to some American traders lying at Greenock, and lost his life in attemping to escape from a brutal Southern driver.

This story, and other circumstances, gave an interest to the glen, which would once have rendered a visit to it an undertaking requiring some courage.

THE GARELOCH.

A narrow and indifferently kept road, notwithstanding the number of turnpikes on it, runs from Row Point to Garelochhead. At many points two carriages can hardly pass abreast, and when its rises above the level of the beach, wall or fence often insufficiently interposes to protect the incautious traveller from being precipitated on the stones beneath. It is badly drained, and there is no footpath for humble pedestrians, and in wet weather is generally submerged in mud to a depth varying from two to five or six inches. With all these drawbacks, however, there is compensation to be found in the scenery through which it passes. Many a smooth and unexceptional highway leads the weary miles past a dreary and uninteresting country, without one refreshing feature or suggestive object anywhere arising to attract the eye or gladden the heart of the toiling traveller, while many a rough and rugged road penetrates the fairest scenes of nature. The smoother the journey the less the pleasure it confers—the glowing panorama of glen and mountain, lake and forest, is only witnessed after the toilsome ascent. As in the roads through life, with toil and trial are most of our pleasures won, and not found in our journey on smooth and easy levels, so it would seem the roughest roads in nature often lead through the most varied and longest remembered of our pleasant experiences: and the road here has this advantage. The road winds around all the little bays and creeks; rises here steeply in front; presents there a sudden turn; at this point reveals the whole loch to the eye; at the next passes in front of some handsome villa or fragrant garden, shutting out the hills from view, or diverges beneath a clump of trees, or between a hedgerow, but nowhere lingers so long as to create a monotony or suggest a wish for change. The distance from Row to Garelochhead is about six miles. The loch varies in breadth from half a mile to a mile, is in some places very deep, and to the eye is completely locked in on every side, the narrow outlet at Row Point being hardly perceptible at a distance. On both sides of the loch, and at its head, rise a barrier of heath-clad hills, generally sloping at an easy declivity down to the water; overtopping those at the head of the loch, the high, bold, rocky mountains that stretch across the head of Glen Croe, and above Ardentinny, present their clear, sharp outlines in the sky, and form a pleasant background to the picture. Like most Highland lakes, Gareloch, a few years since, to the travellers eye, showed but few signs of civilised life. The hills are clad with heath, and towards the margin of the loch, when partially reclaimed from morass and brush-wood, a scanty cornfield, and unplastered heath-thatched hut here and there told of human life and enterprise. At the head of the loch, a little clachan of these huts gathered together, inhabited chiefly by fishermen, formed the village. Railways and steam navigation, however, have changed all that; the aborigines are as nearly extinct as any doomed tribe of red men, or have become amalgamated with the in-vaders of their territories, and are now undistinguishable, and their huts and corn patches have passed away with them.

There are few buildings of any antiquity, or memorials of the past possessing interest enough to detain the stranger, or induce him to wander from the beaten track. Blair-vadic Castle, situated about a mile above the Row, a stately modern castle, built by the late Sir James Anderson, occu-pies the site of an older mansion built by the late James Buchanan, Esq., of Craigend. Perhaps the oldest house on Garelochside is Faslane House, which was a summer resi-dence last century. On the hill above Ardchapel, at Shan-don, enthusiastic and imaginative explorers have found the remains of an old dry dyke, but nothing like the founda-tion of a sacred edifice, even although the tradition is supported by the name yet retains. A much less equivocal building, surrounded by remains of an ancient churchyard can be plainly distinguished at Faslane, a little farther north. Here worshipped generations, now long slumbering in dust, of the Celtic tenants and vassals of these glens. Here, doubtless, some jovial Friar Tuck held saints' fast days o'er other fare than parched peas and holy water; or,

Faslane Chapel.

perhaps, anchorite Cistercian imposed penance on the lawless Macfarlane or Colquhoun, or chanted midnight mass for the unshriven soul of dead freebooter and outlaw. The little chapel with its broken shrine and remote churchyard is worth a visit. It occupies a peculiarly lovely and sequestered spot on a rising knoll almost surrounded by a burn. Adja-

D

cent stood, in old times, Faslane Castle, the foundations of which can hardly now be traced among the mossgrown stones and grassy hillocks covering its site.

But if there are few ancient buildings, there are many modern ones well deserving more than a passing glance. At Shandon there is a collection of villas unsurpassed in beauty and picturesqueness of situation by any on the Frith of Clyde; and occupying a prominent position near the loch, is West Shandon House, the princely mansion of Robert Napier, Esq., a marvel of masonry and decorative art, and containing an attraction of rare treasures of ancient and modern art not equalled almost in Scotland, as a private collection. A greater treat to the art student or vistuoso than an inspection of Mr. Napier's mansion and collection, can hardly be enjoyed. There are both abundant modern curiosities and

> " Fouth o' auld nick nacketts,
> Rusty airn caps and auld steel jackets,
> Wad haud the Lothians three in tackets
> A towmond guid."

The house was built in 1857, but improvements are still going on. In close proximity, and not much inferior in attraction is Shandon House, a much older building, sometime the residence of Walter Buchanan, Esq., M.P. From Shandon to Garelochhead, about two miles distant, the road winds along some beautiful little bays—in particular we notice Faslane Bay, as possessing peculiar attractions, and we wonder that it has not caught the eye of any building speculator as a desirable site for villas. Here the village of Garelochhead first appears in view, and a few minutes' walk takes you to that memorable wooden pier where on a quiet Sunday afternoon some years ago, the battle of the barricades was faught, a battle

West Shandon House.

which ended in the subsequent expenditure of no insignificant sum in the Court of Session, in vindication of the right of the proprietor to exclude Sunday excursionists, and preserve the good order and quiet of the village. The village itself is prettily situated at the head of the loch, and now stretches in a semicircle around it, and seperates the head of the Gareloch from Lochlong. At the top of the hill is the "wee public," called Whistlefield Inn, a welcome resting place for the fatigued pedestrian, and from whence a magnificent view of Gareloch, Lochlong, and Lochgoil, with their rugged and hoary guardian mountains, can be obtained The locality is a favourite resort of holiday parties, and there are few fine summer days in which it is not visited by crowds from some pleasure excursion steamer. In the fishing season a little stir is created in the village, and ample employment for all the girls and boys afforded for a month or two. In June and July fleets of fishing crafts harbour about the head of the loch, nightly dispersing through it in search of herring, of which great quantities are sometimes captured. The loch generally used to be somewhat celebrated for fishing, but seems of late years to have fallen rather into disrepute, probably from the same mysterious causes which have operated in diminishing the supply of fish all along the west coast. To this the season of 1867 was exceptional, when it was visited by such shoals of herring and other fish, as had not been seen in memory of man.

CARDROSS.

Helensburgh is bounded on the east by Cardross parish, which you enter immediately on leaving a long dull wall at the extremity of the town. So dismally secluded is this part of Helensburgh from any possible view of the Frith, that between the highway and the rising ground on the north very few buildings for years had been erected. It is with a feeling of relief you emerge from this end of the burgh again into the open country, and to the ever cheerful view of the sea. A little way beyond the toll-house, on the north side of the road, stands the mansion-house of Colgrain, a plain, unpretending, but commodious building, surrounded by some fine old wood, and occupying a very picturesque situation. It used to be very much neglected—the grounds untrimmed, the fences dilapidated, and the whole premises had that sad, deserted aspect peculiar to many old country houses not regularly occupied, but the enterprising proprietor, Mr Colin Campbell, of Cambus-Eskan, aided by an enterprising tenant, has not only wrought immense improvements on the farm connected with it, but also exercised great taste in renovating the building and lawns. The land here is a rich *alluvium*, and for several miles along the road the gently rising upland is highly cultivated, and bears very heavy crops. There are some of the farms on this and the adjoining Cambus-Eskan estate not surpassed for fertility or good husbandry by any in Dumbartonshire. Adjoining Colgrain, the policies of Cambus-Eskan, stretch down towards the road. A handsome freestone lodge and gateway stand at the approach to the mansion, which occupies a commanding position on the rising ground, and is sheltered from the east wind by a high screen of hill and plantation. Below the road, and towards the river, is a stretch of land of considerable width, and which will, in all probability, in a few years, be occupied by villas, as it commands a beautiful view of the Frith, and is easily accessible by railway. The Cambus-Eskan grounds extend along the road about two miles, after which you pass Keppoch, the property of James Donaldson, Esq., with its comfortable and well-sheltered mansion-house, commanding a wide and varied prospect. Then, a little beyond, Lyleston, belonging to Wm. M. Donald, Esq., nestling under a wood, looks down on the bay and Frith. Here the road rises gradually till you reach Ardarden Hill, from which point a view of the Frith of Clyde, including Helensburgh and the high range of hills to the west, strikes the eye of the tourist. There is, perhaps, not a lovelier prospect in Scotland, and we have heard travellers affirm that nowhere had they seen it surpassed in the old or new world. Beneath lies the well-known promontory of Ardmore, connected with the mainland by a very narrow isthmus. If the tourist can afford leisure, he will find it worth his while to go a little out of his way to visit this beautiful spot. The whole pro-montory is about a mile and a half in circumference. Its centre is a circular wooded rock of some fifty or sixty feet in height, called the Hill of Ardmore, on which a good house is erected, but which is not visible till you approach very closely to it. On various of the higher points rustic moss houses and bowers have been placed by the owners of Ard-more, commanding an ample prospect on either hand. At the base of the rock on the east, the gardens and orchard are situated ; and as the rocks are full of fissures, and clad with ivy and other creeping plants, they strike the eye with a picturesque effect. A rock-bound coast runs all round the promontory, save where little coves occasionally stretch in towards the land, and in stormy weather the waters of the Frith beat furiously against it. Ships breaking from their moorings at Greenock have frequently been dashed to pieces on these rocks; and on such a lee shore escape for an vessel in this hapless plight is almost impossible. On the west corner of the grounds stands the Ferry-house, formerly much frequented by travellers and cattle-dealers as being the almost only means of communication with Greenock and the opposite shore. In stormy weather the passage across was sometimes attended with a considerable degree of peril, and lives have frequently been lost. Many years ago, on attempting to make the passage home one wintry night, the ferryman and his two sons perished when almost on shore, and the first object that met the gaze of his anxious wife next morning were the dead bodies of her husband and sons lying on the beach, almost at the threshold of their own door, where they had been cast up by the tide. A somewhat kindred story, though of less melancholy end, is told of another ferryman who lived here some time, one Jacob Brown, a solitary individual of rather an eccentric turn of mind. During the great French war a boat containing a military band which was being conveyed from Greenock to a transport ship accidentally upset, and the whole band perished. They were washed ashore subsequently near the ferry-house, and interred in the ground immediately behind it, now forming the kailyard. There they slumbered peacefully for many years save on the anniversary night of their death, when it was said the sounds of martial music was regularly heard echoing among the rocks around the lonely point. One night as Jacob was lying in bed he was awakened by an unwonted noise within and around his house; on starting up, his heart quailled and his blood curdled as he saw a whole line of thin airy figures all arrayed in military garb, but through whom the pale moonbeams flitted, perched on the top of a dyke, and playing the Dead March in Saul, opposite his window. The music was weird and unearthly in sound, and the deep notes of the huge trombone as it stretched occasionally till it touched the window of Jacob's room, and the hollow rumble of the drum, froze every drop of blood in his veins. Jacob could not cry, he could not move, he had not even strength to utter an inward prayer, but lay there, spell-bound, staring at the spectral band, till unconsciousness happily released him. When he came to his senses the next morning the band was gone, the sun shining brightly on the waters, and on the graves of the drowned musicians, all undisturbed by their midnight orgies; but Jacob made his escape from the cottage with all convenient despatch, and no persuasion could induce him again to set foot in it, nor till his death did he cease to believe in the reality of the ghostly company who that night serenaded him.

On both sides of the narrow isthmus, connecting Ardmore with the mainland, the tide ebbs a long way, leaving a great tract of sand and marine deposit. These tracts, in the hands of any enterprising party, could easily be embanked and much valuable land reclaimed, and we understand such an operation has been for some time projected. The beauty of the hill and neighbourhood would be greatly increased were this scheme carried out. In the meantime these banks are, in winter, the haunts of various tribes of wild flowers, and are resorted to by numerous sportsmen—professional and amateur. The birds seems to find food amongst the marine grasses and crustacea with which the banks abound, and though not nearly so numerous as they were twenty or thirty years ago, before steam navigation existed to the extent it now does on the river, there are still large quantities found resorting to them each winter. Tribes of wild duck first make their appearance about the end of October, at first in small families, gradually increasing as winter advances, into large and compact flocks. The teal, sheldrake, and common mossduck first appear on the approach of frost or stormy weather, and later in the season flocks of Norwegian duck and barnacle haunt the bays and creeks. At ebb tide the sands at these and various other favourite feeding grounds are almost covered with curlew, gray and golden plovers, and small sand-larks.

On returning to the highway again, the tourist passes on the right hand the properties of Ardarden and Brooks, and on the left Mollandhu. The last was purchased by a legacy of a Mrs. Jane Moore, bequeathed about two hundred years ago to be invested in trust, for behoof of the poor of the parish of Cardross, lying between Lyleston and the burn of Auchenfro. It was then of comparatively small value, but now yields a rental of upwards of £300. The story of Jane Moore may be briefly told, as follows:—Jane Moore was born in Cardross parish, about 1620, in very humble circumstances, and, like most girls in her rank, went out early to domestic service, as the almost only available means of securing an independent livelihood. She was engaged by the family of Keppoch, where one wet afternoon, when baking in the kitchen, a miserable applicant for charity presented himself at the door. Actuated by the first impulse of benevolence, Jane handed the wet and famished man a cake, and bade him dry his rags near the fire. It was carried to the ears of the mistress of Keppoch that night that her servant had given away the bread of the family, and entertained a beggar; and as the lady looked on the matter from a somewhat different point of view from the domestic, as ladies are apt sometimes to do, she immediately turned her out of doors amid the pelting, pitiless, rain, and falling darkness. The poor girl

wandered homewards, but by the time she reached the burnfoot of Auchenfro the stream was a raging torrent, which
she dared not, in the darkness, cross. To return to Keppoch
was vain, and no friendly roof was nigh to shelter her. Such
poor cover as the bushes afforded was her only protection during the long, weary darkness, and storm of the night. But the
wrath of the mistress of Keppoch, and the penance of Jane
Moore were, as many untoward accidents of our lives are,
the turning point of a brighter chapter. In her future
career we find her in London. She was there when the
great plague broke out in 1665—a spectator and sufferer in
that divine purifying of the moral and sanitary condition of
the metropolis. She was attacked by the disease early, and
was one of the few infected who recovered from the fell
malady—a widow and friendless. The benevolence of the
woman, who helped the beggar at Keppoch, who was not ex-
hausted by her own trials, but exalted and purified; she
devoted her energies to nursing the sick and tending the
dying around her while the pestilence lasted. Many had
none left to claim their effects when they died, and bestowed
their gold and treasures on Jane Moore. Wealth flowed in
upon her, but only to be applied to charities; and amongst
others she remembered the home of her youth. Before her
death she appointed a sum to be invested for two purposes—
viz., the erection of a bridge at the burnfoot of Auchenfro,
where she had been arrested in her flight by stress of weather,
and for relief of the poor of Cardross, resident between the
clachan of Lyleston and the burn of Auchenfro. By con-
fining the benefit of her bequest within these limits Keppoch was excluded. The lands of Mollandhu were afterwards purchased by this bequest; but, as in late years, the
poor entitled to receive the benefit were exceedingly few in

number, and gradually diminishing, the Parochial Board of
Cardross parish raised the question whether they were not
the proper administrators of the fund, and after a good deal
of litigation, it was ultimately decided in their favour. The
fund is more beneficially applied than it could have been
under the former arrangement. A beautiful avenue of trees
overarches the road as it passes Geilston, and supplies a cool
and shady walk of about a quarter of a mile in length.
The mansion-house of Geilston stands at a little distance off
the road on the left side, and can only be partially seen from it.
The scenery in the neighbourhood of the house is very fine.
Behind it flows the Geilston Burn, which rises in the moor
some miles above. On this burn are some pretty bits of
rock and waterfall for the pencil of the artist; and were it
not that its course is through very broken and rugged ground,
it would be more frequently visited. A little beyond Geilston stands the village of Cardross—a very ancient village,
consisting of some dozen of houses, an inn, picturesque parish
church, manse, and unpretending Free Church meeting-
house; over-hanging the Parish Church are the beautiful
grounds and manse of Bloomhill. The population of the
village probably does not exceed fifty, and cannot have in
creased within the memory of the oldest inhabitant. It
lies in a sheltered warm situation. There are many beautiful walks in the neighbourhood, and the roads being light
and gravelly, are always dry and pleasant. There are not
many points of interest likely to attract the traveller out of
the regular road. The ruins of an old chapel and churchyard a little way to the north, and the remains of Kilmahew
Castle, are the two objects usually pointed out as worthy of
examination. This chapel was subordinate to the ancient
church of Cardross. The castle was the residence of Napier

of Kilmahew, a branch of the great Napier family who occupy such a prominent position in Scottish annals. The ruins of the old church of Cardross are still remembered on the point opposite Dumbarton Castle. The Lords Commissioners, at the disjunction of Row in 1643, ordained the kirk of Cardross to be transported to a more commodious place; and on 12th September following, the ground was marked out for the new kirk and manse, in the situation now occupied by the present buildings. Kilmahew had not, however, been always united to Cardross. Immediately after the reformation, and for many years after, qualified ministers were not sufficient for the parishes, and often one minister had to hold a plurality of kirks, by the help of readers. In the register of ministers and readers of 1574, "Rosneith, Kilmahew, and Bulhill (Bonhill)," appear united under Malcolm Stevenson as minister, assisted by Ninian Galt as reader at Roseneath, and Adam Hutcheson at Kilmahew, At a farm called Castlehill, two miles nearer Dumbarton, once stood a residence of King Robert Bruce, and the place where he breathed his last after the stormy vicissitudes of his life had passed, and his kingdom had enjoyed a measure of rest and freedom. What an affecting sight it must have been to have seen that lion-hearted old king bowed down by disease and premature age sunning himself on the fair Clyde, or in view of his coming end, detailing to his nobles and barons those wise and prudential measures for the protection and preservation of a kingdom lying so near his heart, and which had cost him such a trouble to preserve! and then the record of his death here, there is scarcely a more touching incident in all Scottish history. How he bequeathes to his tried and noble friend the Douglas—whose friendship had been of that rare and enduring character which no misfortune or disaster could diminish—his heart when it should beat no more; and enjoins him to bear it to Jerusalem to fulfil his vow, in place of his body; and how as every schoolboy knows, the Douglas, old though he was undertook the commission, and afterwards, tossing the golden casket containing that precious heart into the midst of the Saracen host, perished in following it. There was a sincere piety in all this which we must not judge of or measure by the standard of our own times, and which ignorance or bigotry alone would censure. In Scottish history there are but two epochs that relieve it from a dry record of barbarism —of traitorous nobles and an oppressed people—the record of our struggle for national independence, and the Reforma- tion. With the former of these Cardross, as we have seen, is intimately associated, and will ever remain a place of note insignificant though it otherwise be, as connected with the life and death of a true king. In the parish of Cardross the grandfather of the historian, Macaulay, was minister during considerable period of his life. Another distinguished his- torian and novelist, Tobias Smollett, was born in it, and near the place of his nativity, at Renton, a relative has erected a column in his memory, on which a familiar Latin inscription records the virtues and life of the author of "Roderick Random."

GLEN FRUIN

This most interesting and beautiful glen may be approached by several routes from Helensburgh. The most usual is by the road to Luss, which approaches very close to it at one or two points, and ultimately crosses the stream. The best, however, for one who has leisure and a desire to explore it thoroughly, is by crossing the range of hills on the Gareloch, a little above Shandon, whence you decend into the upper part of the glen, not far from its sources. The ascent is pretty steep, but amply is the toil repaid as the traveller reaches the summit. Beneath him on the one hand stretches out Gareloch, like a sheet of molten silver overtopped by the purple hills. To the east can be traced the track of the

Glen Fruin, near Dunfin Mill.

Clyde, its towns, villages and wooded hills, till Dumbarton rock hides it from view. On the left hand, the vale of Fruin slopes away through moorland, wood, and corn-field till it reaches Lochlomond shores. For many miles through it the eye follows the windings of the stream as it gushes through the rocks, or pauses amid the meadows, or struggles through the arms of the leafy hazels that strive to hide it as it dashes along. The descent from the brow of the hill is easy and short, and the pedestrian soon stands upon the borders of the stream. The upper part of the glen embraces a large semicircular tract of pasture meadow, hemmed in on three sides by heath-clad hills. Through the meadows flow numberless little streams,, the limpid parents of the Fruin. There is a cart road leading down cne side of the glen; but for the pedestrian who is willing to encounter a little extra fatigue, which will be more than amply repaid by the scenery he must enjoy, the burnside is the best path. On a bright, pure day, the whole picture is one of calm sweet beauty. Lazily the cattle rest on the marsh, or stand fetlock deep in the stream. The long meadow grasses scarce wave to the breeze; there is no sound of man's existence breaking on the ear. The dragon-fly or the bee, humming past you in their flight, the distant whirr of the blackcock, the cry of curlew or plover, or bleat of sheep, alone wake the echoes, while the stream yields an un-wearying song as it journeys towards home—

" Glittering over the deeper pools,
Glittering over the sand"—

rising as it hurries through the stony channel, still louder as it dashes over rocky barriers, and sinking into a quiet lullaby as it circles through the sedgy pool where the gray duck and her dusky brood hide themselves from strange eyes.

One cannot help a certain mournful retrospect at the changes which time must have wrought in this glen. Like most other Highland retreats, it must have been thickly peopled in the days when the war-cry was a familiar sound and clansmen rushed to a summons which would now find only an echo among the gray rocks. Little stretch of imagination is necessary to conjure up clusters of lowly shielings, the straggling patches of ill-fenced corn, and curling peat smoke, and groups of half-clad, noisy children playing among the tall ferns by the burnside, where the greensward and half-effaced traces of ancient foundations now stretch down the hills. These days of Highland clansmen have rapidly passed away. The commercial power is now supplanting the feudal power, and the change of the face of nature has been correspondingly great. The substantial farm-steading, the active husbandman, and the cultivated field, occupy the sites of rude barbarism. And there are not a few farms, monuments of enterprise and energy throughout the glen. The land is not very fertile nor the exposure desirable ; yet the work of reclaiming waste moor, and converting profitless bog into fields of grass and grain has gone on of late years with great rapidity. Nor does it follow that all the romance and poetry of the people are extinct, because feudalism and vandalism are passing away. Romance and poetry never pass away. They are to the soul what the everlasting hills and mountains are to the landscape; only, as man rises in the scale of humanity they become sublimated and exalted in degree. The rural swain still sings as passionately of love—is still as faithful to his mistress, and as bold in danger as ever henchman of belted knight was. And Glen Fruin is somewhat celebrated for the amatory effusions Cupid has inspired. We quote a specimen given in an interesting little book by Mr. Robert Blakely :—

> "I've often seen the roses blaw—
> I've often stray'd the flowers among—
> I've often heard on birken shaw
> The little woodlark's heavenly song—

" I've often mark'd in cloudless sky
    The progress of the rising moon ;
But never aught could yield me joy
    Like roaming on the banks of Fruin.

'Twas here I saw a diamond bright ;
    Her raven hair's the jetty craw ;
Her silvery neck as pure and white
    As is the bosom of sea-maw ;
The living drop frae off the lip
    O' this dear saint in beauty's noon,
An angel's sel' might fondly sip,
    Sae sweet ! the maiden o' Glen Gruin,"

After emerging from the meadow land, a whitewashed
building on the left side of the stream, surrounded by a
score of riotous children, instructs the tourist that even
here the schoolmaster is abroad. Who would not like to be
a scholar in such a school-house! A mountain stream to
revel in summer's play-hours at the very door. Hazel dells
within a stone's throw, where nests and nuts in their season
may be found in any quantity, and the purple heathery hill
behind, crossed with turf-dikes, where the wild bee has her
store, and the blaeberry grows. Doubtless many a stalwart
man and matronly woman far distant now remembers, with a
sigh and a tear, the joyous days spent at this early *Alma
Mater.*

The ruins of an old chapel, some years since, stood close
by the stream ; and the locality is still indicated by the
name of " The Chapel." Many of the stones were built into
the school-house and adjacent farm-steading occupied by Mr.
Jardine. The remains of a lint mill, which stood close by
it, are still distinctly traceable on a rocky knowe close by
the stream. Beneath them, the waters fall over a series of
rocky ledges into a deep pool ; there the rocks and trees
surround a natural basin, sheltered from the winds on every
side. Imagination records a time when the gray monks

E

tenanting the chapel lands may have often, in this unchanging solitude, sat pondering over the vicissitudes of time, and meditating on the few and simple events of their lonely lives. And a fitting spot it is, too, for quiet reverie. The mossy sward, close by the water edge, offers a tempting seat. Shut out from all view of human existence, with the gray rocks rising around you, and beyond, above their summits, the tops of the everlasting hills, with the many voices of the waters darting first impetuously over their opposing bulwarks, in hoarse angry tone, then murmuring in the pool beneath—now again in livelier melody, dancing over the fretted edges of their slaty bed, as they unweariedly sweep past to the bosom of their great parent, with the graceful fern maintaining hardy life on almost barren crevices in the rocks, waving its leaflets to the melody, the tall foxglove, and the modest primrose looking up from its roots, its beauty unnoticed but by the eye of Heaven, and its sweets unknown, save to the wandering bee—in such a nook one could loiter and muse a summer day.

> " For busy thoughts, the stream flows on
> In foamy agitation,
> And sleeps in many a crystal pool
> For quiet contemplation."

What a different scene was enacted here on a bleak February morning in 1603! The hills were clad with snow, and the biting frosty wind sweeping down the glen, when the war pibroch was heard awakening its echoes, and the wild shout of armed caterans startled the deer from his lair among the heather. The Macgregors and Colquhouns met in deadly feud by the river side, and one of the most sanguinary conflicts on record between two rival clans occurred. For many years previous the Macgregors had been a pro-

scribed clan. Enactments had been passed against them
and commissions obtained "to fersen and assege their housis
and strengthis, raise fyre and use all kind of force and wer-
lyke ingyne" against them. Such commissions put into the
hands of crafty and designing statesmen like Archibald, Earl
of Argyll, were not likely to prove a dead letter. There is
rather reason to suppose that, as Breadalbane and Argyll had
grasped at and secured the lands of this clan in the counties
of Perth and Argyll, and were exposed to the retaliative
wrath of the oppressed, these commissions were obtained for
their own particular benefit. That was not an age of parliamentary commissions, or committees of inquiry into the
proceedings of men in power; and the most lawless and
rapacious deeds might, under slight sanction of authority,
be safely perpetrated in a country so little known as the
Highlands of Scotland. How the feud with the clan Colquhoun originated does not very clearly appear from any
account which has been handed down. It is asserted on the
one hand that the Colquhouns, lending a helping hand to
the strong, were the original aggressors; and on the other,
that the murder of Sir Humphrey Colquhoun in the Castle
of Bannachra, in 1592, had been planned and accomplished
by the Macgregors, in company with the Macfarlanes, and
that this was the foundation of the quarrel. But neither of
these statements rest on any broad basis of fact, and can
only be adopted as probabilities in absence of anything more
tangible. There seems, however, to be good reason for
supposing that, for artful and selfish purposes, the original
quarrel was fomented into such a bitter and relentless hate
as clansmen only could cherish, by Archibald of Argyll.
He was then King's Lieutenant, and something more, in
the government of this country; and the use he made of his

power was, according to good authority, to incite the Macgregors to acts of hostility against his own personal foes. If the declaration of Macgregor of Glenstrae can be believed, and there seems no good reason to doubt it, Argyll seems to have acted the part of a very Judas in his dealings with these and other clans.

The immediate cause of the conflict in Glen Fruin is not easily discoverable. It is more than probable that an outrage of some kind was meditated by the Macgregors, of which the Colquhouns had obtained timely notice, and prepared to meet them. Allister Macgregor, chief of the clan, and his brother John, seem to have been accompanied by about three hundred men ; and probably the number of the Colquhouns was not less. It has been reported at eight hundred ; but this is surely a mistake, for it is hardly credible that the Laird of Luss could have raised such a force. Allister's superior military tactics were manifest in the division of his men into two bodies ; one of which, led by himself occupied the upper part of the glen, while the men under his brother lay concealed near its foot. The clansmen met somewhere in the vicinity of the farm now known as Strone, and for a time the struggle was keen and fierce ; but the Macgregors, long accustomed to the guerilla warfare of these Highland recesses, at length triumphed, and the Colquhouns were driven back. They then fell into the ambush laid by John Macgregor, who seems to have been afterwards slain in the conflict, and were pursued with disastrous slaughter to Rossdhu, a distance of about six miles, and a fearful scene of bloodshed and plunder ensued after the fight. The farm houses and shielings in and near the glen were entered, their inmates cruelly butchered, the houses burned, and the cattle carried off. In the indictment laid against their chief, the cattle are described as six hundred kye and oxen, eight hundred sheep and goats, and fourteen score of horse. There were killed of the Colquhouns about one hundred and forty—in the battle or retreat—while the loss of the Macgregors seems, by all accounts, not to have exceeded a few men.

Tradition assert that the victorious Macgregors, inflamed with victory, wantonly murdered in cold blood some thirty or forty boys, students in the Collegiate Institution at Dumbarton, who had been spectators of the fight. These had been gathered together in a house near Bannachra, and were placed under a guard for protection; but at the close of the day, when the chief of the Macgregors inquired after them, he found that certain of his followers, in the absence of the guard, had butchered the whole of them. There may be some exaggeration in the statement; but the subsequent criminal trial of various of the clan, and their depositions contain allusions which clearly place beyond doubt the fact of some such circumstance having occurred.

The Macgregors returned to their native fastnesses with their booty, where they were welcomed by the plaudits of their clan; but the retributive arm of the law, weak as it then was, soon followed them thither. Sir Alexander Colquhoun appeared before King James VI., at Stirling, followed by a mournful procession of the widows of the slain men, bearing their husbands' bloody plaids and armour. Such a spectacle was not presented in vain before the weak king. It was followed by an act of the Privy Council, advising extermination to the clan, making it even an offence punishable with death to give any of them food or shelter. They were consequently pursued and hunted in every corner, their leaders executed, their possessions destroyed, and their children either put to death, or committed to the tender mercies of some lawless chief, and forbid to bear the name of Macgregor.*

After leaving the chapel, the stream follows a winding irregular course through the glen, till it reaches a point where it is crossed by the road to Luss. Here, and for some distance along its banks, it is densely wooded. On the right-hand side, a little beneath the bridge, stands on a command-

Bannachra Castle.

ing situation the old castle of Bannachra, once possessed by the Colquhouns, and in which Sir Humphrey Colquhoun was

---

* We have been indebted for many of the foregoing particulars, regarding the battle of Glen Fruin, to Irving's History of Dumbartonshire.

murdered under circumstances of peculiar barbarity by some of the Clan M'Farlane. The castle itself is worth a visit; but as it is rather out of the way at present, we only observe that it has been a superior building to the majority of the old keeps in the Highlands. From its situation it commands a magnificent view of Lochlomond, and the country beyond. A more modern mansion, belonging to the Buchanans of Arden, now the property of James Lumsden, Esq., of Arden, has been built beside it, which is now let to the farm tenant. Beneath the castle the river winds picturesquely along till it reaches Dunfin mill, where it falls over a rocky breastwork of considerable height. This is a favourite spot for artists in the summer season; the mill, the waterfall, and the wooded rocks form a very beautiful scene, worthy the pencil of M'Culloch or Donald. In autumn, during flood, the trout may be seen in considerable numbers ascending this fall. It is interesting to witness their patient, persevering effort to overcome the natural barrier to their progress—effort almost invariably crowned with the success it deserves. After taking another curve, the stream runs in an almost straight line to Lochlomond, which receives its waters, after a course of eight or nine miles through varied and beautiful scenery. Alike to botanist, geologist, and naturalist, a visit to Glen Fruin cannot fail to be interesting and profitable, nor less so to the simple rambler, who, in the contemplation of nature, has his thoughts exalted to Him whose handiwork he surveys, who has clothed the earth with beauty, and everywhere teaches us to reverence and love His power, wisdom, and goodness.

The Fruin being the largest stream in the parish, is much frequented by the brethren of the rod in summer. It is a very tempting water, but rarely fulfils the promise of a basket. The trout run small in it, and from the frequency with which it is fished are very shy. Late in the season a number of sea trout find their way into its pools, chiefly in the upper ranges; but seem to be caught only by an initiated few. Salmon do not ascend the stream till very late in the season and then only for a short distance to spawn and retire again to the more congenial waters of the loch. It is now, along with Lochlomond and other tributaries of the loch, under the management of an angling club; but the old fishers to the "manner born," say that protection has not improved it as a fishing stream, although the number of fish may be increased. Probably notoriety has injured it, as it has injured many better things. When it was unprotected it was comparatively little frequented; protection has given it a name, and from the frequency with which it is now fished the fish have become wary and shy. The Luss water, distant a few miles, is well reported of as a superior stream. Small dark coloured flies with teal drake or landrail wing are most suitable for the native trout, and red or yellow for sea trout. The high ranges of both streams are best. The fish become scarcer as you near the foot of the streams.

ROSENEATH

Roseneath Castle.

Is perhaps the favourite spot beyond all others in the neighbourhood for pic-nic parties, and deservedly so, for no other
presents, within the same easy access, so much lovely seclusion and such a variety of shady strolls, and luxurious scenes
of natural beauty. Among its shady paths, and by its pebbly
shores one could loiter unweariedly a summer day. The
stately woods, with their richness of colour, graduating from
the dull, dark yew, to the brown beech, closing in everywhere around ; the evervarying features of the hills, and the

musical restlessness of the waters of the loch, mirroring the unfathomable blue depths and floating clouds of heaven on their bosom; the glimpses of distant scenery through the overarching trees; the plash of the tiny waterfall, and many-voiced songsters among the broom and brush-wood, yield a rich harvest of quiet delight. To one who can appreciate beautiful scenery, and whose mind is susceptible of those influences it is calculated to produce, a stroll through the eastern part of the parish cannot but be both pleasant and profitable. The water here is deep, and the beach shelving rapidly down to it, so that a boat, at almost any stage of the tide, runs high up upon the shore and disembarkation is easily effected. Right before you stands the Castle of Roseneath, a beautiful mansion, belonging to the Duke of Argyll, built of polished freestone, in the Roman Ionic style. It was begun in 1803, and has been gradually advancing towards completion, but parts of the interior are not yet finished. Another castle used to occupy a green knoll nearer the water, but which was destroyed by fire some sixty years since. The design of the modern building, which was furnished by Bononi of London, is very imposing, and the effect is increased by its position. It commands an extensive view of the Gareloch in front on the north, Ardencaple and Helensburgh towards the east, with the surrounding hills as a background. In front, the ground on the immediate vicinity of the castle is laid out as a lawn, interspersed with patches of copse wood and evergreen, stretches down to the beach. It is surrounded on all other sides by woods of great age, through which a variety of walks and drives have been formed with great taste. Campsail Bay, in front of the castle, is one of the most lovely bays on the Clyde. From its sheltered situation it is peculiarly adapted for winter harbourage of numerous cutters and small craft. During the French war it was used as a harbour for a considerable portion of the fleet at one time, and in later times its friendly shelter was sought by her Majesty, for a night during one of her visits to Scotland. From this circumstance it is almost as well known as the Queen's Bay as by its other title. The night and following morning in which her Majesty visited Gareloch were very stormy. It is told of an Helensburgh baker, who had received orders to provide the royal table with bread, that in order to immortalise himself, he baked a great cake worthy of royalty, and intended as an offering to her Majesty; and in the morning, dressed in his best, he accompanied the cake, in charge of two apprentices. But luckless apprentices and unfortunate gift! In ascending the side of the royal yacht one of them stumbled, his hold gave way, and the cake was precipitated into the water, food for fishes instead of royalty. There is not much in the interior of the castle to attract visitors. Inverary, which is the principal seat in Scotland of the Argyll family, contains almost all those relics of a past age interesting to antiquaries and curiosity hunters. In the fire which destroyed the former building, also perished almost all the old furniture, paintings, and ornaments which would otherwise have formed a very valuable collection. Any one curious to examine the house may, however, in absence of the family, easily obtain admittance, and to those who delight in spacious apartments, well appointed in every respect, such a visit will be satisfactory. But on the whole, the gardens and grounds are the chief attractions in connection with the buildings. These are kept in excellent order, and laid out with great taste; and the gardener who is quite an enthusiast in his profession, is most obliging and attentive to visitors. Things are much improved since our first visit years ago. Then there was an air of decay and dilapidation everywhere witnessed. It almost seemed as if decay of the noble house of Argyll, so long prominent both for good and evil in the history of our country, had fallen upon its outskirts. Our old cicerone, a boatman, was perhaps not the most fitting guide that could have been selected to the spot, yet he was an original in his own way. His ideas of the wooded seclusion in the neighbourhood of the castle seemed to be regulated by their adaptation for the unlawful purpose of defrauding her Majesty's revenue, and he was drawn into a narration of various "ploys" and hairbreadth escapes of his younger days connected with the smuggling, and which he seemed to look back upon with a peculiar relish.

The shores of Campsail bay are in some parts rocky, with little natural coves running into them. These are a favourite resort of strollers and such little pleasure parties as in hot summer weather seek a quiet retreat for an hour or two. They are very picturesque, and afford, even in the most boisterous weather, a pleasant shelter. At the extremity of the bay you quit the policies connected with the castle, and emerge on the highway, which runs northward up the Gareloch, and diverges on the left accross the hill to the opposite side of the parish, and nearly at the mouth of Lochlong. The walk up the hill is a very romantic one. The whole distance does not exceed two miles. For about half a mile, before the ascent begins, the road runs through a glen, and passes some picturesque little cottages almost hid among roses and trailing plants of various kinds. One is almost tempted to think if love in a cottage, and love amongst the roses, were ever realized, they might find a fitting abode here, so great is the profusion of these two favourite conditions of Cupid's existence. A little further in advance the traveller passes a Free Church, a neat little building embosomed amongst the trees, and on the hill-side above it stands the manse. A country pastors life, away from the excitement, bustle, and unrest of the city existence, might almost be expected to be fully realized here. The church, however, seems rather awkwardly situated, as it stands neither in the village of Roseneath, nor near enough to the modern villages of Kilcreggan and Cove to be easily accessible on a wet Sabbath, and on a summer day so far distant that the walk may be supposed to excite the soporific tendencies of the congregation. The hill, once ascended, the view that breaks upon the eye is very grand. On the one side is the Gareloch, on the other the Firth of Clyde, with many smiling little villages along its shores, screened behind by high ranges of hills, behind which the blue peak of Goatfell towers up to the clouds. At all times studded with steamers and sailing vessels of every kind, the Firth presents an animated and busy appearance, and the distant white feather of the locomotive suggests that unwearying human industry whose wealth and energies have reclaimed all these coasts from a rude wilderness, and impressed them with the evidences of taste and comfort. Almost immediately at the base of the hill stands the modern village of Kilcreggan, which has sprung into existence during the past six years and about a mile further west, and nearly opposite Lochlong, the kindred village of Cove. In both of these, villas are built in good taste, with considerable pretensions to architectural design, and the gardens and lawns are neatly laid out. The feus are held from the Duke of Argyll at much more reasonable terms than at many of the neighbouring watering-places. The villages are not likely to increase much in size, however, unless his Grace gives off ground for building further east, as much of the available ground near the water is already occupied. The road runs in front of these villas and along the shores of Lochlong towards Arrochar. As the parish of Roseneath is not very extensive—stretching little more than seven miles from east to west, and from one to four miles broad—the pedestrian may easily survey the whole of it in one day, by keeping along the road till he reaches Peaton, the estate of J. D. Campbell, Esq., or onwards to Portincaple, whence there is a road across the hill which brings him again close upon the Gareloch and joins the road leading from Roseneath Bay to the loch, near Rahane Mill. Continuing his walk down the loch, the pedestrian passes Barreman House, the property of R. C. Cumming, Esq., who is also proprietor of a considerable part of the land on this side of the parish. On his grounds a number of very handsome houses have been built, and till the more recent villages started on the Lochlong shore, they were a favourite resort, being, in fact, the only summer quarters for the visitors in the parish. To one great drawback, however, the houses are liable on this side of the Gareloch, and that is, they occupy a northerly position,

"And the spring comes slowly up this way."

The high screen of hills behind the houses must also have considerable influence in shortening the summer day. On Barreman there is an excellent slate quarry, which was worked for several years past by an enterprising firm in Glasgow. It appears to be a continuation of the seam which has for long been quarried at Luss. It breaks out in the range of hills at the head of Glen Fruin, where there are traces of old workings, appears again above Row, and in

the same line at Roseneath. The slate is slightly darker in
colour than that found at Luss quarries, but seems nothing
inferior in quality. The lands of Barreman terminate a
little to the west of Roseneath Ferry, where the Argyll
property on this side of the parish commences. Opposite
the ferry the loch narrows from about a mile and a half to
little more than three hundred yards, a long neck or point
running out from Row far into its waters. At ebb or flood-
tide, the rush of the stream here is very great, and if any
wind is blowing, its waters at times boil and beat furiously.
A pier has been erected at the ferry for the accommodation
of steamers, at which they can land their passengers in all
weathers. A small tax, but which must amount to a very
handsome rent in the course of the year, is exacted by his
Grace from passengers landing or embarking. A little
above the Ferry-house stands Clachan House, belonging to
the Argyll family. There is here an avenue of yew trees
leading from the house to the old church, believed to have
been planted in the time of Charles II. These, along with
two immense silver firs in the woods at Campsail—supposed
to be the first of their species planted in Scotland—are the
chief sylvan glories of the parish, and amply worth a visit.
Passing up from the ferry, the parish church, a neat little
building in the early English style, strikes the eye. It was
erected in 1853-4 from a design by D. Cousin, Esq., of Edinburgh, and originally consisted simply of nave and chancel,
but in 1862 another aisle accommodating 130 sitters was
added—making the whole number 500. In the chancel are
the pulpit, communion table, and font—the latter a gift to
the church. The space on the wall of the chancel below the
window is filled by a large illuminated table of the com-
mandments drawn and coloured from mediæval designs by

W. A. Muirhead, Esq., Edinburgh, and to the left a smaller of the Lord's prayer—both gifts from the artist. To the right is a monument in Ayrshire stone and white marble, containing a medallion by Wm. Brodie, Esq., R.S,A., dedicated by his parishioners and friends to the revered memory of the late Robert Story, minister of Roseneath, whose pastorate of forty-two years closed in 1859. In the neigh-

Roseneath Church.

bourhood of it is Roseneath village or clachan—immortalised by Sir Walter Scott. It probably has not increased since the times of Jeanie Deans, and consists of less than a score of little low-roofed cottages, occupied by a primitive and contented population, who hold themselves secure under the shadow of the great MacCallum More's wing.

The old parish church stood nearer the clachan than the present one. It was a plain old building, as may still be seen,—old enough to be associated with the labours of Reuben Butler, and valuable, as affording building spaces among its timbers to hordes of swallows and bats. On a very wet day the congregregation we are told, had to select their seats with a view to avoid the drip from the ceiling, and the necessity of an umbrella over the precentor's head often suggested itself to strangers. This state of things, has, however, happily passed away, and the congregation now worship in comfort in any kind of weather. For some time prior to the beginning of the thirteenth century, the church was a free parsonage, and under patronage of the Earl of Lennox; but about this time it was given to the monks of Paisley in perpetual alms, and continued as one of their curacies till the Reformation. At removal of part of the last church, the bell was found to bear an inscription in Latin to the effect that it had been made in Holland early in the seventeenth century. It is suspended in the new building, and has a wonderfully musical tongue to have wagged so long. As in most other romantic spots on the borders of the Scottish Lowlands, tradition associates Roseneath with blind Harry and Sir William Wallace, and near the castle there is pointed out to the credulous a rock called Wallace's leap. These traditions doubtless invest the spot with some degree of interest, however much our sober judgment may feel disposed to reject them. There is probably more truth in the story of several of the persecuted Covenanters having found shelter and protection from Argyll here in times of hardship and trial, and till a recent date it is said certain descendants of the renowned Balfour of Burley were found living in the neighbourhood.

F

One peculiarity connected with the parish is deserving of notice and of the attention of naturalists. A writer in the old statistical account of Scotland says:—" Here rats cannot exist; many of these have at different times been accidentally imported from vessels lying upon the shore, but were never known to live twelve months in the place. From a prevailing opinion that the soil of this place is hostile to that animal, some years ago a West India planter actually carried out to Jamaica several casks of Roseneath earth, with a view to kill the rats that were destroying his sugar-canes. It is said this had not the desired effect: so we lost a very valuable export. Had the experiment succeeded, this would have been a new and valuable trade for the proprietors; but perhaps by this time the parish of Roseneath might have been no more." How far the existence of animal life in this form is still unknown in this parish, the present writer is unable to determine; but if it is singular in this exemption, it is also singular in another—the absence of such a thing as a public-house. Although there is an inn at Roseneath Ferry, and a temperance hotel at Kilcreggan, both much frequented, there is not an inn, lodging-house, or shop, in the parish where a single lawful glass of whisky can be obtained—no great deprivation, probably, to any one, but an illustration at home of the possibility of a pretty large and populous parish thriving under the Maine liquor rule, which the advocates of temperance seem to have altogether forgotten. This has been the case now for some time, and we suppose as long as his Grace the present Duke of Argyll, continues to rule on his own lands, it will remain so. There have been a few celebrated men born in this parish, amongst whom we may notice the mathematician, Matthew Stewart, father of the distinguished philosopher, Dugald

Stewart, and Dr. Anderson, the founder of the Andersonian University, Glasgow. Both Dugald Stewart and Dr. Anderson were children of parish ministers of Roseneath, and they are still referred to with no little pride by the older inhabitants, as samples of what the parish could produce. Besides the parish church, of which the Rev. Robert Herbert Story, ordained in 1859, is minister, there is the Free Church already mentioned—Rev. J. M'Ewan, minister; Craigrownie Chapel, in connexion with the Establishment, erected to meet the wants of the population of Cove, Kilcreggan, and Craigrownie—Rev. David Shanks, minister; and a wooden building erected by the United Presbyterian body near Kilcreggan, in which the Rev. Joseph Corbett is pastor. The population of the parish, according to last census, was 1600. The resident Justices of the Peace are R. C. Cumming, Esq., Baremann, and Alexander Abercromby, Esq. of Craigrownie Castle.

COVE AND KILCREGGAN.

Middle aged readers will remember Kilcreggan Ferry house, with its thatched roof and whitewashed gables standing by the pleasant little bay, sheltered by the grassy knowe behind and projecting headlands on each side. Many of them will remember it with kindly feelings as the goal of boyish rambles from Gourock and Helensburgh, during summer holidays, where homely oat cakes and bowls of fresh milk—and such milk it was, rich and fragant as nectar—were always to be had from the good wife, who had a special regard for the whole race of boys. Even ripe gooseberries and the more luscious strawberries and cream were not awanting in their season. How the elders of the party fared, when there were elders amongst them, we care not to enquire, but for boyhood, no better baiting place than the old ferry existed, and no pleasanter ramble than up the hill to the little clachan, or by the sea shore to examine the salmon nets and hunt for nests among the broom. These days have passed away. The ferry house still stands, the thatched farm steading is still there, but the delightful privacy, the primitive hospitality, the joyous sense of freedom from all constraint or possible interference are gone. Modern civilization has placed its fetters on the Arcadian freedom of the spot. The road maker, the builder, the gardener, and worse than all, the Police Act has been abroad, and there is no lodge in the wilderness with any contiguity of shade left, no more wandering at sweet will by the solitudes of the sea shore, possible to the wayfarer.

Cove and Kilcreggan though two distinct villages are classed together. They are embraced as one police district under the provisions of the General Police Act, and very soon will form one continuous line of villas and gardens. Standing on the south-western part of the peninsula of Rose-neath they have an admirable exposure—are warm, dry, and healthy places of resort, and possess facilities for sea bathing which no other place so near Glasgow enjoys. If only a little of the attention were given to the convenience and comfort of sea bathers, which exist so abundantly in our English and foreign watering places, by the employment of bathing machines and placing them under proper regulation, Kilcreggan and Cove might become the most fashionable resort on the Clyde. But the Scotch mind is slow to appropriate ideas foreign to the groove in which ancestral practice has worked, and the growth of a watering place unfortunately brings no increase of comfort or convenience.

The estate of Roseneath, on which these villages are built, it is almost needless to say, belongs to the Duke of Argyll. The lands were offered to feu about the year 1848, and since then the places may be said to have sprung into existence. A pier was erected at Kilcreggan in 1850, and one at Cove in 1852. There are two churches. The Established at Craigrownie, pleasantly situated on the hill side, and built in 1853, and the United Presbyterian, a wooden erection, put up in 1858. A new stone building, to supersede this wooden house, is now being erected.

The principal drives are to Roseneath village, four miles distant through a beautifully wooded dale ; to Coulport, five miles distant by the shores of Lochlong, and round the parish by Rahane and Peaton about twelve miles.

There is not much in the neighbourhood to interest the antiquarian. Tradition points to Balfour of Burley having made it his retreat after the defeat of the Covenanters at Bothwell Brig, and his descendants are said still, or lately, to have been found *living* in the parish. Scott's " Knockdunder Tower," immortalised in the *Heart of Midlothian*, stood somewhere on the west extremity of the now conjoined Burgh, and the site is said to be occupied by a wooden house. Celtic arms, cists, human remains, and ancient coins have in recent times been discovered in various parts of the district, but not to any great extent.

LUSS.

A pretty stiff ascent of about a mile, and you are over
the summit of the Black Hill, looking down on Helensburgh, up at the heavens, or straight forward across a
moor, through which the road winds onwards to Lochlomond. If the day is hot, you long to keep company with
the herd of black cattle standing knee-deep in the pond, or
the sheep sheltered beneath the long heather; for the sun
pours down mercilessly on your shelterless head, and glows
on you as only on the moor the sun can glow and burn.
But if the wind stirs from any point of the compass, you
gratefully feel it here. Even when the firth below is calm
and unruffled, and the white gull "floats double" on its
bosom, the bog cotton is nodding its head, and the tall
grasses rustling their spears together to the passing zephyr,
on this high table-land. By the time you have reached the
summit of the ascent, you are fain to rest and look before
you, unless bent on a more lengthened walk. The blue
heavens are overhead, the purple heath beneath, and everywhere around you, the distant Grampian range in front,
with a little peep of Lochlomond, like a glittering stone,
shining somewhere between the wooded knolls below you;
the air made musical with unnumbered songs, from the chirp
of the grasshopper at your side to the wail of the circling
plover above you. How pleasant to rest and feel the glow of
life and beauty that flows from God's works, and seems to fill,
and purify as it fills, the thirsting soul! A broken moor,
flanked by hills, and embracing the valley of the Fruin,
stretches from this point away down to the shores of Lochlomond, some five miles distant. Very much the same aspect

must this unreclaimed bog and meadow have borne long centuries ago, when the tourists who frequented it were not
young ladies botanising, or young gentlemen rambling with
kit or creel but kilted caterans of the clans, who loved
nature best when in her darkest moods, and the road best
when the stocking of a Sassenach byre was marching on
before them.

Past a clump of wood, past corn fields, then out into more
waste moor, dotted over with little stacks of peat, with the
peewit wheeling in the air, and the snipe starting from the
ditch at your feet; past low-lying, sheltered farm homesteads, that the winter wind, as it howls down the glen,
never in its maddest fury reaches—where bee-hives are
planted thickly in the garden, and the honeysuckle climbs
about the door, and the collie basks sleepily in the porch;
past a dark shady glen, the haunt of the roe-deer and rabbit,
in whose recesses the pigeon chants its mournful song—

> " Where the denser grove receives
> No sunlight from above ;
> But the dark foliage interweaves
> In one unbroken roof of leaves,
> Underneath whose sloping eaves
> The shadows hardly move."

Past a sparkling stream, making melody to the wild flowers
and woods, as it dances and leaps on its way to the lake
beneath ; past another ascent, up a little hill, not so difficult
or so long as the first, with a high primrose-covered bank on
each side, and then suddenly before you stretches out a
noble prospect. The lower waters of the loch are seen, and
a wide range of hill and dale, meadow and moor, are spread
out before you,—such a view as the eye cannot take in at a
glance, but return to again and again, gathering fresh pleasures at each fresh discovery of its beauties, till the gazer

is tempted to give utterance to the feelings awakened, in words of deepest and delighted wonder.

A long low wall, clad in many places with patches of maidenhair fern, and others, which encloses the policies of Rossdhu, now prevents the pedestrian, for some time from seeing much that is interesting, continuing for above a mile, and then Lochlomond is seen in its beauty and grandeur, with the island of Inchtavannach opposite. It bursts upon you at once; you breathe the fresh atmosphere of liberty; your eyes dwell upon a vision of loveliness, and you draw a long involuntary inspiration of delight. You have been wondering for half an hour past, how it looked on close approach, and vainly conjecturing the beauties that might be visible were you on the other side of that endless wall; but now, all this is forgotten, and you revel in the unexpected panorama of slyvan and romantic beauty that lies before you.

> " A dewy freshness fills the silent air;
> No mist obscures, nor cloud, nor speck, nor stain
> Breaks the serene of heaven."

The islands, and their o'erhanging woods, seem to sleep upon the tranquil waters, whose stainless bosom reflects their beauties, and mirrors the blue sky, and each broken white cloud, on its placid depths. Each step reveals new features, and brings to light new points in the landscape, more lovely, if possible, where all is lovely. With slackened pace and enraptured sight, the spectator leisurely lingers, and notes every fresh object of interest that the windings of the road reveals to him. "The courting-tree," a wide-spreading and densely leaved monarch of the wood, familiar in the dreams of Luss lads and lasses for many generations, attracts attention to it itself as you pass, and little glimpses of the lake and mountains obtained through long tunnels of interweaving branches, stereoscopic in minute beauties and effects, arrest your steps at almost every turn. Less than half an hour brings you to the old village of Luss, situated almost on the banks of the loch, and picturesque from its position and age. It is a little cluster of cottages and gardens, amongst which several modern cottages have, of late years, been erected by Sir James Colquhoun, much superior in appearance and comfort to the houses of the old village. Luss contains one inn, at a little distance from the village, a respectable and commodious house, and favourite resort of anglers and tourists, and worthy of more patronage than it receives, commanding a lovely and uninterrupted view of its islands and opposite shores, with the dark shadow of Benlomond, like a giant, rising almost in front. The parish church stands a little to the right, embowered among trees, a plain building, about a century old; but, judging from the dates of the tombstones in the churchyard, erected near the site of an older church. In summer, when the neighbourhood is thronged with visitors, it is found rather small for the accommodation of the worshippers, but otherwise sufficiently large. Its appearance is in keeping with the locality. It is almost impossible to conceive a finer situation for a rural church. On the confines of the Luss water, and partly surrounded by lofty trees—overlooking, from its eminences, the village, and overlooking the lake, hoary with age, and hallowed by the memory of past generations of worshippers, whose dust lies mingled around its walls, it forms one of the best remembered features of the scene.

The tourist to Luss should not neglect obtaining two of the best views of Lochlomond and its scenery that can be had. One of these is from the rising ground on the opposite

island of Inchtavannach; the other, from Stonehill, behind
the village.   Both are within easy access; and from either
point, on a clear summer day, a landscape spreads out before
the eye which scarcely any parallel can be found to in the
scenery of earth's fairest gardens, and which will leave its
impress upon the memory ·of the spectator through coming
years.   If you wish to see the lake properly, and form a
thorough idea of the many glimpses of fairy land to be
obtained amongst its islands and creeks, take a small boat at
Luss, and row through the passages behind the islands opposite.   If you wish a more extensive view, and one which, in
our opinion, is not equalled by the far-famed prospect from
the top of the mighty Ben itself, ascend the hill behind For-
kin toll, a few miles above Luss.   There, after half an hour's
climb, you will reach a hill lochan, or tarn, called the
Fairy's lake, the waters of which seem, in particular lights,
to glow with all the prismatic colours of the rainbow, and
in which, in olden times, the good-wives dipped their yarn
over-night, and found it dyed the desired hue in the morning.   Look back now towards the loch, and your eyes will
be feasted with a vision of loveliness scarcely equalled in
Scotland.   Luss, like almost every old parish of note, had,
in former days, its tutelary saint—one St. Keasog, who is
said to have suffered martyrdom in the sixth century.   History and tradition seem alike silent in regard to his life;
for, so far as we can learn, none of his deeds have survived
the lapse of years since his decease.   His memory is perpet-
uated by the remains of a large cairn of stones in the neighbourhood—the place of his reputed burial—called Cairn-na-
Cheasoig, and a stone effigy dug out of the assumed ruins
of this chapel, which is now removed, and carefully preserved
by the lord of the manor, who takes a deep interest in the

memorials of the past history of the parish. During the thirteenth century Haco, of Norway, better known than the tutelary saint, ravaged the islands of Lochlomond and Luss and put most of the Celtic inhabitants to death. Probably then these islands were inhabited by numbers of savage free-booting Highlanders, who found in them protection and comparative immunity from danger, till the undaunted Norwegians rooted them out. Since that time they have been tenanted chiefly by deer and game. The two largest of them, Inchmurrin and Inchtavannach, each of them extending upwards of a mile in length, and several of the smaller ones—such as Inchlonaig and Inchfad—would be capable of supporting several parishes. They are generally fertile, and, if cultivated, would yield luxuriant crops; but then their sylvan beauty would be lost, and that romantic attraction which they possess, arising, as it does, to a considerable extent from their natural luxuriousness, would be lost for ever. The most utilitarian spirit of this age could hardly desire to see them clothed with corn instead of the dark yew, the oak, heath, and fern, or trimmed into grassy slopes, pasturing sheep in place of the timid deer and rabbit. The Colquhouns acquired the lands of Luss, and certain of the islands from the Lennox family, in the fourteenth century and have since retained them, adding to the original estates many other properties on the shores of Lochlomond, and adjacent to it, and at this date, the present Sir James Colquhoun, is one of the most extensive landholders in Scotland; many parts of his estates are daily increasing in value to an extent which, half a century since, would have been deemed fabulous. Rossdhu House, the beautiful residence of the Colquhoun family, stands close by the shore of the loch about a mile below Luss. An older castle stood here, part of the ruins of which are still preserved, and lend considerable attractions to the view. One of the finest views of Lochlomond and the Ben, not so extensive as those alluded to, but, if possible more lovely, is obtainable from Rossdhu Bay. The Colquhoun family trace decent from a younger son of the old Earls of Lennox, who is said to have obtained a grant of the lands and barony of Colquhoun for military service, in the reign of Alexander II., in 1230-50. The names of the descendants of the first Colquhoun appear in a succession of charters from that period down to 1465 ; shortly after which, Sir John Colquhoun, one of the most distinguished men of his age, obtained a grant of the lands of Kilmardinny, Roseneath, Strone, &c. Subsequent history connects the representative heads of the family with various feuds of the M'Farlanes and M'Gregors. These turbulent clans were at last, however, subdued, and ample compensation given to the Colquhouns for the injuries they had sustained by repeated plunderings and oppressions they had been the victims of. There have been many very distinguished men in the long succession traceable downwards of this family, which occupies a prominent and honourable position in Scottish history.

A little steamer, with holiday crowd on board, comes gliding across the lake— a white puff and a roar from the steampipe, a little bustle on deck, and it is moored to the pier at the end of the village; the bell rings. Fellow-traveller, who has rambled about so long with us, if as pleasantly to thee hitherto as to us, we rejoice—wilt shake hands, and step on board? We could gladly accompany thee, but our holiday is ended, and our gossip must cease ; and as the moorings are loosened, and the pilot takes his stand at the wheel, with one last wave of the hand we bid you farewell.

EXCURSIONS.

It has often been asked, What short excursions from Helensburgh are within the compass of a day, and how can they be managed? Probably the best reply to the question is to hand the inquirer a railway time-table; but even this contains information only for those who know where to seek it, we may mention two or three routes which may be selected by the visitor. By taking the early steamer to Greenock, Rothesay and the Kyles of Bute can be visited, and return home effected in the evening of the same day. By the same steamer to Greenock, Lochgoilhead, Ardentinny or Arrochar may be gained, and at the latter, the tourist may return by Lochlomond to Balloch, and thence home by rail. By early train to Balloch, Lochlomond and its various points of interest may be seen and explored, and return effected in the evening. If, however, a visit to Benlomond is intended, the tourist should start in the afternoon to Balloch, take steamer to Rowardennan, and remain there over night, ascending the mountain before dawn, or he may proceed by Luss and take a small boat across the loch to Rowardennan on the opposite shore and return the same day. The view from Benlomond height at dawn is a thing never to be forgotten—seen later in the day, half its glories are lost. A pleasant excursion may also be made to Stirling by the Forth and Clyde Railway, allowing ample time to inspect this old Scottish town and return; or the Lake of Menteith, or any of the interesting spots on the line of this railway may be visited in the same way. Loch Katrine, by way of Lochlomond and part of the Trossachs, may also be been within the compass of the day; but it is doing injustice

to the noble scenery there to hurry through it in such a
fashion. For the sketcher, who does not object to walk a
mile or two, the Glens of Luss, Douglas, and Falloch are all
accessible and worthy of a visit. They should be explored
from the foot upwards. The highlands in the neighbourhood are thus almost all accessible within the compass of a
day. As for the more immediate walks and drives, these
have been sufficiently discussed.

SKETCH OF THE GEOLOGY OF THE DISTRICT.

BY A MEMBER OF THE GLASGOW GEOLOGICAL SOCIETY.

The western and north-western tracts of the county are
composed of rocks that belong to the Silurian system, and
are supposed to be equivalents of the fossiliferous Silurian
rocks of the south of Scotland, and which exist in the north-
west Highlands in a much higher crystalline or metamorphosed condition than they are found in the southern tracts
of this country. The principal varieties of these old crystalline stratified rocks, found in this county, are rocks of a
gneissage structure, passing into mica, chorite, talc, and
clay slates, and which are sometimes associated with beds of
quartz rock and crystalline limestone. These rocks often
rise into hills of considerable altitude, and form the highest
points of elevation in this part of the country. Their
rugged peaks, wild radines, and coast sections, impress their
features on the scenery over nearly every part of the west
Highlands. They are often pierced or cut through by veins

or dikes of felstone porphyry and other intrusive igneous rocks, and in many parts of the district, (especially about Luss), the schistoze rocks are very much contorted and twisted. Crystals of quartz and other siliceous minerals, besides metallic ores, are occasionally found in this group of rocks. But no organic remains have yet been found; their absence is attributed to the highly metamorphosed condition of the rocks. If any organic remains originally existed in them, they seem all to have been destroyed. The red sandstone of this country forms part of that belt of old red sandstone which stretches across Scotland from sea to sea, along the whole front of the Grampians, and rests unconformably upon the older crystalline schists already noticed. It forms the whole of the rock along the coast between Helensburgh and Dumbarton, and also forms the tract of land which stretches up the valley of the Leven, the islands in the lower reaches of Lochlomond being also composed of it. Its prevailing colour is bright red, and it affords a good durable building stone in many localities. It belongs to what is termed the middle division of the old red sandstone, and in the west of Scotland it has yielded as yet few recognisable organic remains.

Resting conformable upon the old red sandstone, there occurs near Dumbarton, on the east side of the valley of Leven, an interesting group of thin bedded rocks, known to geologists as the Levenside limestones; they are composed of thin bands of nodular limestones, interstratified with a dark gray marly shale, which crumbles down rapidly on exposure to the weather. This formation is capped by beds of white coloured sandstone, which is overlaid by the trap rock which forms the higher parts of the Kilpatrick hills. The best sections of these thin bedded rocks are to be seen in Auchenreoch glen, on the Levenside grounds, where they form very lofty eminences on each side of the glen, and present to the geologist some of the finest veins of stratification to be seen in this country side. The strata is traversed by several intrusive dykes of greenstone and felstone, which being harder then the surrounding beds, often stand up as natural walls across the glen. Between partings of the strata are to be found, at one or two points, some thin veins of a fine, white, crystallised gypsum, from which fine specimens are to be obtained. The limestones seem never to have been worked for any economic purposes, and the only organtic remains yet found in these beds are some obscure fragments of plants and *scales of fishes*, which occur in one of the gray sandstones near the base of the group. At present these beds are disputed among geologists, as to whether they belong to the |upper old red sandstones or to the lower coal series, fossil evidence being wanted to enable them to be linked to either group. The rocks which form the eastern part of the county of Dumbarton, belong to the Carboniferous system. The long ridge of the Kilpatrick hills bounds the coal-field to the north. This group of trappean heights, which terminate in *Dumbarton Castle rock*, and and the heights above Bowling, belong to that chain of trap hills of volcanic origin which run across Scotland from Ardrossan on the south-west to near Montrose on the northeast. The Kilpatrick division of the range has long been famous among mineralogists for the fine series of zoolitic minerals found in veins, &c., of the rocks. In the Bowling quarry and the rocks of the Long Craigs, very fine specimens of Prehnite, Thomsonite, Stilbite, Newlandite, and other minerals of the same group are to be found, and are much sought after by collectors. The features impressed by these trap hills upon the surrounding scenery are often very fine, and in few localities do they lend such a charm as on the banks of our own noble river in the neighbourhood of Bowling, where the lofty and well-marked terraces of trap set high upon the hill-side are surrounded at their base by the natural watchtowers of Dumbarton and Dumbuck, and other small eminences, the whole imprinting such a charm, on the landscape that, when once seen in all its beauty, is not easily thereafter effaced from the memory.

BOTANY OF HELENSBURGH DISTRICT.

The district around Helensburgh, extending from Bowling Bay to Roseneath, abounds with the commoner plants, including some rare species. At Bowling, Turritis glabra occurs, along with the rare moss, Glyphomitrium Daviesii, found in 1842 and 1863. On Dumbarton Castle rock the following plants abound :—Smyrnium olusatrum, Carduus marianus, Malva sylvestris, M. moschata, Conium macula-tum, Carex muricata, Poa maritima. Along the banks of the Clyde, Mimulus luteus is of frequent occurrence; it is a native of Chili, and has become naturalised within the last twenty years in different parts in Scotland. The most characteristic plant in the neighbourhood of Helensburgh, and on the banks of Gareloch, especially at the upper extremity, near Fernycarry, is Bartsia (Trixago) viscosa, a rare species in other parts of the country, but remarkably abundant here. Senecio saracenicus has been observed at the east end of Helensburgh, but was probably an escape from a garden. It has long been known to occupy a spot at Bothwell Bridge. Carum verticillatum, a rare plant in England, is common in the moist pastures and salt marshes from Bowling to Helens-

G

burgh. Lythrum salicaria grows in profusion in the marshes in the neighbourhood. Epilobium hirsutum is found in the vicinity of Helensburgh ; Valeriana Pyrenaica on the sides of a stream in the Roseneath woods ; Trollius Europæus at Garelochhead; Convolvulus sepium on the shores of the loch; Sedum anglicum and S. acre on Dumbuck and in many other places, and S. Telephium is not unfrequent ; Saxifraga aizoides beside the upland streams, as at Glen Fruin; Solanum Dulcamara in the hedges west of Helensburgh ; Linum catharticum in all the fields. Amongst other species more or less frequent are the following:—

Anemone nemorosa
Corydalis claviculata
Arabis hirsuta
Cardamine amara
Cochlearia officinalis
Draba verna
Lepidium Smithii
Parnassia palustris
Silene maritima
Stellaria Holostea
Hypericum Androsæmum
———— humifusum
———— perforatum
———— pulchrum
———— quadrangulum
Geranium pratense
Oxalis acetosella
Prunus communis (spinosa)
Vicia hirsuta
Rubus saxatilis
Circæa alpina
———— Lutetiana
Montia fontana
Chrysospenium alternifolium
———————— oppositifolium
Daucus carota
Œnanthe crocata
Sanicula Europæa
Adoxa moschatellina
Lonicera Periclymenum
Aster Tripolium
Eupatorium cannabinum

Sonchus oleraceus
Vaccinium Myrtillus
———— Vitis-Idæa
———— Oxycoccos
Gentiana campestris
Anchusa sempervirens
Melampyrum pratense
Veronica anagallis
———— scutellata
Galeopsis Tetrahit
———— versicolor
Lycopus Europæus
Scutellaria galericulata
Pinguicula vulgaris
Anagallis arvensis
———— tenella
Glaux maritima
Lysimachia nemorum
Plantago maritima
Chenopodium album
Salsola Kali
Epipactis latifolia
Gymnadenia conopsea
Habenaria viridis
Orchis latifolia
———— maculata
———— mascula
Agraphis nutans
Triglochin maritimum
———— palustre
Zostera marina

In Ardenconnel Glen, Hymenophyllum Wilsoni occurs amongst the ferns, the commoner species of which are abundant in the woods and valleys, viz. :—

Asplenium Adiantum nigrum	Lastrea dilatata
———— Trichomanes	Polypodium vulgara
———— Filix-fœmina	———— Phlegopteris
Blechnum boreale	———— Dryopteris
Cystopteris fragilis	Polystichum lobatum
Lastrea Filix-mas	Scolopendrium vulgare
——— Oroeopteris	

The two silver firs in Roseneath woods are interesting botanical objects, each measuring about nineteen feet in circumference. The Robinia Pseudo-acacia thrives indifferently in most parts of Scotland, but accommodates itself to the climate of this neighbourhood, where it flowers. The Wellingtonia gigantea (the mammoth tree of California) is also hardy in this quarter. As a proof of the mildness of the climate, it may be mentioned that in the memorable frost of December, 1860--the most severe experienced in the present century—the Arancarius, Deodars, the Laurustinus, the Rhododendrous, and Laurels remained uninjured, although without protection, when plants of the same description perished almost universally in the upper parts of the Clyde valley, and in the interior of the country generally.

NOTES ON MOSSES AND LICHENS, (BY A CORRESPONDENT.)

Those who are fond of collecting mosses and lichens will find not only a wide field in the district, but will, in the course of their researches, meet with many specimens of a rare and superior order, such as—

Glyphomitrum Daviesii	Dydymodon flexuosus
Buxbaumia aphylla	Aulacomnium palustre
Orthotrichum rupestre	Spagnum recurvum.
Hypnum stramineum (cum fruit)	

These are all rare and very interesting species. The Glyphomitrium aphylla grows on Trapean rocks. The Buxbaumia aphylla has never been obtained, we believe, near Bowling since Lyon's time ; and to our young lady collectors we may say generally, that they can fill their books, if they please with

The beautiful feather mosses	The hair moss
The bog mosses	The shining moss Hookeria
The fork mosses	The silky Lubia, &c., &c.

In "Lichens" there are many species, and possibly you may find on rocks or stones—

The Romalina scapulorum
The Petsidea Palydactile
The Gyrophora Probarcida
The Romalina farinacea, &c., on trees
The Gladonia furcata, &c.. on walls.

In regard to interesting ferns, and particularly the Osmunda Regalis, or royal flowering fern, which has been so greatly in demand as to occasion its extirpation in many places along the Clyde coast. If our young friends, however, will only travel as far as Lochranza, Arran, they will find plenty of them under the rocks as you enter by the steamer on the left hand side, from two or three inches to three or four feet in height. They are also being cultivated in some of the gardens at Helensburgh in great perfection.

ZOOLOGY OF THE DISTRICT.

The range of quadrupeds is comparatively limited, embracing only those common throughout the Highlands of Scotland, and no variety is abundant. The fox, badger, and polecat—found in considerable numbers some fifty years ago —are rapidly disappearing through the energetic efforts of the numerous gamekeepers, who wage a ceaseless war of extermination against them, and what is more to be deplored, against the rare and beautiful birds of prey, hawks, falcons, jays, kites and owls, once frequently to be met with. In a few years these will only have a traditionary existence. They will be exterminated to make room for larger families of grouse and partridge.

Of smaller birds there is considerable variety. The woods, moors, sea shore, marshes, and fresh water lakes, each exhibit their peculiar tribes in more or less abundance.

Of the owl family three varieties are at least frequently to be found—the short-eared, the white, and tawny owl. The first frequents the neighbourhood of Lochlomond. The other two are seen and heard occasionally in Ardencaple woods, Rossdhu policies, and amongst the plantations bordering Glen Fruin and Luss Glen.

Of smaller birds the curlew is abundant on the hills in summer, and in flocks on the sea shore in winter. The golden plover, the ringed plover, and red shank, also breed on the hills above Helensburgh and Lochlomond, and gather in flocks on the sea shore in winter. In time of snow particularly, great numbers of the golden plover are observed seeking a resting place and food, where the ebb tide has left

the sea beach bare. Woodcock and snipe are at times abundant, and are said to breed frequently on the islands or in
the neighbourhood of Lochlomond. By the pools on the
Luss and upper reaches of the Fruin, and other tributaries
of Lochlomond, the wild duck, teal, coot, and moor hen
breed. On the Loch, and on the waters of the Frith opposite Cardross, flocks of these ducks congregate in winter, and
along with them specimens of the pochard and golden eye,
and other more rare varieties are frequently found, as also
large groups of Barnacle which arrive later than the others,
and do not leave for their remote breeding places till the
month of April. The island of Inch Moan on Lochlomond, is
a favourite breeding place for a variety of gulls, ducks, and
aquatic birds, and for several months of the year is largely
colonised by them. In and around Helensburgh, black-
birds, thrushes, chaffinches, robins, and various tits are very
common, and wherever there is a house with empty chim-
neys or crevices in the eaves the starling is certain to take
up his abode and discourse noisily from the roof. In the
woods near Bannachra and on Garelochside, there are a good
many bullfinches still exist. They are, however, kept down
by prejudice of gardeners against them, taking the form of
fire-arms whenever opportunity occurs. The goldfinch—that
most beautiful of our songsters, we have frequently seen on
Garelochside, in the neighbourhood of Blairvadick. They
are also met with in Camis-Eskan woods. The grey linnet,
sisken, redpole, wagtail, and chaffinch, are distributed through
the parishes of Row and Luss and breed in various places.

There is a heronry in Roseneath woods, and one or two
in Lochlomond; and in Ardencaple woods and Roseneath
are populous rookeries.

Other birds, occasional visitants of our coast, might be

mentioned, but these the ornithologist will find for himself; and it is probable that many summer and winter varieties of winged visitors from foreign countries might be discovered by the keen eye of a naturalist in pursuit of his favourite study.

PASTIME AND SPORT.

While the district affords a wide field for the research of the botanist and the geologist, there is a class of our readers who seek recreation in other pastimes, and it is only fitting that a word or two should be devoted to their interests.

CRICKET.

Some years since by the munificence of Sir James Colquhoun and several gentlemen resident in Helensburgh, several acres of ground were set apart in the east end of Helensburgh as play-ground. A charter to the land was granted to the magistrates, and it has been enclosed and laid off for cricket, quoits, and kindred games. It is much frequented in the summer season. It is open to all without charge, and the habitual players have formed various clubs, admission to any of which can be obtained on the easiest terms. We have as yet no distinguished cricketers, the game having been but recently introduced; but the enthusiasm and zeal with which it is followed encourages a hope that a year or two hence some of the players will be able to distinguish themselves in friendly competition with older clubs.

BOWLS.

The want of a good bowling-green was long a drawback to the cultivation of social and friendly intercourse amongst the gentlemen of the neighbourhood, which only the public news-room partially prevented total extinction of. By the indefatigable efforts of ex-Provost Drysdale and a few others a grant of land was obtained, and at a very great expense three admirable greens were formed. They are under the management of a club formed of subscribers. The greens are situated adjacent to the Luss Road, on the rising ground, and surrounded by shrubbery, form a favourite promenade in the summer season. To the attraction of the game, bands of instrumental music are sometimes added, when the grounds are frequented by a very animated and gay assemblage of the fair sex.

CURLING.

Nor do the votaries of the "roaring game" lack a field for their wintry sport. There has been a curlers' club, including several crack players, in existence for many years. In very hard frost the mill-dams and Lochlomond itself are in requisition for a rink or two, but the club posseses a good pond adjacent to the public park, which a night's frost generally suffices to produce sufficient surface of ice on to afford a game. For several weeks at a time during winter there is often continuous playing on it. An attempt has been made to secure a suitable spot for a larger sheet of ice for skaters which we hope will prove successful.

SHOOTING.

Game is usually preserved throughout the district, and

consequently it is abundant. The lower grounds contain hares, pheasant, and partridge ; grouse and black game on the hills, and roe-deer in the woods are common. The shootings are to some extent let in the neighbourhood, but most of the proprietors reserve them in their own hands. There is a class of sportsmen, however, who devote their attention to the wild-duck and sea-fowl shooting, for which there is a fair field in the neighbourhood. At the approach of winter, flocks of golden plover, (*Charadrius pluvialis*,) redshank, peewit, sand-piper, curlew, (*Numenius arquata*,) and other birds of the class of waders, leave the hills and collect on the sands about Ardmore and Cardross. Later, the mallard duck, (*Anas boschas*,) widgeon, (*Mareca penelope*,) and teal appear in order, and occasional flocks of barnacle, or brent geese, from their Norwegian homes, alight upon the shores. The ducks and geese feed chiefly during day on the marine grasses with which the long sandbanks are clad, and at night in the adjacent fields. There is also another species of duck, of which vast flocks sometimes appear in very intense frost, the *Harelda glacialis*, black on the back or chocolate-coloured, and the rest of a dusky white or gray. It appears, however, to feed a good deal on fish, and is not esteemed of much culinary value, although probably affording in its pursuit as much sport as the other varieties. Wild geese used to visit the district, but of late years very few of them have been seen. Indeed, within the last twenty or thirty years, there has been a rapid and very decided diminution of the numbers of wild fowls on these shores; and many who earned a comfortable livelihood by shooting them during winter have been obliged to give up their calling. Various causes may contribute to this, but chiefly, we suspect, the increased traffic on the river and shores, and disturbance to which the birds are subjected on their feeding grounds, so that they no longer lead that life of seclusion and quiet here which in other less busy regions it is possible they may enjoy. Still, wild-duck shooting is a common and popular pursuit in the winter months, on this part of the river and amongst its bays. There are numerous parties who earn a livelihood by it. We have heard of one man killing in the course of a winter, ducks to the value of £80; and not uncommonly the proceeds of a season amount to more than half that sum. It is by no means an easy task to obtain a shot at a flight of ducks, and requires a more thorough knowledge of the habits of this wary bird than seems at first necessary. The sportsman must make up his mind to fatigue, cold, and repeated disappointment if he would earn success. There are two methods of following them generally employed, which we will attempt to describe. The first is by sailing boat. A bright day with a smart breeze blowing is preferred. Armed with guns of larger calibre than are generally used on the moor, and using No. 1 shot, or B. B., the sportsman endeavours to manage his boat so as to keep the sun betwixt him and the birds. The lights thus prevents his approach being noticed so early as it would be were it behind him, and a sailing craft glides much more noiselessly and rapidly down upon the object than under oars. If he can get within ninety yards of the flock, success is almost certain. A few outer birds rise first, the others are alarmed and swim rapidly off, turning their heads every way, apparently planning the best mode of escape from danger; suddenly a rustle of a multitude of wings, a rush of water, and the whole are under flight. Now is the moment. Fairly risen from the water, with out-spread pinions, the gunner draws upon them once or twice,

as their distance may admit, and a successful shot shows
half a dozen of them dropping with a helpless flap into their
native element. The slain are immediately picked up and
chase given to those only wounded, who oftentimes are difficult to recover, and afford a long hunt before all are captured. If not carefully watched from the very first, they
disperse about by swimming and diving in various directions,
and the pursuit soon becomes utterly hopeless. Few things
require more careful watching than a wounded duck in the
water.

The other, and perhaps more successful, mode of duck-
shooting is followed by moonlight, at low tide, upon those
banks where the birds feed. When the moon is full, or
nearly so, with a gray sky overheard the sport may be pursued with some prospect of success, varying, of course, according to the knowledge and practice of the shooter. A
blue sky is quite unsuitable, as, however near the birds may
be, you cannot see them with the distinctness necessary to a
fair shot. The mode of proceeding is thus:—On arriving
at the bank, the shooter selects a stone in a likely spot—the
drier the more comfortable—squats down upon it, and in-
vokes patience to his aid. If the ducks are in migratory
mood—which they are not always—his reverie will be soon
broken, and his congealing blood startled into circulation by
the whistling of the teal, or the melodious quack of the mallard approaching him. Cocking his gun, and rapidly
scanning the horizon, his eye catches sight of the birds. If
they are only within doubtful range, an old hand will let
them pass without risking a shot, knowing that in all probability, they may return again more closely to him. If a
fair shot offers, the birds are allowed to pass beyond the
sitter, who should on no account fire at advancing birds, as

the chances against his killing any of them, no matter how near, are twenty to one. Once past, however, he selects a bird from the centre of the group, and fires. If they are anything compact, three, four, or five birds may fall. Now is the value of a good dog known. If the shooter rises to collect his birds, he will get the slain, but may have a weary and difficult chase after the wounded, and probably lose some of them in the dark. What is perhaps worse, the time he is dancing about he is scaring other flights of birds, and losing chances he may never again have. The rule seems to be, never to let him rise from his seat if he can avoid it, and the dog saves any necessity for running after wounded birds; but if he have none, let him regain his post as soon as possible. If the night is favourable, the sport may be pursued as long as the shooter can endure the cold and the tide admits. When once the water flows to his knees it is time for him, at all hazards, to take himself off, and seek the shortest road to land. This sport is chiefly followed at Cardross and the bays at Hill Ardmore.

ANGLING.

We have already alluded to the deep sea fishing of the neighbourhood. It of course takes precedence, being followed not only as a recreation, but as a business by a considerable number of the population. To many anglers sea-fishing is the only form of angling they are devoted to or desire to follow; and sea-fishing, although [despised by votaries of the higher branches of the sport, is by no means a contemptible amusement. Boats and lines are easily procurable; for bait the log worm, or hairy worm found in the sand at low tide, mussels and other shellfish are used. The great secret of success rests not on the skill of the fishers so much as in a knowledge of the haunts of the fish at particular stages of the tide and in particular seasons. The only advice we can give on this head is, get a boatman who is practically a fisherman, or take one acquainted with the ground with you. Sea fish of all kinds have of late years been uncertain in their supply. There is neither the quantity nor varieties found that used to exist on these shores. To trawling on the banks during the spawning season, which has of late been greatly on the increase, has been generally attributed the extinction and disappearance of fish. But of cod, whiting, flounder, and lythe there is a fair supply; and very abundant during the spring and autumn months, particularly among shallow currents of the loch, is the sethe, a coarse-grained greenish-complexioned fish. Of these, great quantities are caught in the bays and about the currents of Rose-neath Ferry, in the evenings and mornings, with a bit of white feather dressed on a hook after the similitude of a fly. A bunch of hazel rods, numbering from ten to twenty, are projected from the stern of a small coble; beside them sits the fisher, while another rows the boat, over such ground as sport is expected from. The fish play a good deal on the surface, and thus serve to guide the sportsmen to the proper ground. The boat has thus the appearance of an animated spider, of unusual dimensions, traversing the water in eccentric courses. The fish are dragged in *sans ceremonie* as soon as possible when hooked—the only interest in the proceeding arises apparently from the quantity caught. They are generally about the size of small herrings, though much larger specimens, sometimes weighing eight or nine pounds, are often killed ; but these patriarchs are seldom tricked by a feather— they require more substantial fare. The large sethe, which passes under the name of stenlock, large lythe and cod are taken in considerable quantities by trolling with the sea-worm, (Phyllodoce laminosa.) These long unsightly worms are strung on a strong gut tackle. armed with three or four Limerick hooks, and trolled from a boat with a short line of fifteen or twenty feet. A better plan, however, is to moor the boat in the strong run of some current, where the water is not more than twelve feet deep, above such a tangled bed as these fish haunt, and allow the bait to play under the surface, by dipping the point of the rod two feet or so. Large quantities are sometimes then taken, particularly in the morning or evening, and we can assure you it is no mean sport to kill a ten or twelve pound lythe or cod with the rod in a strong current. The former fish especi-ally, fights hard and gives great play at times. During the greater part of the year there is a considerable sprink-ling of sea-trout to be found all along the shores of the loch: In some places they may be found with more certainty than at others, but in general they haunt the creeks and shore currents throughout it. They are never found in deep water but seem to prefer it of a range from two to seven or eight feet. Probably the small streams and springs that abound on the margin of the loch, conveying food to them, lead them to haunt the shallows chiefly. In the early part of the season, during February and March, they are often caught on shore-lines baited with the common earth-worm, or or sand-worm, for then the trout, recently descended from the fresh water after spawning, enjoys a voracious appetite, and refuses almost nothing at all edible. Later in the season they become more fastidious in their choice of food, and refuse such vulgar fare. The favourite, and, indeed, almost only approved mode of trout-fishing in Gareloch, is by trolling from a boat. The baits used are the sand-eel, minnow, and sprat. Indeed, any kind of small fish, if at all clear in the colours is suitable. When there is a stiff breeze, from fifteen to twenty yards of line is sufficient; but if the day be quiet, double this quantity is not too much; the further you are from your bait the more chance of success. A stiffish rod and plenty of line are necessary, as the sea-trout, if anything large, fights fiercely after being hooked. In general it is a bad plan to land from the boat after hooking a fish, as you are almost sure to lose him amongst the tangle in shallow water; keep him rather in deep water, if possible, and be sure to have a landing-net or gaff with you; either of these is absolutely indispensable. The trout caught in the loch, ranges from half a pound to six pounds, and sometimes heavier. On a good day from half-a-dozen are sometimes taken by a single rod; at other times the temper, patience, and resources of Piscator may be severely put to a test by not a single bite rewarding his diligence. It is said that the modern Yankee invention, the spoon bait, has proved very·attractive during the past season or two. One or two Helensburgh anglers are reported to have done great execution with it. but we cannot personally vouch for its efficiency, never having tried it, and would be rather indisposed to forsake the minnow for any modern invention. If if you wish to enjoy a day's sport, your best way is to engage some one of the regular fishermen of the loch, to all of whom the best spots are known, and on whose candour you can safely rely. The sea-trout, notwithstanding the doubts which have been expressed on the subject, will also rise at a fly on salt water. Whether they accept it as a fly or some marine bait we cannot determine, but can vouch to their being frequently taken by a large fly of gaudy complexion.

Almost all the streams and brooks in the neighbourhood
contain trout. As the streams are small, however, their
inhabitants seldom attain a respectable size, and only in the
larger burns are worth the angler's attention. Beginning
with fresh-water fishing—

Lochlomond commands our first notice. It is easily accessible from Helensburgh, and contains not only plenty of
fish, but a great variety of them, Salmon, sea-trout, brown
trout, perch, roach, pike, and a peculiar fish called powan,
a species of herring, abound in its waters. The fishing is
held by a Club, who pay a sum yearly to Sir James Colquhoun, who bought up the salmon fishings on the rivers
Leven and Clyde, in order to allow free access of these fish
to the loch. The right to angle on the loch and its tributaries
is obtained by purchase of annual tickets, but we believe
there is no restriction as regards the loch itself. There
are plenty of experienced boatmen to be had at Luss well
acquainted with the best parts of the loch, though not to be
indiscriminately recommended as fishermen, as any angler
may experimentally satisfy himself. Although the fish are
abundant, the loch, from its extent and variety of ground
feeding, affords uncertain sport. It is the fairest and most
fickle of all Scotch lakes. Sometimes a very unpromising
day is crowned with success; at other times a succession of
promising days to the angler's eye end in weariness and vexa-
tion. The months of April, May, and latter part of August
and September are reckoned best. The flies used are infinite
in variety, but the experienced on this lake seem to restrict
themselves to three or four, regulating the size according to
the state of the weather, &c.

1. *Green Drake.*—Body yellow mohair, ribbed with tinsel ; legs
red, or ginger hackle; wing mottled mallard or teal.

2. *Black Palmer.*—Ribbed with silver twist on body of ostrich feather; tail yellow tilk; wing brown turkey feather.

3. *Stone Fly.*—Body mixed with yellow and brown mohair, yellow towards the tail; wings, dark mottled feather of teal drake, mixed with blue jay feather.

4. *M'Niven's Favourite.*—Boddy reddish purple or mauve mohair, ribbed with white tinsel, red or black hackle, and light turkey feather wings.

5. *Smith's Fly.*—Body of alternate dark-blue, red and yellow mohair, yellow towards the tail, black hackle; wings, teal drake or pheasant's tail.

6. *Dark Fly.*—Body black silk, ribbed with tinsel, and over with black hackle ; wing, light turkey cock ; tail, strand of speckled feathers.

7. *Brown Fly.*—Body fiery brown mohair and red hackle; wing, teal drake, speckled. This is often a deadly fly.

8. Green body of pigs wool and teal drake wing, and occasionally a perfectly white fly is found captivating.

These should be dressed on pretty large hooks. There are other popular flies used. An acquaintance with the loch will soon put the angler in possession of their qualities and appearance.

It has been matter of surprise that the Club have not introduced char and greyling into the loch ; they could easily be imported and would thrive rapidly in it. Experiments are now being made by Sir James Colquhoun, Bart., on a stream near Rossdhu policies, in the artificial propagation of salmon, the success of which is hopefully and earnestly looked forward to by many anglers.

The perch and pike fishing of the loch are very good, and not so precarious as the trout. Since the removal of the salmon nets, perch have increased very much, and may be found throughout almost all its waters.

The pike fishing is best along the south shore, from the termination of Rossdhu policies down to Belleretira. About the mouth of the river Fruin, and where this stream, at a former period, flowed into the loch, are several good and

H

favourite haunts of this tyrant of the lake. In the reedy
channels behind the islands, near Luss shore, they are also
found; but towards the head of the loch they are more abundant than at any other part. They are taken with spoon
bait, par-tail, and minnow, but the best bait of all is a small
silvery roach. An epicurean pike will dash at this when he
spurns every other delicacy of the season. Pike are in season
in the loch from August till January. In spring they are
not worth taking. The powan was long considered peculiar to
to Lochlomond, but there are other Highland lochs, chiefly
in proximity to the sea, where it is found. It has many points
of resemblance in common with the herring, and, indeed, as
Lochlomond may have been subject to the same tidal influence as the Clyde, at one period of its history, there is
every reason to assume that the powan is the herring accli-
matised to fresh water. Herring still ascend the Clyde
occasionally, as far as Dumbarton Rock: we have seen them
even higher. A very slight change of level, and that such
change has taken place seems confirmed by traces of a
former sea-margin along the shore of the Clyde, would carry
flood tide up to Lochlomond, and thus introduce sea-fish
into it. The powan, like the herring, seems to feed chiefly
on minute larvæ or zoophytes. It is not, or but rarely,
taken with the rod, though formerly largely fished with the
net. When well cooked, it is not a contemptible fish, and
has often, in former times, passed current and probably still
graces the Cockney tourist's breakfast table as Lochlomond
trout. A good many salmon are found in the Loch from
May onwards, but they are as a rule shy. To ensure success a strong breeze of south-west wind is necessary, and a
knowledge of their favourite haunts. The flies used for sea
trout are in general suitable.

If you should be unfortunate enough, as often happens to the angler, to visit the loch on a day unsuitable for trout fishing, the next best thing to be done is to devote your attention to perch—a fair basket of these may be taken in ordinary circumstances with the small red worm or minnow, by fishing either from the shore or a boat. If you are conversant with the haunts of the fish, wherever the water is tolerably deep, and the bottom weedy, you may almost calculate with certainty on finding perch, and if you find one, remember the other branches of the family are not far distant. Perch fishing is best in morning and evening, but they may be taken at any period of the day. They are not fastidious.

The tributaries of the loch are the Endrick, Falloch, Luss, Douglas, and Glen Fruin waters. The Endrick is the largest of these. It is easily accessible by railway, but, save late in the season, when the sea-trout ascend it, is almost worthless as a fishing stream. It has a traditionary excellence, but the trout seem to have been much thinned by night-poaching and netting. The only really good part of the stream is from Fintry to Balfron. Of the other streams, the Falloch is the best, and Luss Water next in order. The native trout in these streams are abundant, but not large. In autumn, considerable numbers of sea trout are found in them. The flies used for river-trout are chiefly dark, with a lightish wing of small size ; for sea-trout, yellow or red on No. 4 or 5 hook. Bait-fishing is prohibited by the rules of the Club, though apparently without any very good reason, as the verdict of most of the angling patriarchs frequenting these streams is, that the fish do not readily take the bait, save in very heavy floods. The chief reason given against it is the facility it affords to dishonest fishing in low clear streams with rake hooks amongst trouts huddled together in the pools.   Otherwise it seems unobjectionable.

All these streams and their tributaries, which generally abound in small trout, may be easily reached in an hour or two by rail or steamer, and most of them are within easy ing range.

There is also a small loch above Rahane, on the Gareloch, in which perch are very abundant.

These embrace the chief fishing localities in the district, and it will be hard if some of them do not yield to the visitor a fair amount of sport.   If in haunting the loch's reedy shores, or the dancing, hurrying streams of the brook, and listening to their melody, and breathing the pure exhilarating mountain air, you should be content even with a light pannier if you secure a share of the good gifts old Izaak endows angling with :—" Indeed, my friend, you will find angling to be like the virtue of humility, which has a calmness of spirit and a world of other blessings attending upon it."

THE COMET, THE FIRST STEAM BOAT IN BRITAIN. 1811

HENRY BELL.

It seems to be only a fitting appendix to a Guide Book to Helensburgh to add a notice of one whose labours had given it much of the eminence it enjoys. Helensburgh and Henry Bell will ever be associated in the history of the industrial commerce of our land. It was not his birth place, but it was the field of his labours and the scene of his triumphs; and the "mad innkeeper," as those who failed to understand him, called him, has stamped his name indelibly on the place. Henry Bell was born at Torphichen, in the neighbourhood of Linlithgow, in the year 1767, of humble parentage. He was first apprenticed to a stone mason. We afterwards find him working as a millwright, and after a short interval acquiring a measure of engineering knowledge with Mr. Inglis, at Bellshill, and more fully, when he was about 22 or 23 years of age, with the celebrated Sir John Rennie, of London. He never, however, obtained a thorough knowledge of mechanical science, and all through his subsequent life complained of the disadvantage this defect placed him under. After leaving London, where his stay was comparatively short, he entered into business in Glasgow with a Mr. Paterson, under the firm of Bell and Paterson, builders, and undertook and successfully completed several large and very important contracts. During this period his fertile mind seems to have run in engineering enterprises and projects.

About the end of last or beginning of the present century his thoughts were directed to the propulsion of vessels by steam. The subject was not entirely a new one, for it had received the attention of other scientific men, and various experiments had been made, all demonstrating its feasibility. But it had been abandoned by the earliest pioneers, and was even denounced by Watt and other eminent engineers as impracticable to any extent, when Bell took it up. In 1803, we find him bringing a scheme for steam navigation under notice of the Board of Admiralty, but with that wisdom and foresight which have eminently characterised this department of Government, they condemned the scheme as purely visionary. Indeed, it was twenty years later before the Government was educated into the belief that steam navigation was practicable, or if practicable, a prudent thing for a constitutional Government to recognise. Bell's plans, were, however, favourably received by the American Government, who exhibited an interest in them, as they have always done in projects affecting the commercial advantages of the country, and they availed themselves to some extent of his ideas. Hence we find steam navigation of the American rivers almost cotemporaneous with our own.

About 1806, Bell settled at Helensburgh, where he built the Baths—now Queen's Hotel—to which numerous visitors were attracted by the conveniences it offered them, then rare at watering places, and by the celebrity of the host, whose name was already become a household word. Here he planned the first Clyde steamer, through many perplexities and anxieties, and had her built by Mr. John Wood, of Port-Glasgow, from whose dock the *Comet* was launched in in 1812. Here culminated the thoughts and energies of years, the skill and patience and perseverance and triumphs over difficulties, which with his imperfect engineering skill might have been held insurmountable.

At this late date, with an advanced mechanical skill, the difficulties of Henry Bell can hardly be understood or appreciated in the construction of this little pioneer of commerce and civilisation, which was mis-named the *Comet*, for its course has been steady and onward since. Coupled with mechanical difficulties, and greatly increasing them were the limited resources of Bell, and a lack of skilled labour. The same battle which Palisy and Watt, and a host of others had to fight for years, encountered him at every step. Often times at his wit's end for want of funds, and as often unexpectedly obtaining fresh supplies. Trying the patience and temper of his faithful and cheerful good wife oftentimes, and getting hold of her little stores, hoarded past to meet the the current expenses of the hotel, which were swept into the unsatisfying maw of the boat, to her dismay and chagrin, and almost wearying the good nature of friends willing to aid,— at length the gaol was reached, and Henry Bell was famous.

The first *Comet* was about 40 feet long. Her paddles were about 18 inches broad by 12 deep, amd her tall funnel, which also did duty for a mast, ran up from the deck at an angle for some distance before ascending. Her engines were three horse-power. For a time she plied between Glasgow and Greenock, accomplishing the distance in about four hours when the tide was favourable. The interest she created was intense. Great crowds of people lined the shores from the Broomielaw downwards to witness her departure and arrival, but of the hundreds of wonder seekers, few recognised in her the advent of a revolution in the maratime enterprise of the world. Few comparatively even believed in the success of the little vessel itself, or regarded it with other feelings than they would have experienced had any marine monster made its appearance in the river. People were afraid of entering it, and regarded it with a degree of superstition and terror, and generally with aversion. In a foot note to Mr. Smile's Life of Boulton and Watt, the following illustrative anecdote is given:—

"The masters of small sailing crafts regarded the *Comet* with apprehension and dismay. The old Highland gabbert men were especially hostile, denouncing the new vessel as being impelled by the "teevil's wun'." The story is told of the steamer one day coming up with a fly boat, tacking against the tide, when the crew began to jeer the skipper of the fly, calling upon him to come along with his lazy craft. "Get out o' ma sicht," he cried in reply; "I'm just gaun as it pleases the breath o' the Almichty, an I'll neer fash ma thoom how fast ye gaug wi' your blasted reek."

Success, though delayed, did come. The *Comet* was afterwards lengthened 20 feet, and her engine power increased, and the British public began to appreciate the invention and avail themselves of it. The trips of the *Comet* were extended to Lochfine, and intermediate ports. In Lochfine, somewhere about Lochgilphead, the first *Comet* was wrecked. She was succeeded by another larger steamer of the same name, also wrecked off Gourock; but by this time the steam navigation of the Clyde was an accomplished fact. The reward of the application of skill and industry was not to Bell, however, who lay suffering under ill health, and struggling with crippled resources, died comparatively poor, at the Baths Hotel, in 1830.

In person, Mr Bell was about middle size, a stout-built, fresh-complexioned man, hearty and genial in his manner. His features were regular and expressive, impressing a stranger at a glance with a good opinion of him as a shrewd, pawky Scot, an impression which ten minutes' conversation stamped as sound. His general knowledge was extensive, and he had a peculiar aptitude for seizing the salient points of any new invention, and making himself master of the subject. He was a great talker, when excited by any favourite hobby, and nothing delighted him more than an intelligent listener, to whom he would descant all night on any of his multifarious plans and schemes. There were always some leading projects in view. The construction of a canal betwixt east and west Tarbet, in Lochfine, was a favourite one. He had also a scheme for the partial drainage of Lochlomond, and reclamation of the land, about which he had an extensive correspondence with the Duke of Montrose, who did not receive it favourably. The introduction of water to Helensburgh from Glenfruin, he had also in view. The reclamation of waste lands in Scotland, and even the Suez Canal, he discussed and urged its practicability despite the opinion of many eminent engineers. Of all his plans he was exceedingly sanguine, neither the indifference of others, the want of resources, partial failure, or any of the thousand embarrassments that haunt projectors, daunted him. Whatever the failure or disappointment met, he was always hopeful of ultimate success. With a large measure of Watt's inventive faculty he possessed in a good degree the energy and knowledge of men which Watt's partner, Boulton, enjoyed. To the many doubts and disbelief of scientific and unscientific men, that steam vessels would never accomplish much, Bell's reply was always, "they will yet traverse the ocean," and his prophesy now being fulfilled, living men who heard it can verify.

The life of Bell is a study, and his energy, zeal and courage a model for young men of to-day.

NOTE.—The crew of the original *Comet* consisted of William M'Kenzie, sometime teacher in Helensburgh afterwards, Robert Bain, master, an engineer, a pilot, and a fireman. The fare from Glasgow to Greenock was four shillings and three shillings, for first and second cabin, and it sailed from each port three times a week.

BATTRUM'S

GUIDE AND DIRECTORY

TO

HELENSBURGH AND NEIGHBOURHOOD.

SEVENTH EDITION.

HELENSBURGH :
PRINTED AND PUBLISHED AT 50 & 52 EAST PRINCES STREET.

1875.

PREFACE.

In issuing the seventh edition of the Helensburgh Directory, the publisher tenders his sincere thanks for the generous support hitherto accorded the publication ; and as every effort has been made to make the Directory worthy of the public, he trusts that it will be found to merit a similar reception.

Although not a perfectly got up work, still it is hoped that, as a book of reference, it will be found very useful. This year it is larger, and contains more names, and bodies of societies than any formerly published.

The map this year has been improved, showing the new feus, houses, and streets that have been made.

August 20th, 1875.

NAMES OF THE NEW POLICE COMMISSIONERS.

Alexander Breingan.
Andrew Provan.
Thomas Steven, *Chief Magist.*
Finlay Campbell.
William Bryson.
J. W. M'Culloch, *Junr. Mag.*

John Cramb.
Donald Murray.
John Dingwall.
John Stuart, *Junr. Mag.*
R. S. M'Farlane.
Martin M'Kay.

CONTENTS OF DIRECTORY.

Abercromby Street	King Street, east
Adelaide Street	King Street, west
Alma Crescent	Lomond Street
Argyle Street, east	Luss Road
Argyle Street, west	Maitland Street
Campbell Street	Milligs Street, east
Charlotte Street	Milligs Street, west
Clyde Street, east	Montrose, Street, east
Clyde Street, west	Montrose Street, west
Colquhoun Square	North King, street
Colquhoun Street	North Sutherland Street
George Street	Princes Street, east
Glasgow Street	Princes Street, west
Glenfinlas Street	Queen Street
Grant Street	Sinclair Street
Granville Street	South King Street
Hanover Street	Stafford Street
Havelock Street	Suffolk Street
Henry Bell Street	Sutherland Street
James Street	Sutherland Crescent, Up.
John Street	Sutherland Crescent, Lo.
King's Crescent	William Street

HELENSBURGH STREET DIRECTORY.

ABERCROMBY STREET.

Wemyss, Robert, Bennochy
Mitchell, Mrs, Locksley
Napier, James A., Omaha.
Orr, William, Ardenlade
Wemyss, Miss
Easton, Mr
new houses

ADELAIDE STREET.

1 Stewart, Adam, labourer
2 Fairman, J. A., Elmbank House
6 Baylis, Mrs, Giffnock Cottage
8 Stewart, Mrs, East Thorn
9 Telfer, James, gardener
9 Ross, David, coachman to Miss Allan
10 Elizabeth Borland, Janelee Cottage.
11 Sharp, James, Ardenclutha
12 Hunter, John, house-agent, Parklee Cottage
14 Lang, Mrs, Duart Cottage
16 Galloway, George, seed merchant, Galloway Cottage
18 Mackie, William, Park View Cottage
20 Thomson, Mrs, Glenorchy Villa
22 Ogston, Mrs, Glenorchy Villa

ALMA CRESCENT.

Muir, Robert, Hazelwood
Topping, William, Marion Villa
Watt, Mrs, Taybank
Burr, Thomas, gardener
Lightbody, Thomas, Skerryvore
Barron, Alexander, Gowanlea
Gemmill, William M., Ruhe

ARGYLE STREET, EAST

3 Colquhoun, Andrew S. D., drysalter, Rosemount
5 Ritchie, Miss, Rosemount Cottage
8 M'Farlane, Miss, Dailnabruich Cottage
10 Smith, David, plumber
12 Robb, Hamilton, mason
16 Fraser, John, teacher, Seaview Place
18 Stewart, Captain William, Seaview Place
29 Holdsworth, John, Clifton Cottage
30 Auld, Mrs, Glenlea
33 Kay, Thomas, joiner, Chapelfield House
35 M'Lellan, Miss, East Woodend House
37 Donald, W. Macalister, J. P., of Lyleston, Hawthorn Bank
46 Alexander, Miss, Milligs Cottage

ARGYLE STREET, WEST.

4 Sloan, Miss, Craigie Lea
8 Batty, Mrs Richard, Laurel Bank
10 Dickie, Hugh, teacher
11 Campbell, Mrs Archibald, Lillybank
12 Swan, Mrs, Oakbank
14 Bayly, Miss, Woodend Cottage
16 Turnbull, Duncan, merchant, Woodville
18 Doddrel, D. T., Beechwood Villa
   Stables and Coachhouse—David Black, cab hirer
19 Hillen, Miss, dressmaker
20 Stewart, Edward, Westwood Villa
22 Roberts, William B., Woodlee
24 M'Callum, Donald, draper, Fairbank
25 White, John J., dentist, Woodbank
27 Allan, Mrs, The Lodge
29 Hutchison, Miss, Sunnybrae
29 Taylor, Miss, Sunnybrae,
29 Malcolm, Mrs, Sunnybrae
33 Stewart, Mrs, Greenoak

BELL STREET.

1 Lennox, Peter, Oakfield
2 **Thomson, Alexander George, I.A. civil engineer**

Montgomery, William, farmer, Laigh Stuck
M'Lachlan, William, farmer, High Stuck

CAMPBELL STREET.

1 Gemmell, Mrs, Bellevue House
7 Lennan, Peter, gardener to Miss Foot
8 Wallace, Matthew, coal dealer, Rosebank Terrace
10 Taylor, William M., Rosebank Terrace
11 Gow, Mrs, Clarkfield House
12 Phillips James, drawing-master, Rosebank Cottage
13 Millar, Miss, Clarkfield House
14 Allan, Miss, Rosevale Cottage
15 M'Nab, Mrs, Greenbank
17 M'Phun, W. R., bookseller and publisher, Maryfield
19 Cowan, Miss, Garnet Bank
20 Buchanan, Miss, Burnside House
21 Watt, Miss, Hopetoun Park
22 Shanks, Miss, Burnside House
24 Arthur, Rev John, Burnside Cottage
26 Oswald, Andrew, Glennan Bank
28 M'Lachlan, Mrs Walter, Glenmore
M'Micking, Thomas, J.P., Burnbrae
Campbell, Hugh, gardener to T. M'Micking

CEMETERY ROAD.

Helensburgh Cemetery—George Combs, gardener
Helensburgh Hospital
M'Auslane, James, farmer, Kirkmichael

CHARLOTTE STREET.

2 Bakehouse—John M'Nicol,
4 M'Dougall, Miss
4 Dewar, Peter, mate
4 M'Nicol, John, baker
6 Smith, Mrs
7 Bain, David, weaver
8 Whittle, Mrs
10 Traill, Anthony, mason
12 Brown, Barbara

12 Finlay, Archibald, seaman
13 Wilson, William, mason
14 M'Farlane, Malcolm, shoemaker
16 Sutherland, John, shoemaker
16 Wilson, Gilbert, painter
15 Park Free Church—Rev. W. H. Carslaw, M.A.
17 Carslaw, Rev. William Henderson, Park Free Manse
18 Ferguson, Thomas, slater
19 M'Farlane, Robert, Rowanbrae
21 Christie, Mrs Thomas, Janeville Lodge
22 Stuart, John, Thistle Bank
23 Spence, William, architect, Ardlui
25 Nicol, Miss, Kintyre Villa—Ladies' Boarding School
30 Marshall, Robert, Birkfell
32 Cuthbertson, John, Cranley Lodge
34 Barton, William, Devaar Lodge
36 Proudfood, Miss, Egremount House
38 Lindsay, Rev. John, The Manse

CLYDE STREET, EAST

1 Reid, Mrs, refreshment rooms
2 and 4, M'Farlane, R. S., seed and grain merchant
3 M'Lachlan, L.,—house, 1 Young's Place, Colquhoun Sq.
5 M'Callum and Sons, drapers
7 M'Callum, Mrs P.
8 Hart, Mrs
8 Rhodes, Mrs
9 and 11, M'Lellan, Adam, ironmonger
10 Service, Mrs
12 Paton, John, bootmaker
13 Pettit, Afred, joiner, china and toy merchant—house, 17
14 M'Nicol, Alexander, bootmaker
15 Ingram, Thomas, butter and egg store
17 Waldie, John, coach proprietor
18 Russell, Mrs
19 Imperial Hotel—James Fraser
20 Caldwell, William, tailor and clothier
22 Murray, Mrs, stoneware and china warehouse

24 Martin, Miss, Greenburn Lodge
25 Warnock, John, flesher—house, 31
26 Henderson, Dr Francis, Seabank
27 Fowler, James, wine and spirit merchant
28 Brown, James, clerk
28 Bennet, Mrs, Newark Villa
32 Dale, James J.
33 M'Dougall, John, green grocer
34 Harvie, Thomas, druggist
34 M'Callum, Daniel, Methven Villa
34 Sword, John, Methven Villa
34 Wilson, Robert, tobacconist, Methven Villa
34 Glen, William, Methven Cottage
37 Paterson, Mrs, refreshment rooms
38 Hall, Robert H., shoemaker—house, 20 George Street
39 Waddell and Jack, wine and spirit merchants
40 M'Allister, Mrs
40 M'Killop, George, saddler,
40 Smith, Robert, gardener
40 Stephen, Mrs John
40 M'Dougall, Alexander, collar maker
40 Robertson, David, mason
41 Elliot, Robert, shoemaker
42 M'Farlane, Miss, dressmaker
43 Gardner & Lindsay, grain merchants
  Established Church—Rev. J. Lindsay
  Established School—John Fraser
45 Gardner, Duncan M,
45 M'Lellan, Daniel
45 Dickie, Robert
47 Begbie, Robert, gardener and seedsman
48 Wheeler, Miss
48 Waugh, James B.
48 Brown, Peter, engraver
48 Johnston, Mrs
49 Rankin, John, haircutting and shampooing rooms
50 Cameron, Neil, grocer
51 M'Kinlay, William, plumber—house, 53

53 Taylor, William, joiner
54 Gilmour, Agnes, grocer
55 Rennards, J. R., apothecary—house, 59
56 Cameron, Miss
56 Donald, Archibald
57 Finlayson, Miss, confectioner
58 Whyte, John, plasterer
59 Bain, John, joiner
59 Livingstone, John, grocer
60 Kerr, Gordon, vanman
63 Swanson, William, bootmaker—house, 59
64 Blackwood, Mrs William
64 Hodge, George, N.B.R. collector
64 Ferguson, Mrs
64 Bruce, Miss
65 Little, Mrs, draper—house, 71
66 M'Nicol, Robert
66 Tyson, Mrs
67 Hamilton, Mrs, confectioner
68 Gore Booth, Mrs, East Seaside
69 Robertson, Miss, confectioner
70 Hamilton, Miss
71 Buchanan, Thomas, joiner
71 M'Pherson, Mrs
72 Smith, Miss, The Baths
72 Buchanan, Walter, J.P., The Baths
73 Maclachlan, David S., baker
74 Queen's Hotel—Alexander Williamson
75 Bain, Walter
75 Bain, Mrs
75 M'Farlane Duncan
75 M'Kay, William, plasterer
76 Stirling, James, J.P., Rockend House
76 M'Millan, George, gardener
76 Patrie, John, butler
77 M'Farlane, Andrew, shoemaker
78 Wilson, Andrew, Rockville
79 Gillies, William, Helensburgh and Glasgow carrier

79 Gillies, Margaret, grocer and confectioner
80 Walker, Mrs Robert, Rockbank House
81 Campbell, Miss, confectioner
82 Rintoul, Andrew, grain merchant, Rockbank
82 Stevenson, John, coachman
83 Forrester, William, plumber
84 Teacher, William, Rockfort House
84 Kerr, Robert, gardener
85 Gillies, Mrs, dairy
87 Macleod, Donald, tailor
89 M'Auslan, Mrs, wine and spirit merchant—house, 91.
93 M'Aulay, Captain Robert, Eastburn House
93 Gordon, Alexander, painter
93 Laurie, Mrs
95 Dempster, Donald, slater
97 Dickson, Mrs
99 Stevenson, Charles, porter
99 Jarvie, James, goods clerk
99 Lennox, Mrs
99 Robertson, J. S., excise officer
99 Robertson, Thomas, joiner
99 M'Leod, Miss, dressmaker
99 M'Naught, Alexander, baker
99 M'Lellan, Donald, lorryman
101 Walker, William
103 Buchanan George—joiners' workshop
107 Niven, Mrs
109 Anderson, Miss, spirit dealer
111 Davidson, Thomas
113 Torrance, Miss
123 M'Murrich, Daniel, blacksmith
127 Weir, Duncan, gardener
129 Somerville, Mrs
131 M'Nicol, John, baker
133 Smith, Mrs P., grocer and wine dealer
137 Buchanan, George, joiner
139 M'Allister, Angus, colporteur
141 Buchanan, Alexander, engineer

143 Houston, William
147 Davie, Miss Catherine
151 Kyle, Andrew, spirit dealer
153 Yates, Mrs
153 Service, Mrs
157 Peddie, William, gardener
157 Brown, Robert, clerk
157 M'Kirdy, James, plumber
157 M'Nicol, John, joiner
157 Walker, Mrs
159 Miller, David, mason
161 Laurie, Thomas, butler
161 Morrison, Miss Ann
165 Drummond, William, joiner
167 Gray, Miss
169 Flint, James, mason
171 Kater, John, joiner
173 M'Intosh, Mrs
175 Young, George, engineer
177 Bain, Mrs
177 Menzies, Miss
179 Taylor, William, joiner
181 Sellars, Peter, gardener
189 M'Farlane, Alexander, gardener
189 Brown, Miss, washer and dresser
191 M'Gilvary, Mrs
193 Lightbody, Mrs
197 Pollok, Robert, commercial traveller
197 Ferguson, Miss, Barncroft
199 Hamilton, Charles, Oakfield
201 Kinghorn, James, Windsor Cottage
203 Kemp, Miss, Albert Cottage
205 M'Aulay, Alexander, Eastbank Cottage
209 Beattie, John, Rocklee House
211 Robertson, J. C., Eastwood House
217 Walker, R. D., Maple Bank
　　　Reid, Rev. S. W., Rockfort Place
　　　Drumfork Toll—William M'Lellan

Cameron, Mrs, Old Toll House, Drumfork
Caldwell, James, farmer, Craigendoran

CLYDE STREET, WEST

1 Watt, Robert, draper
2 Brash, John, tailor and clothier—house, 3 Colquhoun St.
3 Ponds, James, wine and spirit merchant
4 Temperance Hotel and Restaurant—WilliamGatenby
5 Robb, David, tobacconist
6 Ærated Water Manufactory—Alex. Williamson, junr.
6 O'Rake, Barney, labourer
6 M'Ginnes, Patrick, labourer
6 Billiard and Smoking Room—Wm. Waters
7 M'Callum, C. & M., milliners
8 Lennox & Chapman, family grocers and wine merchants
9 M'Nair, William, family grocer and wine merchant
10 Bank of Scotland—Alexander Breingan, agent
11 Houston, Mrs
13 Suttie, Mrs A.
14 Service, Mrs, refreshment rooms
15 Dingwell, Roderick
15 Elliot, Robert, shoemaker
16 Ross, James, watchmaker
17 Dixon, Robert, baker—house, 15
18 Dickson and Veitch, grocers
19 Macneur, Alexander, bookseller—house, 20
20 Ireland, George
20 Reid, Alex., plumber
21 Urie, Mrs, china warehouse—house, 20
22 Roy, Gabriel, watchmaker
23 Young, Miss, fruiterer and confectioner
24 Campbell, Finlay, grocer and wine merchant
25 Moir, Mrs, fishmonger—house, 39
26 Porter, Miss, milliner
27 Allan, A. P., bookseller
28 Reid, D. Stevenson, pharmaceutical chemist
29 Parlane, Mrs, umbrella and staymaker—house, 32
30 Holms, Mrs, draper—house, 65

32 Spence, Mrs
32 M'Laren, John, joiner
32 M'Laren, Mrs, dressmaker
33 Arroll, Walter, poulterer and fruiterer
34 M'Kinlay, Mrs
34 Arroll, Mrs,
34 Craig, Robert, joiner
35 Patterson, William, tailor and clothier—house, 34
36 Waters, William, upholsterer and cabinetmaker
37 Morris, Mrs, baker—house, 39
38 Stevenson, Robert, boot and shoemaker
39 M'Garrigle, Hugh, labourer
39 Neil, Henry, gardener
39 Brough, William, painter
39 Burns, Mrs
39 Kerney, Edward, coachman
39 Aitken, Mrs
39 M'Donald, Archd., yachtsman
39 Dempster, Mrs
39 Williamson, John, upholsterer
39 Wilkie, Robert, labourer
40 Freebairn, Mrs, jeweller
41 Donald, Archibald, butter, ham, and egg merchant
42 Wilson, John, flesher
43 Glen, Peter, tobacconist—house, 44
44 M'Donald, Mrs
44 Smith, Alex.
44 Melvine, Mrs
44 Holliss, Charles
46 M'Kim, Adam, bookseller
47 Kyle, Andrew, spirit merchant
48 Russell, M. C., confectioner
49 Buchanan, James, grocer
50 Thomson, R. & J. drapers, Argyle Place
51 Watt, J. A., china merchant, Argyle Place
52 Paterson, & Son, upholsterers
55 M'Callum, Donald, grocer
56 Watson. John, baker

56 Fraser, Miss
56 M'Leod, Mrs
57 M'Donald, Miss
58 M'Culloch, J. W., painter
59 Wardlaw, David, baker—house, 61
60 Jamieson, James, flesher
61 Williamson, Alex., junr., ærated water manufacturer
61 Grant, A. W.
61 Napier, Mrs
63 Angus, George, painter
64 Gairdner, Cathrine, dressmaker
65 Jack, John, builder
65 Hay, James, wood merchant
66 Clark, John, draper
67 Young, Gavin, surgeon dentist
68 Forewell, Henry, druggist, Flower Bank
69 Leggat, Mrs, Flower Bank
70 Forrest, Mrs, Flower Bank
71 Robertson, Miss, Ardmore
72 M'Ewan, Mrs, Ardmore
73 Falconer, Miss
74 Burns, Adam
76 Kerr, Miss, Bellevue House
77 M'Millan, Mrs, Ivy House
78 Bunten, Mrs, Claremont Villa
79 Gibb, Dr. G., Lorn House
80 Baird, Rev. John, West Bay Cottage
81 M'Donald, Mrs, West Bay Cottage
82 Scott, Mrs James
83 Brown, John, J.P., Brandon Grove
84 Fullerton, Gavin, Farnie House
85 Martin, Joseph Russell
86 Oughterson, Miss Dahlbeg
88 Aitchison, Miss
89. Reid, Dr Douglas, Easterton House

COLQUHOUN SQUARE.

1 M'Lachlan, Lachlan, baker, Young's Place

2 Bryde, Archibald, coach-builder
3 Dempster, Donald, slater
4 M'Aulay, James, boat-hirer
6 Bain, Mrs, box mangle keeper
6 Ingram, James, mason
7 Walker, Robert
7 Walker, Mrs, ladies' nurse
7 Fraser, Janet
8 Eman, John, coal merchant
8 Galloway, William,
17 National Bread Company
18 Lorimer, Mrs
18 M'Pherson, Mrs
18 Cairns, Alex., grocer
18 Shaw, William, grocer
19 M'Pherson, & Carson, painters
20 Beveridge, Miss, milliner
21 M'Pherson, Malcolm, painter
21 Morton, Miss
21 Bayne, Thomas, teacher
21 Barclay, Andrew, builder
22 Missionary Hall, and Penny Savings Bank
24 Union Bank—Wm. Drysdale, agent
25 Glover, John, ticket collector
25 Glover, Mrs, dressmaker
25 Newlands, Thomas, beadle of West Free Church
25 Gairdner, John, corkcutter
26 Dow, John, joiner, Pine Grove Cottage
27 M'Callum, Peter, house painter, Colquhoun Place
27 Brown, Mrs　　　　　　　　　　　　　　　"
27 Dingwell, John, joiner　　　　　　　　　"
27 Vere, Thomas, coach builder　　　　　"
27 Murrie, John, blacksmith,　　　　　　"
28 Oddfellows' Hall
29 Todd, Peter S., boat builder

COLQUHOUN STREET.

1 Brash, John
2 Currie, George, cabman

2 Reid, Mrs James
2 Jardine, Marion
2 M'Ewan, M. & W., milliners and dressmakers
3 Cavana, Bernard, tailor
4 Milk Shop—Mrs Dow.
5 Drummond, Robert
5 Rifle Volunteer Drill Hall
6 Caldwell, Mrs, pastry baker·
7 Hamilton, Alexander, mason
7 Lyon, James, mason
8 Bakehouse—L. M'Lachlan
9 Printing Office—William Campbell
10 Osborne, Thomas, carter
10 M'Master, James, mason
11 Buchanan, Thomas, tailor
12 Ingram, James,
12 Ingram, Thomas, butter and egg merchant
12 Murray, Thomas, water inspector
13 Buchanan, Miss, dressmaker
15 Watson, James, mason
16 M'Lean, Alexander, joiner
17 Burnett, John, slater
18 Drysdale, William, J.P,, agent, Union Bank
19 Coal Depot—John Eman
20 Miller, Mrs James
21 Kerr, William, contractor
22 Hastie, Janet
   West Free Church—Rev. Alexander Anderson
23 West Free Church School—Miss K. Mitchell, teacher
24 M'Dougall, Mrs
24 M'Lean, Miss, dressmaker
26 David S. Allan, teacher of music
26 Hunter, Mrs
27 Miller, Miss, cloak and dressmaker
27 Yuille, Archibald B., Brownhill
28 Hamilton, Alexander, guard
29 Cramb, Duncan, Larch Villa
29 Cramb, James, artist,   „

29 Cramb, John, artist, Larch Villa
30 Crawford, Hugh, baker
31 Notman, Mrs Robert, Colquhoun Villa
32 M'Dougall, John, gardener
32 Arroll, John, gardener
34 White, James, joiner
35 Larchfield Academy—Alex. Mackenzie, M.A., headmaster
37 Mair, George, teacher, Galloway Cottage
39 Smith, Captain M. H., Beaulah Lodge
46 Breingan, Alexander, J.P., banker, Madgefield
48 Cree, Mrs, Merlefield
50 Smellie, Miss, Ellangowan
    M'Lean, John, D. L., High School, Glasgow, Edenbank
    Jeffrey, Miss, Torwood Villa
    Houston, Adam, Baronfrow

GEORGE STREET.

1 Davidson, Mrs, dressmaker
1 Shearer, Miss
1 Smith, Mrs John
5 Paton, James, wholesale grocer
7 Beck, George
7 M'Donald, Robert Parker, baker
9 M'Aulay, Mrs
11 Paton, John, wholesale stationer
19 Marsland, Sergeant James
20 Kettle, Sergeant
20 M'Lachlan, Hugh, mason
20 Hall, Robert, shoemaker
22 Boswell, John, painter
22 Ralston, Alex., Town Missionary
24 Orr Mrs James, Park House
28 Paterson, Misses, Holm Glen
30 Duncanson, Miss, Rockland Cottage

GLASGOW STREET.

1 Miller, David, gardener to John Brown
2 Tassie, Miss, Craigbank
3 Campbell, Robert, coal merchant, Wellcroft

4 Shields, William, joiner
7 Wallace, Mrs, Westwood
9 Fraser, Mrs, Beauly Cottage
10 M'Nair, William, Willowburn Cottage
11 Forrester, Mrs, Porton Cottage .
12 Black, David, coach proprieter
14 Anderson, H. L., Ava Cottage
15 Gray, Mrs, Govane Bank
15 Govane, Miss, Govane Bank
16 Gray, John, Easterton.
17 Smith, Patrick, Westfield
18 Risk, Mrs, Elmwood
19 Andrew, Thomas, Yew Bank

GLENFINLAS STREET,.

2 Carlow, Wm.
8 Mackenzie, John, tailor
8 Burns, Mrs
8 M'Gregor, Mrs
10 Chapman, Mrs, ladies' nurse
12 M'Leod, Mrs
14 Rathbone, Mrs, laundress and mangle keeper
16 Stewart, Christopher, saddler
17 Mitchell, George, Blairkip
18 Turnbull, Mrs, Rannoch Villa
20 Walker, Robert, J.P., Eskville

GRANT STREET.

5 Burgh Slaughter House
7 Barclay, Andrew, builder
11 Industrial School—George ''air & Miss Malcolm, tec oher
15 M'Gehan, Henry, engine driver
19 M'Menemy, Peter, byre and stables
50 M'Dougal, Mrs, Ardbeg Cottage
52 Mackay, Martin, writer, Osborne Villa
54 Primrose, Thomas, Hawthorn Hill

GRANVILLE STREET.

1 Falconer, Thomas, J.P., Parkhill
3 Graham, M. C., Huntly Villa

5 Wotherspoon, Miss, teacher of music, Pomona Villa
7 Kirkwood, Mrs Alexander, Clarefoot
9 Hamer, Job, Carden Bank
10 Murdoch, John, Dalblair
11 MacGoun, Misses,·Killearn Lodge
13 Mitchell, John, Brooklee
15 Mirrlees, Miss, Burnshill
17 Vannan, Robert, tea and wine merchant, Blawlowan

HANOVER STREET.

2 Monteith, Adam, Eastbank
4 Henderson, Mrs, Eastbank

HAVELOCK STREET.

1 Fisken, Archibald, Birkhall
3 Gilmour, Mrs, Edgemount
5 Stewart, Alexander, Collinslee
7 York, Miss, Fairthorn

JAMES STREET.

1 Dewar, Donald, gardener
1 Ogilvie, Mrs
2 Roy, Gabriel, watchmaker
2 Thomson, Alexander, plumber
8 Buchanan, Thomas, tailor
10 Clydesdale Bank—R. D. Orr, agent
12 Orr, R. D., J.P., banker
13 Burgess, James, gardener
14 Lamont, Hugh, dairyman and carter
15 Ballantyne, James, shoemaker
16 Smith, William, baker
17 Allan, James, gardener
19 Provan, Andrew
19 M'Kay, Miss, dress and cloakmaker
20 Wilson, Mrs
20 Jardine, Bryce, coal merchant
20 Kennedy, Mrs
21 M'Coll, Duncan, joiner
22 M'Kinlay, Mrs

22 M'Connel, David, Roseneath post
22 M'Lachlan, Mary
22 Orr, Andrew, labourer
23 M'Millan, Hamilton
23 Melville, Robert, mason
23 Gillespie, William, engineer
23 Litster, Mrs
23 Campbell, Mrs
24 Black, John, slater
24 Gordon, James, house painter
24 Ferguson, James harbour-master
24 M'Neil, Hugh, carter
24 M'Kay, James, joiner
24 Smith, Mrs
32 Henderson, John, dairyman
32 Henderson, Joseph, boatbuilder
35 M'Naughton, John, dairyman and carter
37 Neilson, Mrs, washer and dresser
37 Brabender, Andrew
37 Henderson, Wm., mason
37 Allan, Walter, blacksmith
37 Ward, John, tinsmith
37 Forsyth, Mrs
39 M'Gregor, Gregor, mason
39 M'Kinnon, Peter, labourer
40 Yuile, Miss, Prospect Cottage
41 Ferguson, George, painter
42 Marquis, Miss, Argyle Park
43 Campbell, Robert, grocer and coal merchant
44 Patterson, R. J. B., Dalglenan Lodge
44 Patterson, Mrs J. B., Dalglenan Lodge
46 Walker, Miss Lydia, Hilsrig
48 Samuel, Miss, Dunbeg
50 M'Clure, Robert, writer
51 Springfield Academy—Thomas Harker, head-master
52 Lindsay, Alexander, Leven Villa
53 Harker, Thomas, Springfield Academy
61 Sloan, Charles, Springbank Cottage

63 Smith, James, Methill Field
65 Anderson, Mrs, Violet Bank
67 Thomson, Miss, ladies' boarding and day school, Glenfruin House
69 Brown, Miss, Middledrift
71 Urie, Rev. William, Sefton Cottage
71 Urie, Miss, Sefton Cottage
    Anderson, John, Clarendon Villa
    Reid, D. S. Hartree
    Duff, Rev. David, M.A., L.L.D., Glenan Manse

JOHN STREET.

1 Thomson, J. & R., drapers
2 Adams, Mrs, dressmaker
2 Leitch, Miss Jane
2 M'Farlane, John, joiner
3 Fubister, Miss, furrier
3 Ewing, Peter, coal merchant
3 Nimmo, John, baker
4 Bride, Archibald
4 Short, George, shoemaker
5 Craig, John, mason
6 Lindsay, John, gardener
7 Grant, Miss Mary
7 Arroll, James, gardener
8 Hannah, Mrs Thomas
9 Martin, Miss Christina
9 Brabendar, Archibald, porter
9 Scott, Mrs
9 Robertson, James, mason
9 Kennedy, Miss
9 Murray, Miss
10 M'Innes, Robert, shoemaker
10 M'Dermid, Margaret
10 Robertson, David, bootmaker
11 and 13, Hill, Samuel, grocer
12 Service, Janet
15 Cochran, Captain James

17 Young, William
22 and 24, Ferguson & Shields, joiners
23 Bryce, William, Burnbank Cottage
23 Aitken, John
27 Kinniburgh, Alexander, inspector of poor
29 Dingwell, John, The Glennan
30 M'Allister, John, joiner, and Established Church beadle
30 Colquhoun, Mrs
30 M'Isaac, Hugh, mason
30 Moody, Miss
30 M'Taggart, Miss, dressmaker
31 Templeton, James, Drumgarve
32 Finlay, Captain, Portland Place
33 Donaldson, Mrs P., Lenylea
33 Sinclair, Alexander,   ,,
34 M'Kenzie, Mrs Alex.
34 Finlay, Alexander, clerk
34 Owler, Mrs
35 Robertson, Miss, Annat Lodge
36 Bisland, Alex., painter
37 Mathieson, Mrs, Glendarroch House
38 Anderson, Miss J.
39 M'Culloch, John C., Woodburn House
40 Colquhoun, Captain
40 Bain, Andrew John, teacher
40 Grant, Mrs C.
40 Assafrey, A. T.
42 Dickson, James
44 Arroll, Robert, gardener
50 M'Callum, Peter, Sunnyside Cottage
56 Dunlop, Robert, writer, Springfield House
58 Kerr, John, coachman
60 Hannah, Mrs Thomas, Laurel Green
62 Pollock, Robert, Cornwall House
Rennie, Mrs William, Wellcroft

JOHN STREET LANE.

Barr, Gavin, Hartfield
Troup, Rev. James, M.A., Seirra Cleare

Mylius, Major Rodney, Dallglennan Cottage
Henderson, James,   ,,

KING'S CRESCENT.

1 M'Auslan, Archibald, Park Cottage
2 Wright, Rev. T., Towerville
3 Lochhead, John, Ronbank
3 Fuller, J. S,
4 Laird, Alexander A., Clyde View

KING STREET, EAST.

4 Hodgson, Parker, police sergeant, Gay's Cottage
20 Murray, Patrick, joiner
21 King Street Hall—James Lennox, keeper
37 Chiene, Patrick John, Eastburn Cottage
40 Jardine, James, bootmaker
42 Paton, Mrs
47 Eastburn School—Miss Davie, teacher
47 M'Gregor, Gregor, mason
47 Carruthers, Richard, cartwright
51 Lindsay, M., (of Gardner & Lindsay), grain merchant
53 Lindsay, John, contractor
62 Rowson, Rev. Samuel B., R.C.C.
64 Niven, James, landscape gardener
66 Ponds, James, Whinbrae
68 Sinclair, Mrs,   Eastburn Place
68 Robertson, William, tailor   ,,
68 Douglas, Alex., gardener   ,,
68 M'Lachlan, Hugh, railway porter   ,,
70 Waters, Wm., upholsterer   ,,
72 Shearer, William   ,,
74 Cameron, Duncan, gardener   ,,
76 M'Leod, John, beadle of Park Free Church ,,
78 Kirkmichael, John, railway porter   ,,
78 M'Lachlan, Mrs A,   ,,
78 M'Kellar, John, gardener   ,,
78 M'Lachlan, James, mason   ,,
78 Livingstone, Mrs, washer and dresser   ,,
78 Crocket, Mrs,   ,,

78 M'Cabe, John, coal merchant   Eastburn Place
78 Robertson, John, mason   ,,
78 Lang, Alexander, mason   ,,
78 Paterson, John, mason   ,,
82 Somerville, James, grocer   ,,
84 Allan, George, grocer
88 Brown, John, mason and grocer
    Kerr & Bishop, joiners
90 M'Menemy, Peter, dairyman
94 Pollock, James, grocer
95 Town Mission Reading Room
100 Cornall, F., coal merchant—depot 17 Princes street, **w.**
104 Douglas, Mrs, washer and dresser
110 Stevenson, Robert, plasterer
118 Wood yard—Archibald M'Auslan, joiner
124 Stirling, Mrs,   Woodside Place
126 Mason, Miss   ,,
126 M'Skimmon, Captain   ,,
126 Turner, Mrs   ,,
126 Kenny, Captain   ,,
129 M'Dougal, Mrs, Cora House
130 M'Naught, Archibald, farmer
131 Campbell, Colin, Cora House
133 Crow, Mrs, Braefoot
135 M'Auslan, Miss, Enmore
137 Buchanan, Moses, Aberdale
142 Purvis, T. A., station master
144 Gray, James, Park House
118 Fox, Wm. H., leather merchant, La Belle Villa
150 Comrie, Alexander, builder,   ,,
152 Stirrat, Mrs,   ,,
154 Orr, Mrs, Lauder Villa
156 Finlay, Mrs, Mayfield
160 Richmond, John, Doune Cottage
164 Tweedle, Robert, Parkend Cottage
170 Sloan, Dr S., M'Master's Cottage
    Mitchell, Miss, Millerslee Villa
    Elsworth, John,   ,,

KING STREET, WEST

1 Colquhoun, Mrs, Moss Cottage
2 Anderson, Rev. Alexander, West Free Manse
3 Thomson, Mrs
3 M'Ewan, Thomas, mason
3 Hunter, James, plasterer
3 M'Arthur, Peter, gardener
3 M'Lachlan, Henry, painter
12 Murray, Donald, joiner—house 14
16 Wilson, John, Devar Cottage
16 Jenkins, Miss, Devar Cottage
18 Lamond, Miss, Sunnyside
20 Campbell, Miss,   ,,
20 Grant, Mrs,   ,,
20 M'Callum, Donald, tailor
25 Bulloch, James, gardener
26 Ronald, Mrs, Dover Cottage
27 Ferguson, Miss
28 Smith, Mrs, Rossdhu Villa
29 M'Pherson, Wm., gardener
30 Snell, Miss, Rossdhu Villa
31 Harvie Miss
32 M'Laurin, Miss
33 Brown, Alexander, St. Clair Villa
35 Warren, Timothy, St. Clair Villa
38 Waddell, David, Eva Cottage
40 Adams, Mrs, Mossbank Cottage
42 King, Mrs, Valleyfield
42 King, John, Valleyfield
43 Drysdale, Mrs, Mossgrove
46 Thomson, Misses, Union Villa
48 Duncan, Mrs J.,   ,,
49 M'Candy, Mrs
50 Gray, G. W., Carisbrook
51 Webster, John, merchant, Clyde Cottage
52 Nairn, John, Roselea Cottage
52 Cochrane, Miss, Roselea Cottage
53 Tait, William, Netherlee

54 Clark, Miss, Melbourne Villa
56 M'Pherson, Mrs, Ashens
57 Lay, Miss
58 Thomson, John, Woodneuck
59 Shaw, William
60 Auld, Mrs T., Woodneuck
61 Good, John, mason
63 Macduff, Peter, Hayfield Cottage

LOMOND STREET.

2 Battieson, Mrs
7 Rodger, John, carter and dairyman
8 Macindoe, Mrs Walter, Albion Cottage
10 Harvie, George, chemist, Kilinn Cottage
15 Gray, William, railway guard
17 Jamieson, William, yacht master, Dougal's Place
19 Smith, Mrs
19 Graham, Miss
19 Gourlay, Margaret
19 Drew, Miss
23 Dougall, Mrs John, Hopewell Cottage
24 Fowler, James, spirit merchant, Alma Cottage
25 Ramsay, Mrs, Hopewell Cottage
26 Comrie, Alexander, Fairyknowe
30 Williams, Mrs, Stewart Green
30 Vallance, Miss   ,,
30 Macfarlane, Mrs   ,,
32 M'Ewan, James, Brackenhill Cottage
33 Pearson, John, Bloomfield   .
34 Burgess, Miss, Elgin Villa
41 Brown, Robert, Lomond Cottage
43 Dun, stationer, Fruinfield
45 Coltart, John, Larkhill

MAITLAND STREET.

1 M'Laren, Miss
2 Colquhoun, John
  Muirhead, Robert, (of Muirhead and Feddie), painters
  Snodgrass, James

Robb, David
3 Gardner and Lindsay's grain store
4 Brown, Mrs
4 Docharty, Thomas, labourer
4 Stewart, Donald, carter
4 Fisher, Daniel, shoemaker
4 Smith, Robert, mason
4 Service, Mary, washer-woman
5 Temperance Hall
6 M'Farlane, Mrs
8 Paton, John, boot and shoemaker
10 Ruthven, John, saddler
11 Cameron, Archibald, gardener
11 Mackay, James, carter
11 M'Donald, Lachlan, carter
11 Wylie, George, seaman
12 Bulloch, Francis, gardener
12 Purvis, William, carter
13 Glen, Mrs,
14 Strachan, Mrs
14 Gilchrist, Thomas, porter
14 Grehan, John, police constable
14 Stirling, William, tailor
14 Meldrum, George, painter
14 Neil, Henry, gardener
15 Campbell, Alexander, carter
15 M'Leod, Donald, tailor
15 M'Leod, Miss, dressmaker
15 Glen, Mrs
15 Mackay, Mrs
15 M'Farlane, Mrs
16 M'Innes, Thomas, gardener
16 M'Innes, Mrs, grocer
17 M'Cafer, Miss, washer and mangle keeper
17 M'Pherson, Malcolm, mason
17 Kelly, Mrs
17 Ferguson, Miss
17 Roper, Mary

18 M'Auslane, Robert, shoemaker
19 Millar, John, labourer
19 Paul, Mrs
19 Murphy, John, scavengar
19 M'Neil, John, joiner
19 Rennie, Mrs
19 Doun, Andrew, plumber
19 Thomson, William, gardener
19 M'Farlane, Andrew, gardener
19 Greenlee, John, gardener
19 M'Aulay, Frank, gardener
19 Craig, James, gardener
19 M'Cormick, Mrs, washer-woman
19 M'Cree, Miss
19 M'Vey, Miss
19 Forsyth, Mrs
19 Forsyth, Miss, dressmaker
20 Stirling, Mrs, draper—house, 14
21 Morris, Mrs, mangle keeper
22 White, Alexander, butcher
23 Slorance, George, gardener
23 Smith, David, mason
24 Robertson, Mrs
24 M'Pherson, Daniel, slater
24 M'Kenzie, George, plasterer
25 Murray, Mrs
26 Spiers, William, barber—house, 14

MILLIG STREET, EAST

M'Haffie, Mrs, Belmont
Sharp, William, Glenfeulan
Angus, Ritchie, Lindens, Victoria Road
Snodgrass, Matthew, farmer, East Milligs Farm

MILLIGS STREET, WEST

Murdoch, Misses, ladies' boarding school, Ashmount
Somervail, James, Carron Bank
M'Gregor, John, Ardshiel
Robley, Harrington, Carleton

Robertson, Andrew C., Woodend House

MONTROSE STREET, EAST

1 Chapman, William, Agnew Villa
5 Steven, Thomas, J.P., Ardlui House
7 Peat, Misses, day school, Barwood
9 Wilson, Rev. John, Camden Villa
11 M'Millan, Daniel, Pinlea
13 Dale, Robert G., Braehead
13 Drysdale, Archibald B., Ochil Bank
15 M'Lellan, Duncan, Annock Bank
17 Readman, James, St. Leonards
19 Millar, William, Wellington Lodge
19 Millar, Miss Jane
21 Smith, William, confectioner, Fernbank
23 Gillies, John, merchant, Glenelg Villa
25 Garroway, James, Airdbank
27 Allan, Miss, Greenknowe
29 Corbett, William A., J.P., Carbrook
31 Paterson, George, Dunfillan

MONTROSE STREET, WEST

1 Skene, Mrs J.
2 White, Mrs, Wardfield
4 Neil, Mrs David, Hillside Cottage
6 Robertson, Mrs, Blairnairn House
8 Carslaw, Mrs,   „
9 Ramsay, James, Woodend Nursery
9 Ramsay, Miss, dressmaker
10 Robertson, Matthew, Annsfield
11 Buchanan, Miss
12 Currie, John, Heathfield
14 Gow, Archibald, Ashburn House
16 Fyfe, Miss, Letrewel
16 Frew, John, Elmwood Cottage
20 Orr, Mrs Robert, Ballimore Lodge
22 Kirkwood, Miss, Laurel Villa
24 Todd, Mrs James, Woodlea

PRINCE'S STREET, EAST

1 Hay, Mrs John, draper—house, 5

2 Snodgrass, Andrew, boot and shoemaker, Young's Place
3 Millar, James, carver and gilder,
4 M'Lean, Miss Jessie, furnishing shop, Young's Place
5 Donaldson, Mrs
5 Beveridge, John, gardener
5 Paterson, William, saddler
5 Veitch, John
6 M'Lachlan, George, writer, Young's Place
7 Wilson, Robert, tobacconist
8 Paton, William, gardener, Young's Place
9 Post·Office—William Bryson, postmaster, nurseryman, and seedsman
9 Public Library
10 Millar, James
10 Gray, Mrs
10 Goodwin, Alexander, joiner
11 Millar, Mrs T., bookseller
12 Watt, Miss J. A., china merchant, Rossdhu Place
13 Ferguson, Andrew, painter
14 Gilchrist, William, baker
15 M'Arthur, Mrs, dairy
16 Cuthill, James, flesher
17 Barr, Francis, tailor
17 Adams, William, tailor
17 Cornall, Francis—coal depot
18 Service, H. & M., dressmakers
19 Stevenson, Robert—workshop
20 Berlin Wool Repository—Dickson and Aikman—ho., 79
21 Waldie, John—blacksmiths' workshop
21 Hunter, James—bakehouse
22 Billiard and Smoking Room—T. M'Menemy, proprietor
23 Reid, William, plumber and gasfitter
24 Muirhead & Peddie, painters
25 Parochial Board Office—Alexander Kinniburgh, inspector
26 M'Menemy, Peter, grain merchant
27 M'Lachlan, Mrs
28 Barron, Mrs, refreshment rooms
29 M'Culloch, J. W. & Son, painters and paperhangers

30 Telfer, James, fruiterer
31 Police Office—John Anderson, superintendent
32 Henderson, Miss, flesher
33 Town Hall and Court House
34 Veitch, John, junr., spirit dealer
35 Russell, William, coal merchant
36 Hunter, James, baker—house, 10
37 Ewing, Peter & Co., coal merchants
38 Harvie, George, chemist
39 Railway Station—T. A. Purves, station-master
40 Burgess, James, grocer and provision merchant
41 Glen, John, contractor
42 M'Menemy, Thomas, tobacconist—house, 76
43 M'Menemy, Peter
44 Ure, Miss M., embroidery printer
44 Spalding, James, writer and insurance agent
44 Stamp and Tax Office—James Spalding distributor and
      collector
44 Bain, Mrs
44 Dickson, Mrs
45 Rankin, Mrs, Main Cottage
46 Frame, Helen, fruiterer
47 M'Callum, Mrs, washer woman
48 Provan, Andrew, bookseller and stationer
49 Carson, Mrs
50 Battrum, William, bookseller, stationer, and fancy goods
      emporium—music shop, 7 Sinclair Street
52 Printing Office and Reading Room—Wm. Battrum
52 Allan, Miss
52 Meikle, John
52 Robertson, David, gardener
54 & 56 Muir, Robert, draper
58 M'Donald, David Ross, pastry cook and resterateur
59 Kelly, John, labourer
60 Temperance Hotel—Mrs Sharp
60 Ballantyne, James
60 Allwood, Jonathan, gothic glazier
61 Stewart, William, photographer

62 & 64 Mitchell, A. R., grocer and spirit merchant
63 M'Kimb, James, stationer
66 Sharp, Thomas, butcher
67 Campbell, John, mason.
68 Hamilton, James
68 Orme, William
68 Shearer, James
69 Hosie, Russell, blacksmith
70 Peddie, W., fruiterer
71 Galloway, John, mason
72 Filluel, Charles, fish merchant—house, 68
73 Williamson, William, tinsmith
74 M'Lean, Donald, grocer—house, 76
75 Tait, Miss
76 Anderson, John, joiner
77 M'Pherson, Mrs.
78 Stevenson, Robert, boot and shoemaker—house, 76
79 Cunningham, Matthew, joiner
79 Rumgay, James, joiner
79 Plowright Miss
80 Stewart, Misses, milliners
81 Crawford, Miss, dressmaker
82 M'Crae, Kenneth, wholesale confectioner
83 Tosh, Misses
84 Muirhead, Mrs
84 Love, Robert, mason
84 Murray, Patrick, joiner
84 Cunningham, John, gardener
86 Thomson, Peter, wine and spirit merchant—house, 84
87 Edgar, John, Greenbank Cottage
88 Gas Work—William Smith, manager
93 Anderson, Joseph, tailor
93 Adar, William, gardener to Dr Finlay
93 M'Donald, John, cabinet-maker
93 Brownlee, John, plasterer
93 M'Corkindale, George, carter
95 Campbell, Archibald, joiner
95 Campbell, Miss, dressmaker

 97 Spratt, Miss, Springvale Cottage
115 Volunteer Artillery Drill Hall
117 Service Mrs
117 Agnew, William, painter
117 Cavana, John, painter
119 Bruce, Mrs, Glenfinlas
119 Bruce, Miss, Glenfinlas
121 Smith, Mrs
122 M'Dougal, John
126 Kerr, Mrs
128 Brown, Mrs
130 Kerr, Hugh, joiner
130 Gray, William, engine driver
131 Eddie, Mrs, Walton Cottage
132 Noble, John, mason
137 Martin, Matthew, Bath House
137 Martin, Miss   ,,
134 Connell, George   ,,
137 Sellers, Miss   ,,
148 Aikman, Mrs Peter, Iona Terrace
172 Barclay, James, sculptor
172 Renfrew, Miss
172 Carslaw, William, wood-turner
172 Towers, Miss
180 Bell, James, gardener
182 Rankin, James
184 Grant, Mrs
202 Carter, Mrs, Giffnock House
204 Smith, Mrs, Giffnock House

PRINCES STREET, WEST

 2 Cairns, Alexander, grocer
 4 Allan, George
 4 Campbell, William
 4 Mitchell, Miss
 6 Irvine, John, tailor and clothier—house, 4
 8 Gardner, Mrs
10 Spy, Robert, letter carrier and coal merchant
10 Carson, Robert, painter

10 Frame, J., joiner
10 Muter, William, grocer
10 Mitchell, David,
12 Ramsay, James, florist and seedsman
14 Porter, Clement, upholsterer—house, 16
16 Chalmers, John, joiner
16 Sproul, Matthew, book deliverer
16 Grant, Mrs
18 Grant, James, plumber—house, 16
19 Congregational Church—Rev. James Troup, M,A. .
20 Brown, Jacob, painter
22 Gibbons, Patrick, photographer
24 Ward, C., coal merchant
28 M'Kinlay, Duncan, contractor
30 Smith, William, baker and confectioner
31 Dunlop, William, coal merchant
32 M'Millan, Hamilton, spirit dealer
33 Woodyard—Duncan M'Coll, joiner
34 Maxwell, Mrs
35 Jack, John, stables
36 Russell, William
38 Russell, Mrs, dairy
39 Shanks, Mrs
39 Trought, S. E., portrait and landscape painter·
39 Dunlop, William
40 Deans, John, surfaceman
40 Goodwin, Mrs, washer and dresser
41 Middlemass, Joseph, blacksmith.
41 Hamilton, Mrs J..
42 Rodger, James, carter
42 Park, Alexander, saddler
42 Campbell, William, shoemaker
42 Ingles, John, shoemaker
42 Park, Thomas, slater
42 Robb, John, mason
43 Ross, Misses, milliners and dressmakers·
44 M'Coll, John, joiner
45 Lamont, Miss

46 Bain, Mrs John
46 O'Neil, Michael, gardener
46 Haxton, John, fireman
47 Buchanan, William, joiner
48 Forsyth, James, slater
49 Hill, Samuel
50 Mackay, John, mason
51 Aitken, Miss
52 Cameron, Mrs
54 Chapman, Miss, teacher of music
55 Morrison, Mrs, George
56 Leslie, Captain,
56 Paterson, Miss
57 Boatbuilding and joiners' yard
58 Watson, John
59 Thomson, William, joiner
59 Thomson, Robert, boatbuilder
60 Jack, Mrs A., Holyrood Place
61 Johnson, David, mason
62 Watt, Robart, draper
62 Stewart, Mrs,
63 Fisher, Miss, mangle keeper
64 Jamieson, Joseph
65 Ross, John, mason
66 Pender Miss
66 M'Auslan, Misses, laundresses
68 Glen, John
68 Colquhoun, Mrs
70 Hunter, Mrs
70 Buchanan, James, grocer
72 Bell, Miss
72 Munro, Alex, gardener
74 Wood yard—William Buchanan, joiner
80 Wotherspoon, Mrs, Rosebank Terrace
82 M'Gilp, Miss, Rosebank Terrace
84 Foot, Miss, Rosebank
85 Campbell, Robert, Wellcroft
87 Fisher, Miss, Wellcroft

87 Fisher, Robert M., teacher of painting and drawing, Wellcroft
91 Buchanan, Mrs, Brandongrove Cottage
95 Mackie, Charles, Milton Cottage
96 Perritt, William, Byron Cottage
97 Galloway, Wm, town weigher, Milton Cottage
98 Cameron, Archibald, gardener
99 Anderson, John, Lochview
101 Paton, Mrs
102 M'Culloch, Wm. L., Laurel Cottage
104 Paton, Mrs, Blairburn Villa
106 Colquhoun, Daniel, ironmonger, Westwood Cottage
108 Wallace, Mrs
108 M'Auslan, Mrs A.
110 M'Haffie, James
110 Lang, Miss, Bellview
112 Scoular, William, Leewood Villa

SINCLAIR STREET.

1 Forbes, Mrs, milliner and dressmaker
2 Mitchell, John, grocer, wine and spirit merchant
3 Dickie, R. W., confectioner
4 M'Farlane, R. S.
4 Reid, Miss
4 M'Nee, John
5 Campbell, Lorne, J. M., Central Apothecaries' Hall
6 Pettit, Wm. A., printer, bookseller, and house-agent
7 Pianoforte and Music Warehouse—W. Battrum
8 Orme, Wm., butter, ham and egg merchant
9 and 11 M'Ewan, Miss, Berlin Wool Repository
10 M'Connell, Thomas, ironmonger—house, 12
12 Galloway, George, builder
12 Bryde, Archibald
12 Laurie, James, carter
13 Smith, Mrs, boot and shoemaker
14 Shaw, William, family grocer and wine merchant
15 Anderson, Miss J., furnishing shop
16 Dickson, Mrs, painter and decorator
17 Wheldon, Daniel, carter

18 Mainds, William, painter
18 Paterson, Miss, teacher
19 Spy, Andrew, coal merchant—house, 12
20 Crawford, Thomas, plumber—house, 4
22 Craig, James, refreshment rooms –house, 12
24 M'Kechnie, William, dairyman and green grocer
26 M'Kechnie, William, barman
26 M'Leod, Gabriel, gardener
26 M'Leod, Miss, dressmaker
26 Neilly, Richard, basket-maker
26 Graham, Thomas
26 Strath, David, saddler
26 Gifford, Mark, blacksmith
26 Stewart, Peter, mason
26 M'Lean, Mrs
30 Davidson, John, tailor and clothier—house, 28
31 Helensburgh Inn—John Veitch
32 Rodger, William, blacksmith—house, 34
38 Bell, Miss, refreshment rooms
40 Campbell, Peter auctioneer
41 M'Culloch J. W., & Son, painters' shop
42 Lennox, James, beadle of U. P. Church
42 Lennox, George, painter
45 & 47 Waldie, John, coach proprietor
48 M'Kechnie, Angus, bootmaker and prison keeper
51 Allan, George, slater
51 Falconer, William, labourer
53 M'Killop, Archibald, carter
53 Boyd, Robert, coachman
53 M'Ewan, Henry, plasterer
53 Ross, William, bill poster
53 Ross, Miss, dressmaker
53 Carline, Mrs
53 Paterson, William, mason
53 M'Leod, Mrs
53 Hutchison, William, gardener
54 Sharp, Thomas
55 M'Millan, Dougal, grocer

57 Smith, Mrs, mangle keeper
59 Grierson, John, mason
60 Finlay, Dr. James, M.D., Millbrae
61 Clark, William, mason
61 Young, Miss
61 Allison, James, joiner
61 M'Isaac, John, sawyer
61 Hyndman, William
61 Hyndman, Mrs, washer and mangle keeper·
62 Aitken, James, Oxford Bank
63 M'Donald, Ronald, gardener
63 M'Callum, Mrs
63 M'Callum, Mrs
63 Clark, Mrs
64 Jardine, Mrs, Dovehill
65 Paterson, Joseph, mason
66 Fisher, Peter, Bonnie Brae
   United Presbyterian Church—Rev, D. Duff, M,A., LL.D
67 M'Coll, Mrs, Fountain Bank
69 Bain, James, Fountain Bank
71 Bain, James, blacksmith and horse shoeing forge
73 Lamont, Mrs, Millhill
75 Buchanan, Mrs, ,,
76 Smith, John, Hermitage
76 M'Intyre, Duncan, gardener, Hermitage
76 Arroll, Archibald, gardener
77 Nelson, Robert
79 Skimming, Alexander, cartwright
81 Bow, Mrs, Millview
82 Buchanan, John, Hermitage Cottage
83 M'Laren, Alexander, Millfield
85 M'Gregor, Robert, Ettrick Bank
87 Gray, Hugh, Braeside
89 Hamilton, James, Thornton Lodge
   M'Intyre, John, Cawdor Lodge,   Luss Road
   Deas, Mrs, East House   ,,
   Thomson, James, Fairfield,   ,,
   Wilson, Miss, Chapel Acre,   ,,

Kilty, H., gardener, Chapel Acre Lodge, Luss Road
Young, James, Rockmount,   ,,
Fleming, Mrs, Brownhill,   ,,
Bowling Green,   ,,
Robertson, James, Northwood,   ,,
Jamieson, Miss, Moorlands,   ,,
Zinkeisen, Victor, Dhuhill,   ,,
Reid, William, Dhuhill,   ,,
Millig Toll—William Brock   ,,

QUEEN STREET

Allan, James, merchant, Warriston Lodge
Hamilton, Mrs James, Hayfield
M'Bean, Lachlan, Findhorn
Dick, Alexander, Queensmount
Alexander, James, Rachan House
Donald, Miss, Marian Lodge
Davie, Archibald, ploughman, Glenan Farm
Stoker, Archibald, ploughman,   ,,
Jardon, Marion   ,,
Livingston, Mrs, Ardvuela
Spence, James, gardener, Ardvuela
Stewart, Walter, Glenan
Lindsay, John, farmer, Woodend Farm

STAFFORD STREET.

2 Lennox, Alexander, Albert Villa
4 Hendry, Mrs, Glencairn
6 M'Lachlan, George, Blairlomond
12 Anderson, Alexander, J.P., Wellfield

SUFFOLK STREET.

1 Wylie, Robert, Lochiel Cottage
2 Fulton, Mrs, Farnie House
3 Cook, Matthew, Byron Cottage
4 Andrew, Miss, La Retraite
5 Butt, Edward, Canton Cottage
6 Dorward, Charles, Lochview
7 Craig, Alexander, Oriel Cottage

9 Lindsay, Miss, Valleyfield
9 Hector, Miss, Valleyfield
9 Campbell, Alexander, joiner
11 M'Auslane, Miss, Sunnybrae
11 Oliphant, Miss   ,,
13 Hadfield, Mrs, Oakbank
15 M'Farlane, Mrs, Claremont House
16 Battrum, William, Mossbank House
17 Blair, Mrs, Annsfield Villa
18 Malcolm, William, Mossbank House
19 Walker, Mrs R., Elmtree Villa
20 Reid, Mrs, Anchorage
21 Currie, Captain Henry, Helenslee
22 Webster, Robert, Ardenvahr
23 Thomson, James, Grange
24 Arnot, Thomas, Shawfield
26 Drew, Miss, Holly Villa
   Potter, Mrs, Auchentiel

SUTHERLAND STREET.

2 Kennedy, Fergus
3 Robertson, Mrs, dairy
4 M'Isaac, Mrs, Heath Cottage
6 Jamieson, Mrs Thomas, Jordonhill
7 Ferguson, Andrew B., Woodside Cottage
8 Heggie, Mrs James
9 Campbell, James, gardener, Woodside Place
9 M'Auslane, Mrs,   ,,
9 Millar, Miss   ,,
10 Ure, Miss
10 Watt, Mrs
11 Robertson, Mrs

SUTHERLAND STREET, NORTH.

Smith, Miss, Payta Villa
Leiper William, architect, Tertesie
Hunter, David, Duncairn

SUTHERLAND CRESCENT, UPPER.

1 M'Gregor, John, J.P., Bonnyton
2 Murray, Robert, civil engineer, Woodhill

SUTHERLAND CRESCENT, LOWER.

1 Dennistoun, Miss, Elmtree Villa
2 Edward, Matthew, Sherwood
3 Robertson, James, Elm Park
3 Robertson, Mrs, Elm Park
4 Leslie, Miss, Edenwood,
5 M'Millan, Miss, Woodcliff
6 Bain, James, Argyle Cottage
7 Millar, Dr John, Bute Cottage
8 Parker, James, Underwood

WILLIAM STREET

1 Buchanan, Robert
2 Crawford, William, collector
2 Greer, George
3 Law, Mrs, dressmaker, Treesbank
5 Lamb, James, Dargeeling
7 Gray, Mrs,   „
9 Messer, Dr Fordyce, surgeon
11 Wallace, Mrs
13 Ingleton, Miss, teacher of pianoforte, harmonium, guitar, and singing
15 Campbell, Mrs W.
16 Syme, Rev. J. Stuart, Parsonage
   St. Michael and All Angels Church—Rev. J. Stuart Syme, Incumbent
17 M'Coll, Mrs
17 M'Vey, Miss
22 Buchanan, Mrs
23 Armit, Allan, plasterer
23 Goodman, Mrs
23 M'Farlane, Archibald, mason
22 Keyden, Thomas, sawyer
24 Taylor, Robert, surveyor
25 Blackwood, John, Helensburgh and Glasgow carrier
26 Weir, Mrs
27 Bald, A. H., photographer, Richmond Cottage
28 Young, William, Loch Sloy Cottage
   West Established Church—Rev. John Baird, B.D.

29 Dickson, Mrs, Homeston House
30 Ferguson, Miss
31 Smith, Alexander, gardener
32 Whitelaw, Mrs D., Greenhaugh
33 Ferguson, John, Ebenezer Cottage
34 Ewing, William, Heath Villa
35 Storer, James

GENERAL DIRECTORY.

A

Adams, Mrs, dressmaker, 2 John street
Adams, Mrs, Mossbank Cottage, 40 King street, west
Adams, William, tailor, 17 Princes street, east
Adar, William, gardener, 93 Princes street, east
Agnew, William, painter, 117 Princes street, east
Aitchison, Miss, 88 Clyde street, west
Aitken, James, Oxford Bank, 62 Sinclair street
Aitken, John, 23 John street
Aitken, Mrs, 39 Clyde street, west
Aikman, Mrs Peter, Iona Terrace, 148 Princes street, east
Allan, A. P., bookseller, 27 Clyde street, west
Allan, George, grocer, 84 King st., east—house, 4 Princes
    street, west
Allan, George, slater, 51 Sinclair street
Allan, James, gardener, 17 James street
Allan, James, Warriston Lodge, Queen street
Allan, Mrs, The Lodge, 27 Argyle street, west
Allan, Miss, Rosevale Cottage, 14 Campbell street
Allan, Miss, Greenknowe, 27 Montrose street, east
Allan, Miss, 52 Princes street, east
Allan, Walter, blacksmith, 37 James street
Allison, James, joiner, 61 Sinclair street
Allwood, Jonathan, gothic glazier, 60 Princes street, east
Alexander, James, J.P., Rachan, Queen street
Alexander, Miss, Milligs Cottage, 46 Argyle street, east
Anderson, Alexander, J.P., Wellfield, 12 Stafford street
Anderson, H. L., Ava Cottage, 11 Glasgow street
Anderson, John, J.P., Clarendon House, James street
Anderson, John, joiner, 76 Princes street, east
Anderson, John, supt. of police—ho. 99 Princes street, west
Anderson, Joseph, tailor, 93 Princes street, east

Anderson, Miss, spirit dealer, 109 Clyde street, east
Anderson, Mrs, Violet Bank, 65 James street
Anderson, Miss J., 38 John street
Anderson, Rev. Alexander, West Free Manse, 2 King st., w
Andrew, Miss, La Retraite, 4 Suffolk street
Andrew, Thomas, Yewbank, 19 Glasgow street
Angus George, painter, 63 Clyde street, west
Angus, Ritchie, Lindens, Victoria Road
Armit, Allan, plasterer, 23 William street
Arnot, Thomas, Shawfield, 24 Suffolk street
Arroll, Archibald, gardener, 76 Sinclair street
Arroll, James, gardener, 7 John street
Arroll, John, gardener, 32 Colquhoun street
Arroll, Robert, gardener, 44 John street
Arroll, Walter, poulterer and fruiterer, 33 Clyde street, west
Arthur, Rev. John, Burnside Cottage, 24 Campbell street
Artillery Volunteer Drill Hall, 115 Princes street, east
Assafrey, A. T., 40 John street
Auld, Mrs, Glenlea, 30 Argyle street, east
Auld, Mrs T., Woodneuck, 60 King street, west

B

Bain, Andrew John, teacher, 40 John street
Bain, David, weaver, 7 Charlotte street
Bain, James, Fountain Bank, 69 Sinclair street—workshop 71
Bain, James, Argyle Cottage, 6 Lower Sutherland Crescent
Bain, John, joiner, 59 Clyde street, east
Bain, Walter, 75 Clyde street, east
Bain, Mrs, 44 Princes street, east
Bain, Mrs, 177 Clyde street, east
Bain, Mrs, 75 Clyde street, east
Bain, Mrs John, 46 Princes street, west
Baird, Rev. John, West Bay Cottage, 80 Clyde street, west
Bald, A. H., photographer, Richmond Cottage, 27 William st.
Ballantyne, James, 60 Princes street, east
Ballantyne, James, shoemaker, 15 James street
Bank of Scotland—Alexander Breingan, agent
Barclay, Andrew, builder, 21 Colquhoun square
Barclay, James, sculptor, 172 Princes street, east

Barr, Francis, tailor, 17 Princes street, east
Barr, Gavin, Hartfield, John street lane
Barron, Alexander, Gowanlea, Alma Crescent
Barron, Mrs, refreshment rooms, 28 Princes street, east
Barton, William, Devaar Lodge, 34 Charlotte street
Battieson, Mrs, 2 Lomond street
Battrum, William, bookseller, stationer, printer, and fancy
    goods emporium, 50 Princes street, east ; pianoforte, har-
    monium, and music warehouse, 7 Sinclair street ; house,
    Mossbank, 16 Suffolk street
Batty, Mrs Richard, Laurel Bank, 8 Argyle street, west
Baylis, Mrs, Giffnock Cottage, 6 Adelaide street
Bayly, Miss, Woodend Cottage, 14 Argyle street, west
Bayne, Thomas, teacher, 21 Colquhoun square
Beattie, John, Rocklee House, 209 Clyde street, east
Begbie, Robert, gardener, 47 Clyde street, east
Bell, James, gardener, 180 Princes street, east
Bell, Miss, refreshment rooms, 38 Sinclair street
Bennet, Mrs, Newark Villa, 28 Clyde street, east
Berlin Wool Repositories—Miss M'Ewan, 9 Sinclair street ;
    and Misses Dickson & Aikman, 20 Princes street, east
Beveridge, John, gardener, 5 Princes street, east
Beveridge, Miss, milliner, 20 Colquhoun square
Billiard and Smoking Rooms—Rossdhu place, and Clyde st. w
Bisland, Alexander, painter, 36 John street
Black, David, coach proprietor, 12 Glasgow street
Black, John, slater, 24 James street
Blackwood, John, Helensburgh and Glasgow Carrier, 25
    William street
Blackwood, Mrs William, 64 Clyde street, east
Blair, Mrs, Annsfield Villa, 17 Suffolk street
Boswell, John, painter, 22 George street
Borland, Elizabeth, Janelee Cottage, 10 Adelaide street
Boyd, Robert, coachman, 53 Sinclair street
Bow, Mrs, Millview, 81 Sinclair street
Bowling Green, Luss Road
Brabender, Andrew, 37 James street
Brabender, Archibald, porter, 9 John street

Brash, John, tailor and clothier, 2 Clyde street, west, ho., 3 Colquhoun street
Bray, Tom Cox, Carrick House, 195 Clyde street, east
Breingan, Alexander, J.P., Madgefield, 46 Colquhoun street
Brough, William, painter, 39 Clyde street, west
Brown, Alexander, St Clair Villa, 33 King street, west
Brown, Barabara, 12 Charlotte street
Brown, Jacob, painter, 20 Princes street, west
Brown, James, clerk, 28 Clyde street, east
Brown, John, J.P., Brandongrove, 89 Clyde street, west
Brown, John, grocer, 88 King street, east
Brown, Peter, engraver, 48 Clyde street, east
Brown, Robert, Lomond Cottage, 41 Lomond street
Brown, Robert, clerk, 157 Clyde street, east
Brown, Miss, Middledrift, 69 James street
Brown, Mrs, 128 Princes street, east
Brown, Mrs, 27 Colquhoun square
Brown, Mrs, 4 Maitland street
Brown, Mrs, washer and dresser, 189 Clyde street, east
Brownlee, John, plasterer, 93 Princes street, east
Bruce, Mrs, Glenfinlas, 119 Princes street, east
Bruce, Miss,   do.   do.
Bruce, Miss, 64 Clyde street, east
Bryce, William, Burnbank Cottage, 23 John street
Bryde, Archibald, 12 Sinclair street
Bryson, William, nurseryman and seedsman, 9 Princes st. east
Buchanan, Alexander, engineer, 141 Clyde street, east
Buchanan, George, joiner, 137 Clyde street, east
Buchanan, James, grocer, 49 Clyde street, west
Buchanan, John, Hermitage Cottage, 82 Sinclair street
Buchanan, Moses, Aberdale, 137 King street, east
Buchanan, Thomas, tailor, 11 Colquhoun street
Buchanan, Thomas, joiner, 71 Clyde street, east
Buchanan, Robert, 1 William street
Buchanan, Walter, J.P., The Baths, 72 Clyde street, east
Buchanan, Miss, dressmaker, 13 Colquhoun street
Buchanan, Miss, 11 Montrose street, west
Buchanan, Miss, Burnside House, 20 Campbell street

Buchanan, Mrs, 22 William street
Buchanan, Mrs, Brandongrove Cottage, 91 Princes street, w.
Buchanan, Mrs, Millhill, 75 Sinclair street
Bulloch, James, gardener, 25 King street, west
Bulloch, Francis, gardener, 12 Maitland street
Bunten, Miss, Claremont Villa, 78 Clyde street, west
Burns, Adam, 74 Clyde street, west
Burns, Mrs, 8 Glenfinlas street
Burns, Mrs, 39 Clyde street, west
Burgess, James, gardener, 13 James street
Burgess, James, grocer and provision mer., 40 Princes st. east
Burgess, Miss, Elgin Villa,, 34 Lomond street
Burgh Slaughter House, 5 Grant street
Burnett, John, slater, 17 Colquhoun street
Burr, Thomas, gardener, Alma Crescent
Butt, Edward, Canton Cottage, 5 Suffolk street

C

Cairns, Alexander, grocer, 2 Princes street, west ; house 18 Colquhoun square
Caldwell, James, farmer, Craigendoran
Caldwell, Mrs, pastry baker, 6 Colquhoun street
Caldwell, William, tailor and clothier, 20 Clyde street, east
Cameron, Archibald, gardener, 11 Maitland street
Cameron, Archibald, gardener, 98 Princes street, west
Cameron, Duncan, gardener, 74 King street, east
Cameron, Neil, grocer, 50 Clyde street, east
Cameron, Miss, 56 Clyde street, east
Cameron, Mrs, Old Toll House, Drumfork
Campbell, Alexander, carter, 15 Maitland street
Campbell, Alexander, joiner, 9 Suffolk street
Campbell, Archibald, joiner, 95 Princes street, east
Campbell, Colin, Cora House, 131 King street, east
Campbell, Finlay, grocer and wine merchant, 24 Clyde st. w
Campbell, Hugh, gardener, Campbell street
Campbell, James, gardener, 9 Sutherland street
Campbell, Lorne J. M., Central Apothecaries Hall, 5 Sinclair street—house, Clarkfield, 13 Campbell street
Campbell, Peter, auctioneer, 40 Sinclair street

Campbell, Robert, coal merchant, Wellcroft, 3 Glasgow st.
Campbell, William, printer, Col. st ; ho., 4 Princes st., west
Campbell, William, shoemaker, 42 Princes street, west
Campbell, Miss, Sunnyside, 20 King street, west
Campbell, Miss, dressmaker, 95 Princes street, east
Campbell, Miss, confectioner, 81 Clyde street, east
Campbell, Mrs Archibald, Lillybank, 11 Argyle street, west
Campbell, Mrs, 15 William street
Campbell, Mrs, 23 James street
Carlow, William, 2 Glenfinlas street
Caroline, Mrs, 52 Sinclair street
Carslaw, Rev. William Henderson, M.A., Park Free Manse,.
    17 Charlotte street
Carslaw, Mrs, Blairnairn House, 8 Montrose street, west
Carslaw, William, wood turner, 172 Princes street, east
Carson, Robert, painter, 10 Princes street, west
Carson, Mrs, 49 Princes street, east
Carruthers, Richard, cartwright, 47 King street, east
Carter, Mrs, Giffnock House, 202 Princes street, east
Cavana, Bernard, tailor, 3 Colquhoun street
Cavana, John, painter, 117 Princes street, east
Chalmers, John, joiner, 10 Princes street, west
Chapman, William, Agnew Villa, 1 Montrose street, east
Chapman, Mrs, ladies' nurse, 10 Glenfinlas street
Chapman, Miss, teacher of music, 54 Princes street, west
Chiene, Patrick John, Eastburn Cottage, 37 King st., east
Christie, Mrs Thomas, Janeville Lodge, 21 Charlotte street
Clark, John, draper, 66 Clyde street, west
Clark, William, mason, 61 Sinclair street
Clark, Miss, Melbourne Villa, 54 King street, west
Clark, Mrs, 63 Sinclair street
Clydesdale Bank—R. D. Orr, agent, 10 James street; ho. 12
Cochran, Captain James, 15 John street
Cochrane, Miss, Roselea Cottage, 52 King street, west
Colquhoun, Andrew S. D , drysalter, Rosemount, 3 Argyle
    street, east
Colquhoun, Captain, 40 John street
Colquhoun, Daniel, Westwood Cottage, 106 Princes st., w.

Colquhoun, John, 2 Maitland street
Colquhoun, Mrs, 30 John street
Colquhoun, Mrs, 6 Princes street, west
Colquhoun, Mrs, Moss Cottage, 1 King street, west
Coltart, John, Larkhill, 45 Lomond street
Comrie, Alexander, builder, 26 Lomond street
Connor, George, Bath House, 134 Princes street, east
Congregational Church, 19 Princes street, west—Rev. James
    Troup, M.A.
Cook, Matthew, Byron Cottage, 3 Suffolk street
Corbett, William A., J.P., Carisbrook, 29 Montrose st,, east
Cornall, Francis, coal merchant, 100 King street, east
Cowan, Miss, Garnet Bank, 19 Campbell street
Craig, Alexander, Oriel Cottage, 7 Suffolk street
Craig, James, refreshment rooms, 22 Sinclair st.—house, 12
Craig, James, gardener, 19 Maitland street
Craig, John, mason, 5 John street
Craig, Robert, joiner, 34 Clyde street, west
Cramb, Duncan, Larch Villa, 29 Colquhoun street
Cramb, John,   ,,   ,,
Cramb, James   ,,   ,,
Crawford, Hugh, baker, 30 Colquhoun street
Crawford, Thomas, plumber, 20 Sinclair street—house, 4
Crawford, William, 2 William street
Crawford, Miss, dressmaker, 81 Princes street, east
Cree, Mrs, Merlefield, 48 Colquhoun street
Crocket, Mrs, 78 King street, east
Crow, Mrs, Braefoot, 133 King street, east
Cuthill, James, flesher, 16 Princes street, east
Cuthbertson, John, Cranley Lodge, 32 Charlotte street
Cunningham, John, gardener, 84 Princes street, east
Cunningham, Matthew, joiner, 79 Princes street, east
Currie, Captain Henry, Helenslee, 21 Suffolk street
Currie, John, cabman, 2 Colquhoun street
Currie, John, Heathfield, 12 Montrose street, west

D

Dale, James, 32 Clyde street, east
Dale, Robert, G., Braehead, 13 Montrose street, east

Davidson, John, tailor and clothier, 30 Sinclair st. ; house 28
Davidson, Thomas, 111 Clyde street, east
Davidson, Mrs, dressmaker, 1 George street
Davie, Archibald, ploughman, Glenan Farm, Queen street
Davie, Miss, 147 Clyde street, east
Dick, Alexander, Queensmount, Queen street
Dickie, Hugh, teacher, 10 Argyle street, west
Dickie, Robert, confectioner, 3 Sinclair street
Dickson, James, (of Dickson and Veitch) 42 John street
Dickson, Mrs, 44 Princes street, east
Dickson, Mrs, 97 Clyde street, east
Dickson, Mrs, painter, 16 Sinclair st.—house, 29 William st.
Dixon, Robert, baker, 17 Clyde street, west—house, 15
Deas, Mrs, East House, Luss Road
Deans, John, surfaceman, 40 Princes street, east
Dempster, Donald, slater, 95 Clyde street, east
Dempster, Mrs, 39 Clyde street, west
Dewar, Donald, gardener, 1 James street
Dewar, Peter, mate, 4 Charlotte street
Dingwall, John, The Glenan, 29 John street
Dingwall, John, joiner, 27 Colquhoun square
Dingwall, Roderick, 15 Clyde street, west
Docharty, Thomas, labourer, 4 Maitland street
Doddrel, D. T., Beechwood Villa, 18 Argyle street, west
Donald, Archd., butter and egg merchant, 41 Clyde st., west
Donald, W. Macalister, J.P., of Lyleston, Hawthorn Bank,.
    37 Argyle street, east
Donald, Miss, Marian Lodge, Queen street
Donaldson, Mrs, P., Lenylea, 33 John street
Donaldson, Mrs, 5 Princes street, east
Dow, John joiner, Pine Grove Cottage, 26 Colquhoun sqr.
Doward, Charles, Lochview, 8 Suffolk street
Dougal, Mrs John, Hopewell Cottage, 23 Lomond street
Douglas, Mrs, washer and dresser, 104 King street, east
Douglas, Alex., gardener Eastburn Place, 68 King st., east
Doun, Andrew, plumber, 19 Maitland street
Drew, Miss, 19 Lomond street
Drew, Miss, Holly Villa, 26 Suffolk street

Drysdale, Archibald, B., Ochil Bank, 13 Montrose st., east
Drysdale, Wm., J.P., agent of Union Bank, 18 Colquhoun st.
Drysdale, Mrs, Mossgrove, 43 King street, west
Duff, Rev. David, M.A.,L.L.D., Glenan Manse, James street
Dun, Samuel, Fruinfield, 43 Lomond street
Duncan, Mrs, Union Villa, 48 King street, west
Duncanson, Miss, Rockland Cottage, 30 George street
Dunlop, Robert, Springfield House, 56 John street
Dunlop, William, coal merchant, 31 Princes, street, west—
    house, 39
Drummond, William, joiner, 165 Clyde street, east
Drummond, Robert, 5 Colquhoun street
Drumfork Toll—William M'Lellan

E

Eadie, Mrs, Walton Cottage, 131 Princes street, east
Easton, Mr, Abercromby street
Eastburn School—Miss Davie, teacher, 47 King street, east
Edgar, John, Greenbank Cottage, 87 Princes street, east
Edward, Matthew, Sherwood, 2 Lower Sutherland Crescent
Elder, James, Myrtlebank, 129 King street, east
Elsworth, John, Millerslee Villa, King street, east
Elliot, Robert, shoemaker, 41 Clyde street, east—house, 15
    Clyde street, west
Eman, John, coal merchant, 19 Colquhoun street—house, 8
    Colquhoun square
Ewing, Peter, coal merchant, 13 John st,—depot, 37 Princes
    street, east
Ewing, William, Heath Villa. 34 William street
Established Church—Rev. John, Lindsay, Clyde street, east
Established School—John Fraser, teacher, Clyde street, east

F

Fairman, J. A., Elmbank House, 2 Adelaide street
Falconer, Thomas, J.P., Parkhill, 1 Granville street
Falconer, William, labourer, 51 Sinclair street
Falconer, Miss, 73 Clyde street, west
Ferguson, Andrew B., joiners, 7 Sutherland street
Ferguson, Andrew, painter, 13 Princes street, east

Ferguson, George, painter, 41 James street
Ferguson, James, harbour-master, 25 James street
Ferguson, John, Ebenezer Cottage, 33 William street
Ferguson, Thomas, slater, 18 Charlotte street
Ferguson, Miss, 30 William street
Ferguson, Miss, 64 Clyde street, east
Ferguson, Miss, Baroncroft, 191 Clyde street, east
Ferguson, Miss, 27 King street, west
Ferguson, Miss, 17 Maitland street
Filluel, Charles, fish merchant, 72 Princes st., east—ho. 68
Finlay, Alexander, clerk, 34 John street
Finlay, Archibald, seaman, 12 Charlotte street
Finlay, Dr James, J.P., Millbrae, 60 Sinclair street
Finlay, Captain, Portland Place, 32 John street
Finlay, Mrs, Mayfield, 156 King street, east
Finlayson, Miss, confectioner, 57 Clyde street, east
Fisher, Daniel, shoemaker, 4 Maitland street
Fisher, Peter, Bonnie Brae, 66 Sinclair street
Fisher, Robert M., teacher of painting and drawing, Well-
    croft, 87 Princes street, west
Fisher, Miss, mangle keeper, 63 Princes street, west
Fisher, Miss, Wellcroft, 87 Princes street, west
Fisken, Archibald, Birkhall, 1 Havelock street
Fleming, Mrs, Brownhill, Luss Road
Flint, James, mason, 169 Clyde street, east
Foot, Miss, Rosebank, 84 Princes street, west
Forbes, Mrs, milliner and dressmaker, 1 Sinclair street
Forewell, Henry, druggist, Flower Bank, 68 Clyde st., west
Forrest, Mrs, Flower Bank, 70 Clyde street, west
Forrester, William, plumber, 83 Clyde street, east
Forrester, Mrs, Porton Cottage, 11 Glasgow street
Forsyth, James, slater, 48 Princes street, west
Forsyth, Miss, dressmaker, 19 Maitland street
Forsyth, Mrs, 37 James street
Forsyth, Mrs, 19 Maitland street
Fowler, James, wine and spirit merchant, 27 Clyde street,
    east—house, Alma Cottage, 24 Lomond street
Fox, William H., La Belle Villa, 148 King street, east

Fraser, James, Imperial Hotel, 19 Clyde street, east
Fraser, John, teacher, Seaview Place, 16 Argyle street, east
Fraser, Janet, 7 Colquhoun square
Fraser, Miss, 56 Clyde street, west
Fraser, Mrs, Beauly Cottage, 9 Glasgow street
Frame, John, joiner, 10 Princes street, east
Frame, Helen, fruiterer, 46 Princes street, east
Freebairn, Mrs, jeweller, 40 Clyde street, west
Frew, John, Elmwood Cottage, 18 Montrose street, west
Fubister, Miss, furrier, 3 John street
Fuller, J. S., 3 King's Crescent
Fullerton, Gavin, Farnie House, 84 Clyde street, west
Fulton, Mrs, Farnie House, 2 Suffolk street
Fyfe, Miss, Letrewel, 16 Montrose street, west

G

Galbraith, Miss, Cora House, 131 King street, east
Galloway, George, Galloway Cottage, 16 Adelaide street
Galloway, George, builder, 12 Sinclair street.
Galloway, John, mason, 71 Princes street, east
Galloway, William, 8 Colquhoun square
Galloway, William, Milton Cottage, 97 Princes street, west
Gardner & Lindsay, grain merchants, 43 Clyde street, east
Gardner, Duncan, veterinary surgeon, 45 Clyde street, east
Gardiner, John, corkcutter, 25 Colquhoun square
Gardner, Catherine, dressmaker, 64 Clyde street, west
Gardiner, Mrs, 8 Princes street, west
Garroway, James, Airdbank, 25 Montrose street, east
Gas Work—Wm. Smith, manager, 88 Princes street, east
Gatenby, William, Temperance Hotel, 4 Clyde street, west
Gemmill, William M., Ruhe, Alma Crescent
Gemmill, Mrs, Bellevue House, 1 Campbell street
Gibb, Dr. G., Lorn House, 79 Clyde street, west
Gibbons, Patrick, photographer, 22 Princes street, west
Gifford, Mark, blacksmith, 26 Sinclair street
Gilchrist, William, baker, 14 Princes street, east
Gilmour, Agnes, grocer, 54 Clyde street, east
Gilmour, Mrs, Edgemount, 3 Havelock street

Gillies, John, Glenelg Villa, 23 Montrose street, east
Gillies, William, Helensburgh and Glasgow Carrier, 69 Princes street, east
Gillies, Margaret, grocer and confectioner, 79 Clyde st., east
Gillies, Mrs, dairy, 85 Clyde street, east
Gillespie, William, engineer, 23 James street
Glen, John, contractor, 41 Princes street, east
Glen, John, 68 Princes street, west
Glen, William, Methven Villa, 34 Clyde street, east
Glen, Peter, tobacconist, 43 Clyde street, west—house 44
Glen, Mrs, 13 Maitland street
Glen, Mrs, 15 Maitland street
Glover, John, ticket collector, 25 Colquhoun square
Glover, Mrs, dressmaker, 25 Colquhoun square
Good, John,'mason, 61 King street, east
Goodman, Mrs, 23 William street
Goodwin, Alexander, joiner, 10 Princes street, east
Goodwin, Mrs, washer and dresser, 40 Princes street, west
Gow, Archibald, Ashburn House, 14 Montrose street, west
Gow, Mrs, Clarkfield House, 13 Campbell street
Gore Booth, Mrs, East Seaside, 68 Clyde street, east
Gordon, Alexander, painter, 93 Clyde street, east
Gordon, James, house painter, 24 James street
Gourlay, Margaret, 19 Lomond street
Govane, Miss, Govane Bank, 15 Glasgow street
Graham, M. C., Huntly Villa, 3 Granville street
Graham, Thomas, 26 Sinclair street
Graham, Miss, 19 Lomond street
Grant, A. W., 61 Clyde street, west
Grant, James, plumber, 18 Princes street, west—house, 16
Grant, J & R., joiners, 8 Campbell street
Grant, Miss, 7 John street
Grant, Mrs, Sunnyside, 20 King street, east
Grant, Mrs, 16 Princes street, west
Grant, Mrs, 40 John street
Grant, Mrs, 184 Princes street, east
Grantham, Mrs E. H., 64 Clyde street east
Gray, G. W., Carisbrook, 50 King street, west

Gray, Miss, 167 Clyde street, east
Gray, Hugh, Braeside, 87 Sinclair street
Gray, James, Park House 144 King street, east
Gray, John, Easterton, 16 Glasgow street
Gray, William, engine driver, 130 Princes street, east
Gray, William, railway guard, 15 Lomond street
Gray, Mrs, 10 Princes street, east
Gray, Mrs, Dargeeling, 7 William street
Gray, Mrs, Govane Bank, 15 Glasgow Street   .
Grain Store, 3 Maitland street
Grehan, John, police constable, 14 Maitland street
Greer, George, 2 William street
Greenlee, John, gardener, 19 Maitland street
Grierson, John, mason, 59 Sinclair street

H

Hadfield, Mrs, Oakbank, 13 Suffolk street
Hall, Robert H., shoemaker, 38 Cl. st east—ho. 20 Geo. st.
Hamer, Job, Carden Bank, 9 Granville street
Hamilton, Adam, Baronfrow, Colquhoun street
Hamilton, Alexander, guard, 28 Colquhoun street
Hamilton, Charles, Oakfield, 199 Clyde street, east
Hamilton, James, 68 Princes street, east
Hamilton, James, Thornton Lodge, 81 Sinclair street
Hamilton, William, contractor, 68 Princes street, east
Hamilton, Miss, 70 Clyde street, east
Hamilton, Mrs, confectioner, 67 Clyde street, east
Hamilton, Mrs J., 41 Princes street, west
Hamilton, Mrs James, Hayfield, Queen street
Hannah, Mrs Thomas, 8 John street
Hannah, Mrs Thomas, Laurel Green, 60 John street
Harker, Thomas, Springfield Academy, 53 James street
Hart, Mrs, 8 Clyde street, east
Harvie, George, chemist, 38 Princes street, east, ho., Kilinn
          Cottage, 10 Lomond street
Harvie, Miss, 31 King street, west
Haxton, John, fireman, 46 Princes street, west
Hay, James, wood merchant, 65 Clyde street, west
Hay, Mrs, draper, 1 Princes street, east ; ho. 5

Hector, Miss, Valleyfield, 9 Suffolk street
Heggie, Mrs James, 8 Sutherland street
Helensburgh Cemetery—George Combs, gardener
Helensburgh Hospital, North King street
Helensburgh Inn—John Veitch
Helensburgh Public Library, 9 Princes street, east
Henderson, Dr Francis, Seabank, 26 Clyde street, east
Henderson, James, John street lane
Henderson, John, dairyman, 32 James street
Henderson, Joseph, boatbuilder, 32 James street
Henderson, William, mason, 37 James street
Henderson, Miss, Eastbank, 4 Hanover street
Henderson, Miss, flesher, 32 Princes street, east
Hendry, Mrs, Glencairn, 4 Stafford street
Hill, Samuel, grocer, 11 John street
Hillen, Miss, dressmaker, 19 Argyle street, west
Hodge, George, N.B.R. collector, 64 Clyde street, east
Hodgson, Parker, police sergeant, 4 King street, east
Holdsworth, John, Clifton Cottage, 29 Argyle street, east
Holliss, Charles, 44 Clyde street, west
Houston, Mrs, 11 Clyde street, west
Houston, William, 143 Clyde street, east
Hosie, Russell, blacksmith, 69 Princes street, east
Hunter, James, baker, 36 Princes street east ; house, 10
Hunter, James, plasterer, 3 King street, west
Hunter, David, Duncairn, North Sutherland street
Hunter, John, house-agent, Park Cottage, 12 Adelaide st.
Hunter, Mrs, 70 Princes street, west
Hutchison, William, gardener, 53 Sinclair street
Hutchison, Miss, Sunnybrae, 29 Argyle street, west
Hyndman, William, 61 Sinclair street
Hyndman, Mrs, washer and mangle keeper, 61 Sinclair st.

I

Imperial Hotel—James Fraser, proprietor, 19 Clyde st. east
Industrial School, 11 Grant street
Inglis, John, shoemaker, 42 Princes street west
Ingleton, Miss, teacher of pianoforte, harmonium, guitar,
   and singing, 13 William street

Ingram, Thomas, butter and egg store, 15 Clyde street east ;
 house, 12 Colquhoun street
Ingram, James, mason, 5 Colquhoun square
Ingram, James, 12 Colquhoun street
Ireland, George, 20 Clyde street, west
Irvine, John, tailor and clothier, 6 Princes street, west ; ho. 4

J

Jack, John, builder, 65 Clyde street, west
Jack, Mrs A., 60 Princes street, west
Jardine, Bryce, coal merchant, 20 James street
Jardine, James, bootmaker, 40 King street, east
Jardine, Marion, 2 Colquhoun street
Jardine, Mrs, Dovehill, 64 Sinclair street
Jardon, Marion, Queen street
Jamieson, Joseph, flesher, 60 Clyde street, west
Jamieson, William, yachtmaster, 17 Lomond street
Jamieson, Miss, Moorlands, Luss Road
Jamieson, Mrs Thomas, Jordonhill, 4 Sutherland street
Jarvie, James, goods clerk, 99 Clyde street, east
Jeffrey, Miss, Torwood Villa, Colquhoun street
Jenkins, Mrs, Devar Cottage, 16 King street, west
Johnston, David, mason, 61 Princes street, west
Johnston, Mrs, 48 Clyde street, east

K

Kater, John, joiner, 171 Clyde street, east
Kay, Thomas, Chapelfield House, 33 Argyle street, east
Kettle, Sergeant, 20 George street
Kerr, William, contractor, 21 Colquhoun street
Kerr, Miss, Bellevue House, 76 Clyde street, west
Kerney, Edward, coachman, 39 Clyde street, west
Kerr, John, coachman, 58 John street
Kerr & Bishop, joiners, King street, east
Kerr, Mrs, 126 Princes street, east
Kerr, Hugh, joiner, 130 Princes street, east
Keyden, Thomas, sawyer, 22 William street
Kenny, Captain, 126 King street, east
Kelly, John, labourer, 59 Princes street, east

Kelly, Mrs, 17 Maitland street
Kennedy, Fergus, 2 Sutherland street
Kennedy, Mrs, 20 James street
Kenney, Miss, 9 John street
King, John, Valleyfield, 42 King street, west
King, Mrs, Valleyfield, 42 King street, west
Kinghorn, James, Windsor Cottage, 201 Clyde street, east
King Street Hall, East King street, James Lennox, keeper
Kinniburgh, Alexander, inspector of poor, and Registrar of
    births, marriages, and deaths, 25 Princes street, east
Kilty, H., gardener, Chapel Acre Lodge, Luss Road
Kirkwood, Miss, Laurel Villa, 22 Montrose street, west
Kirkwood, Mrs Alexander, Clarefoot, 7 Granville street
Kyle, Andrew, spirit dealer, 151 Clyde street, east

L

Laird, Alexander A., Clyde View, 4 King's Crescent
Lamb, James, Dargeeling, 5 William street
Lamond, Miss, Sunnyside, 18 King Street, west
Lamont, Mrs, Millhill, 73 Sinclair street
Lamont, Hugh, dairyman and carter, 14 James street
Lamont, Miss, 45 Princes street, west
Lang, Alexander, mason, 78 Clyde street, east
Laing, Miss, Bellview, 110 Princes street, west
Lang, Mrs, Duart Cottage, 14 Adelaide street
Larchfield Academy—Alexander Mackenzie, M.A., head-
    master, 35 Colquhoun street
Laurie, James, carter, 12 Sinclair street
Laurie, Thomas, butler, 161 Clyde street, east
Laurie, Mrs, 93 Clyde street, east
Law, Mrs, dressmaker, Treesbank, 3 William street
Lay, Miss, 57 King street, west
Leggat, Mrs, Flower Bank, 69 Clyde street, west
Leiper, William, architect, Tertesie, North Sutherland st.
Lennan, Peter, gardener, 7 Campbell street
Lennox & Chapman, family grocers, 8 Clyde street, west
Lennox, Alexander, Albert Villa, 2 Stafford street
Lennox, George, painter, 42 Sinclair street
Lennox, James, beadle of U.P. Church, 42 Sinclair street

Lennox, Peter, Oakfield, 1 Bell street
Leslie, Captain, 56 Princes street, west
Leslie, Miss, Edenwood, 4 Lower Sutherland crescent
Lindsay, Alexander, Leven Villa, 52 James street
Lindsay, John, contractor, 53 King street, east
Lindsay, John, farmer, Woodend Farm
Lindsay, Rev. John, The Manse, 38 Charlotte street
Lindsay, Miss, Valleyfield, 9 Suffolk street
Lightbody, Thomas, Skerryvore, Alma Crescent
Lightbody, Mrs, 193 Clyde street, east
Litster, Mrs, 23 James street
Little, Mrs, draper, 65 Clyde street, east ; ho, 71
Livingston, John, grocer, 59 Clyde street, east
Livingston, Mrs, washer and dresser, 78 King street, east
Livingston, Mrs, Ardvuela, Queen street
Lorimer, Mrs, 18 Colquhoun square
Lochhead, John, Ronbank, 3 King's Crescent
Love, Robert, mason, 84 Princes street, east
Lyon, James, mason, 7 Colquhoun street

M

Macduff, Peter, Hayfield Cottage, 92 King street, east
Macfarlane, Mrs, Stewart Green, 30 Lomond street
MacGoun, Misses, Killearn Lodge, 11 Granville street
Macindoe, Mrs W., Albion Cottage, 8 Lomond street
Mackay, James, carter, 11 Maitland street
Mackay, John, mason, 50 Princes street, west
Mackay, Martin, Osborne Villa, 52 Grant street
Mackay, Mrs, 15 Maitland street
Mackenzie, Alexander, M.A., Larchfield Academy, 35 Colquhoun street
Mackenzie, John, tailor, 8 Glenfinlas street
Mackie, Charles, Milton Cottage, 95 Princes street, west
Mackie, William, Park View Cottage, 18 Adelaide street
Macleod, Donald, tailor and clothier, 87 Clyde street, east
Macneur, Alexander, bookseller, 19 Clyde street, west—ho, 20
Mainds, William, painter, 18 Sinclair street
Mair, George, teacher, Galloway Cottage, Colquhoun street
Malcolm, William, Mossbank House, 18 Suffolk street

Malcolm, Miss, teacher, Industrial School, 11 Grant street
Malcolm, Mrs, Sunnybrae, 29 Argyle street, west
Marquis, Miss, Argyle Park, 42 James street
Marshall, Robert, Birkfell, 30 Charlotte street
Marshall, William, Cora House, 129 King street, east
Marsland, Sergeant James, 19 George street
Martin, Joseph Russell, 85 Clyde street, west
Martin, Matthew, Bath House, 137 Princes street, east
Martin, Miss, Bath House, 137 Princes street, east
Martin, Miss, Christina, 9 John street
Martin, Miss, Greenburn Lodge, 24 Clyde street, east
Mason, Miss, Woodland Place, 126 King street, east
Mathieson, Mrs, Glendarroch House, 37 John street
Maxwell, Mrs, 34 Princes street, west
Meikle, John, 52 Princes street, east
Meldrum, George, painter, 14 Maitland street
Melville, Robert, mason, 23 James street
Melvine, Mrs, 44 Clyde street, west
Menzies, Miss, 177 Clyde street, east
Messer, Dr. Fordyce, surgeon, 9 William Street
Middlemiss, Joseph, blacksmith, 41 Princes street, west
Miller, David, gardener, 1 Glasgow street
Millar, David, builder, 159 Clyde street, east
Miller, Dr John, Bute Cottage, 7 Lower Sutherland Cresnt.
Millar, James, carver and gilder, 3 Princes st., east—ho., 10
Millar, John, labourer, 19 Maitland street
Millar, William, Wellington Lodge, 19 Montrose street, east
Millar, Miss,   „   19   „
Millar, Miss, 9 Sutherland street
Miller, Miss, dress and cloakmaker, 27 Colquhoun street
Miller, Miss, Clarkfield House, 13 Campbell street
Millar, Mrs T., bookseller 11 Princes street, east
Millar, Mrs, 20 Colquhoun street
Millig Mill, 70 Sinclair street—Lachlan M'Lachlan
Millig Toll—William Brock, Luss Road
Milk Shop—Mrs Dow, 4 Colquhoun street
Mirrlees, Miss, Burnshill, 15 Granville street
Missionary Hall and Penny Savings Bank, 22 Colquhoun sqr.

Mitchell, David, 10 Princes street, west
Mitchell, George, Blairkip, 17 Glenfinlas street
Mitchell, John, grocer, 2 Sinclair street—house, Brooklee, 13 Granville street
Mitchell, Miss, Millerslee Villa, King street, east
Mitchell, Miss, 4 Princes street, west
Mitchell, Mrs, Locksley, Abercromby street
Moir, Mrs, fishmonger, 25 Clyde street, west—house, 39
Montgomery, William, farmer, Laigh Stuck, Bell street
Monteith, Adam, Eastbank, 2 Hanover street
Moody, Miss, 30 John street
Morris, Mrs, baker, 37 Clyde street, west
Morris, Mrs, mangle keeper, 21 Maitland street
Morrison, Miss, 161 Clyde street, east
Morrison, Mrs George, 55 Princes street, west
Morton, Miss, 21 Colquhoun square
Muir, Robert, draper, 56 Princes street, east—house, Hazelwood, Alma Crescent
Muirhead & Peddie, painters, 24 Princes street, east
Muirhead, Robert, painter, Maitland street
Muirhead, Mrs, 84 Princes street, east
Munroe, Alexander, gardener, 72 Princes street, west
Murphy, John, scavengar, 19 Maitland street
Murdoch, John, Dalblair, 10 Granville street
Murdoch, Misses, ladies' boarding school, Ashmount, Millig street, west
Murray, Donald, joiner, 12 King street, east—house, 14
Murray, Patrick, joiner, 20 King street, east—house, 84 Princes street, east
Murray Robert, Woodhill, 2 Upper Sutherland crescent
Murray, Thomas, water inspector, 12 Colquhoun street
Murray, Miss, 9 John street
Murray, Mrs, 25 Maitland street
Murray, Mrs, stoneware and china warehouse, 22 Clyde street, east
Murrie, John, blacksmith, 27 Colquhoun square
Muter, William, grocer, 10 Princes street, west
Mylius, Major Rodney, Dalglennan Cottage, John st. lane

M‘

M‘Allister, Angus, colporteur, 137 Clyde street, east
M‘Allister, John, joiner, 30 John street
M‘Allister, Mrs, 40 Clyde street, east
M‘Arthur, Peter, gardener, 3 King street, west
M‘Arthur, Mrs, dairy, 15 Princes street, east
M‘Aulay, Alexander, Eastbank Cottage, 205 Clyde st., east
M‘Aulay, Captain, Eastburn House, 93 Clyde street, east
M‘Aulay, Frank, gardener, 19 Maitland street
M‘Aulay, James, boat hirer, 4 Colquhoun square
M‘Aulay, Mrs, 9 George street
M‘Auslan, Misses, laundresses, 66 Princes street, west
M‘Auslan, Mrs A., 108 Princes street, west
M‘Auslan, Mrs, wine and spirit merchant, 89 Clyde st., east
M‘Auslane, Archibald, Park Cottage, 1 King's Crescent
M‘Auslane, James, farmer, Kirkmichael, Cemetery Road
M‘Auslane, Robert, shoemaker, 18 Maitland street
M‘Auslane, Miss, Enmore, 135 King street, east
M‘Auslane, Miss, Sunnybrae, 11 Suffolk street
M‘Auslane, Mrs, Woodside Place, 4 Sutherland street
M‘Bean, Lachlan, Findhorn, Queen street
M‘Bride, Archibald, 4 John street
M‘Cabe, John, coal merchant, 78 King street, east
M‘Cafer, Miss, washer and mangle keeper, 17 Maitland st.
M‘Callum, Daniel, Methven Villa, 34 Clyde street, east
M‘Callum, Donald, Fairbank, 24 Argyle street, west
M‘Callum, Donald, tailor, 20 King street, west
M‘Callum, Donald, grocer, 55 Clyde street, east; ho. 54
M‘Callum, Peter, Sunnyside Cottage, 50 John street
M‘Callum, Peter, painter, 27 Colquhoun square
M‘Callum & Sons, drapers, 5 Clyde street, east
M‘Callum, M. & C., milliners, 7 Clyde street, west
M‘Callum, Mrs P., 7 Clyde street, east
M‘Callum, Mrs, 63 Sinclair street
M‘Callum, Mrs, washer-woman, 47 Princes street, east
M‘Candy, Mrs, 49 King street, east
M‘Clure, Robert, Verreville, 50 James street
M‘Coll, Alexander, miller, 70 Sinclair street

M'Coll, Duncan, joiner, 21 James street
M'Coll, John, joiner, 44 Princes street, west
M'Coll, Mrs, Fountain Bank, 67 Sinclair street
M'Coll, Mrs, 17 William street
M'Connel, David, Roseneath post, 22 James street
M'Connell, Thomas, ironmonger, 10 Sinclair street; ho. 12
M'Corkindale, George, carter, 93 Princes street, east
M'Cormick, Mrs, washer-woman, 19 Maitland street
M'Crae, Kenneth, confectioner, 82 Princes street, east
M'Cree, Miss, 19 Maitland street
M'Culloch, J. W., & Son, painters, 29 Princes street, east
M'Culloch, J. W., painter, 58 Clyde street, west
M'Culloch, John C., Woodburn House, 39 John street
M'Culloch, Wm. L., Laurel Cottage, 102 Princes street, w.
M'Dermid, Margaret, 10 John street
M'Donald, Archibald, yachtsman, 39 Clyde street, east
M'Donald, D. R., restaurant, 58 Princes st., east—house, 60
M'Donald, John, cabinet-maker, 93 Princes street, east
M'Donald, Lachlan, carter, 11 Maitland street
M'Donald, Robert P., 7 George street
M'Donald, Ronald, gardener, 63 Sinclair street
M'Donald, Miss, 57 Clyde street, east
M'Donald, Miss, West Bay, 81 Clyde street, west
M'Donald, Mrs, 44 Clyde street, west
M'Dougal, Alexander, collar-maker, 40 Clyde street, east
M'Dougal, John, gardener, 32 Colquhoun street
M'Dougal, John, 122 Princes street, east
M'Dougal, John, green grocer, 33 Clyde street, east
M'Dougal, Miss, 4 Charlotte street
M'Dougal, Mrs, Ardbeg Cottage, 50 Grant street
M'Dougal, Mrs, 24 Colquhoun street
M'Dougal, Mrs, Cora House, 129 King street, east
M'Ewan, Henry, plasterer, 53 Sinclair street
M'Ewan, James, Brackenhill Cottage, 32 Lomond street
M'Ewan, Thomas, mason, 3 King street, west
M'Ewan, M. & W., milliners and dressmakers, 2 Col. st.
M'Ewan, Miss, Ardmore, 72 Clyde street, east
M'Ewan, Miss, Berlin Wool Repository, 9 Sinclair street

M'Farlane, Alexander, gardener, 189 Clyde street, east
M'Farlane, Andrew, shoemaker, 77 Clyde street, east
M'Farlane, Andrew, gardener, 19 Maitland street
M'Farlane, Duncan, 75 Clyde street, east
M'Farlane, John, joiner, 2 John street
M'Farlane, Malcolm, shoemaker, 14 Charlotte street
M'Farlane, R. S., grain merchant, 2 Clyde street, east; ho,
    4 Sinclair street
M'Farlane, Robert, Rowanbrae, 19 Charlotte street
M'Farlane, Miss, dressmaker, 42 Clyde street, east
M'Farlane, Miss, Dailnabruich Cottage, 8 Argyle st., east
M'Farlane, Mrs, 6 Maitland street
M'Farlane, Mrs, 15 Maitland street
M'Farlane, Mrs, Claremont House, 15 Suffolk street
M'Garigal, Hugh, labourer, 39 Clyde street, west
M'Gilp, Miss, Rosebank Terrace, 82 Princes street, west
M'Gilvary, Mrs, 191 Clyde street, east
M'Ginnes, Patrick, labourer, 6 Clyde street, west
M'Gregor, Gregor, mason, 39 James street
M'Gregor, Gregor, mason, 47 King street, east
M'Gregor, John, J.P., Bonnyton, 1 Upper Sutherland crest;
M'Gregor, John, Ardshiel, Millig street, west
M'Gregor, Robert, Ettrick Bank, 85 Clyde street
M'Gregor, Mrs, 8 Glenfinlas street
M'Haffie, James, 110 Princes street, west
M'Haffie, Mrs, Belmont, Millig street, east
M'Innes, Robert, shoemaker, 10 John street
M'Innes, Thomas, gardener, 16 Maitland street
M'Intosh, Mrs, 173 Clyde street east
M'Intyre, Duncan, gardener, Hermitage, 76 Sinclair street
M'Intyre, John, Cawdor Lodge, Luss Road
M'Isaac, Hugh, mason, 30 John street
M'Isaac, John, sawyer, 61 Sinclair street
M'Isaac, Mrs, Heath Cottage, 4 Sutherland street
M'Kay, James, joiner, 24 James street
M'Kay, William, 75 Clyde street east
M'Kay, Miss, dress and cloakmaker, 19 James street
M'Kechnie, Angus, bootmaker, 48 Sinclair street

M'Kechnie, William, dairyman, 24 Sinclair street

M'Kechnie, William, barman, 26 Sinclair street

M'Kenzie, George, plasterer, 24 Maitland street

M'Kenzie, Mrs, 34 John street

M'Kellar, John, gardener, 78 King street, east

M'Killop, Archibald, carter, 53 Sinclair street

M'Killop, George, saddler, 40 Clyde street, east

M'Kim, Adam, bookseller, 46 Clyde street, west

M'Kimb, James. 63 Princes street, east

M'Kinlay, Duncan, contractor, 28 Princes street, west

M'Kinlay, Wm., plumber, 51 Clyde street, east—house, 53

M'Kinlay, Mrs, 22 James street

M'Kinlay, Mrs 34 Clyde street. west

M'Kirdy, James, plumber, 157 Clyde street, east

M'Lachlan, David S., baker, 73 Clyde street, east

M'Lachlan, George, writer, 6 Princes street, east—house,
　　Blairlomond, 6 Stafford street

M'Lachlan, Henry, painter, 3 King street, west

M'Lachlan, Hugh, railway porter, 68 King street, east

M'Lachlan, Hugh, mason, 20 George street

M'Lachlan, James, mason, 78 King street, east

M'Lachlan, Lachlan, baker, 3 Clyde street, east—house, 1
　　Colquhoun square

M'Lachlan, William, farmer, High Stuck, Bell street

M'Lachlan, Mary, 22 James street

M'Lachlan, Mrs, 78 King street, east

M'Lachlan, Mrs, 27 Princes street, east

M'Lachlan, Mrs W., Glenmore, 28 Campbell street

M'Laren, Alexander, Millfield, 83 Sinclair street

M'Laren, John, joiner, 32 Clyde street, west

M'Laren, Miss, 1 Maitland street

M'Laren, Mrs, dressmaker, 32 Clyde street, west

M'Laurin, Miss, 32 King street, west

M'Lean, Alexander, joiner, 16 Colquhoun street

M'Lean, Donald, grocer, 74 Princes street, east—house, 76

M'Lean, John D. L., Edenbank, 102 Colquhoun street

M'Lean, Miss, furnishing shop, 4 Princes street, east

M'Lean, Miss, dressmaker, 24 Colquhoun street

M‚Lellan Daniel, 45 Clyde street, east
M‘Lellan, Donald, lorryman, 99 Clyde street, east
M‘Lellan, Duncan, Annock Bank, 15 Montrose street, east
M‘Lellan, Miss, East Woodend House, 35 Argyle st., east
M‘Leod, Donald, tailor, 15 Maitland street
M‘Leod, Gabriel, gardener, 26 Sinclair street
M‘Leod, John, beadle, 76 King street, east
M‘Leod, Miss, dressmaker, 26 Sinclair street
M‘Leod, Miss, dressmaker, 15 Maitland street
M‘Leod. Miss, dressmaker. 99 Clyde street, east
M‘Leod, Mrs, 56 Clyde street, cast
M‘Leod, Mrs, 53 Sinclair street
M‘Leod, Mrs, 12 Glenfinlas street
M‘Master, James, mason, 10 Colquhoun street
M‘Millan, Hamilton, spirit merchant, 32 Princes street, west
    —house, 23 James street
M‘Menemy, Peter, dairyman, 90 King street, east
M‘Lellan, Adam, ironmonger, 9 Clyde st., east—house, 11
M‘Menemy, Peter, grain mercht, 26 Princes st. east. ho. 43
M‘Menemy, Thomas, tobacconist, 42 Princes street, east—
    house, 76
M‘Micking, Thomas, J. P., Burnbrae, Campbell street
M‘Millan, Daniel, Pinelea, 11 Montrose street, east
M‘Millan, Dougal, grocer, 55 Sinclair street
M‘Millan, George, gardener, 76 Clyde street, east
M‘Millan, Miss, Woodcliff, 5 Lower Sutherland Cresent
M‘Millan, Mrs, Ivy House, 77 Clyde street, west
M‘Murrich, Daniel, blacksmith, 123 Clyde street, east
M‘Nab, Mrs, Greenbank, 15 Campbell street
M‘Nair, William, family grocer, 9 Clyde street, west ; house
    Willowburn Cottage, 10 Glasgow street
M‘Naught, Alexander, baker, 99 Clyde street, east
M‘Naught, Archibald, farmer, 130 King street, east
M‘Naughton, John, dairyman and carter, 35 James street
M‘Nee, John, 4 Sinclair street
M‘Neil, Hugh, carter, 24 James street
M‘Neil, John, joiner, 19 Maitland street
M‘Nicol, Alexander, bootmaker, 14 Clyde street, east

M'Nicol, John, joiner, 157 Clyde street, east
M'Nicol, John, baker 131 Clyde street, east—house, 4 Charlotte street
M'Nicol, Robert, J.P., 66 Clyde street, east
M'Pherson, Daniel, slater, 24 Maitland street
M'Pherson, Malcolm, painter, 21 Colquhoun square
M'Pherson, Malcolm mason, 19 Maitland street
M'Pherson, William, gardener, 29 King street, west
M'Pherson & Carson, painters, 19 Colquhoun square
M'Pherson, Mrs, 77 Princes street, east
M'Pherson, Mrs, Ashens, 56 King street, east
M'Pherson, Mrs, 71 Clyde street
M'Pherson, Mrs, 18 Colquhoun square
M'Phun, W. R., Maryfield, 17 Campbell street
M'Skimmon, Captain, 126 King street, east
M'Taggart, Miss, dressmaker, 30 John street
M'Vey, Miss, 17 William street
M'Vey, Miss, 19 Maitland street

N

Nairn, John, Roselea Cottage, 52 King street, west
Napier, James A., Omaha, Abercromby street
Napier, Mrs, 61 Clyde street, west
National Bread Company, 17 Colquhoun square
Neil, Henry, gardener, 14 Maitland street
Neil, Mrs David, Hillside Cottage, 4 Montrose street, west
Neilly, Richard, basketmaker 26 Sinclair street
Neilson, Mrs, washer and dresser, 37 James street
Nelson, Robert, 77 Sinclair street
Nicol, Miss, Kintyre Villa, ladies' boarding school, 25 Charlotte street
Newlands, Thomas, beadle, 25 Colquhoun square
Niven, James, landscape gardener, 64 King street, east
Niven, Mrs, 107 Clyde street, east
Nimmo, John, baker, 3 John street
Noble, John, mason, 132 Princes street, east
North British Insurance Office, 50 Princes street, east— William Battrum, agent

Notman, Mrs Robert, Colquhoun Villa, 31 Colquhoun street

O

Oddfellows' Hall, 28 Colquhoun square
Ogilvie, Mrs, 1 James street
Ogston, Mrs, Glenorchy Villa, 22 Adelaide street
Oliphant, Miss, Sunnybrae, 11 Suffolk street
Orme, William, butter, ham, and egg merchant, 8 Sinclair
    street ; house, 68 Princes street, east
Orr, Andrew, labourer, 22 James street
Orr, William, Ardenlade, Abercromby street
Orr, R. D., J.P., banker, 12 James street
Orr, Mrs James, Park House, 24 George street
Orr, Mrs, Lauder Villa, 154 King street, east
Orr, Mrs Robert, Ballimore Lodge, 20 Montrose street, west
Osborne, Thomas, carter, 10 Colquhoun street
Oswald, Andrew, J.P., Glennan Bank, 26 Campbell street
O'Neil, Michael, gardener, 46 Princes street, west
O'Rake, Barney, labourer, 6 Clyde street, west
Oughterson, Miss, Dahlbeg, 86 Clyde street, west
Owler, Mrs, 34 John street

P

Park, Alexander, 42 Princes street, west
Park, Thomas, slater, 42 Princes street, west
Park Free Church, 15 Charlotte st.—Rev. W. H. Carslaw
Parker, James, Underwood, 8 Sutherland crescent lower
Parlane, Mrs, umbrella and staymaker, 29 Clyde street, west
Paterson, George, Dunfillan, 31 Montrose street, east
Paterson, John, mason, 78 King street, east
Paterson, Joseph, mason, 65 Sinclair street
Paterson, William, mason, 53 Sinclair street
Paterson, William, saddler, 5 Princes street, east
Paterson, & Son, upholsterers, 52 Clyde street, west ; ho. 53
Paterson, Mrs, refreshment rooms, 37 Clyde street, east
Paterson, Miss, teacher, 18 Sinclair street
Paterson, Miss, 56 Princes street, west
Paterson, Misses, Holm Glen, 28 George street
Patterson, R. J. B., Dallglennan Lodge, 44 James street

Patterson, Wm., tailor and clothier, 35 Clyde st., w ; ho 34
Patterson, Mrs J. B., Dallglennan Lodge, 44 James street
Paton, James, 5 George street
Paton, John, 11 George street
Paton, John, bootmaker, 8 Maitland st.—ho, 12 Clyde st., e
Paton, William, gardener, 8 Princes street, east
Paton, Mrs, 42 King street, east
Paton, Mrs, 101 Princes street, west
Paton, Mrs, Blairburn Villa, 104 Princes street, west
Patrie, John, butler, 76 Clyde street, east
Parochial Board Office, 25 Princes street, east—William
    Kinniburgh, inspector and registrar of the parish
Paul, Mrs, 19 Maitland street
Pearson, John, Bloomfield, 33 Lomond street
Peat, Misses, day school, Barwood, 7 Montrose street, east
Peddie, William, fruiterer, 70 Princes street, east
Peddie, William, gardener, 157 Clyde street, east
Pender, Miss, 66 Princes street, west
Perrit, William, Byron Cottage, 96 Princes street, west
Pettit, Alfred, joiner, toy and china mercht., 13 Clyde st., e.
Pettit, Wm. A., printer, bookseller, and house-agent, 6 Sin-
    clair street
Phillips, James, Rosebank Cottage, 12 Campbell street
Pianoforte and Music Warehouse, 7 Sinclair st.—William
    Battrum
Plowright, Miss, 79 Princes street, east
Police Office, 31 Princes street, east—John Anderson, supt.
Pollock, James, grocer, 94 King street, east
Pollock, Robert, Cornwall House, 62 John street
Pollok, Robert, 197 Clyde street, east
Ponds, James, spirit merchant, 3 Clyde street, west—house,
    Whinbrae, 66 King street, east
Porter, Clement, upholsterer, 14 Princes street, west ; ho.,16
Porter, Miss, milliner, 26 Clyde street, west
Post Office, 9 Princes st., east—Wm., Bryson, post-master
Potter, Mrs, Auchentiel, Suffolk street
Printing Office, 52 Princes street, east—William Battrum
Printing Office, 9 Colquhoun street—William Campbell

Printing Office, 4 Sinclair street—William A. Pettit
Primrose, Thomas, Hawthorn Hill, 54 Grant street
Proudfoot, Miss, Egremount, 36 Charlotte street
Provan, Andrew, bookseller, 48 Princes street, east—house,
19 James street
Purvis, T. A., station-master, 142 King street, east
Purvis, William, carter, 13 Maitland street

Q

Queen's Hotel, 74 Clyde street, east—Alex. Williamson

R

Railway Station, 39 Princes street, east—T. A. Purvis,
station-master
Ramsay, James, florist, 12 Princes street, west—house, Wood-
end Nursery, 9 Montrose street, west
Ramsay, Mrs, Hopewell Cottage, 25 Lomond street
Ramsay, Miss, dressmaker, 9 Montrose street, west
Rankin, James, 182 Princes street, east
Rankin, John, barber, 49 Clyde street, east
Rankin, Mrs, Main Cottage, 45 Princes street, east
Rathbone, Mrs, laundress and mangle keeper, 14 Glenfinlas st
Readman, James, St Leonards, 17 Montrose street, east
Reid, Alex., plumber, 20 Clyde street, west
Reid, D. S., chemist, 28 Clyde street, west—house, Hartree,
James street
Reid, Dr. Douglas, Easterton House, 89 Clyde street, west
Reid, Rev. S. W., Rockfort Place, Clyde street, east
Reid, William, plumber and gasfitter, 23 Princes street, east
—house, Dhuhill, Luss Road
Reid, Mrs, Anchorage, 20 Suffolk street
Reid, Mrs, refreshment rooms, 1 Clyde street, east
Reid, Miss, 4 Sinclair street
Renfrew, Miss, 172 Princes street, east
Rennards, J. R., apothecary, 55 Clyde street, east ; house 59
Rennie, Mrs, 19 Maitland street
Rennie, Mrs Wm,, Welcroft, John street
Rhodes, Mrs, 8 Clyde street, east
Rifle Volunteer Drill Hall, 5 Colquhoun street

Rintoul, Andrew, Rockbank, 82 Clyde street, east
Risk, Mrs, Elmwood, 18 Glasgow street
Ritchie, Miss, Rosemount Cottage, 5 Argyle street, east
Robb, David, Maitland street
Robb, Hamilton, mason, 12 Argyle street, east
Robb, John, mason, 42 Princes street, west
Roberts, William B., Woodlee, 22 Argyle street, west
Robertson, Andrew C., Woodend House, Millig street, east
Robertson, David, bootmaker, 10 John street
Robertson, David, gardener, 52 Princes street, east
Robertson, David, mason, 40 Clyde street, east
Roberston, James, Elm Park, 3 Lower Sutherland crescent
Robertson, James, Northwood, Luss Road
Robertson, James, mason, 9 John street
Robertson, J. C., Eastwood House, 211 Clyde street, east
Robertson, J. S., excise officer, 99 Clyde street, east
Robertson, John, mason, 78 King street, east
Robertson, Matthew, Annsfield, 10 Montrose street, west
Robertson, Thomas, joiner, 99 Clyde street, east
Robertson, William, tailor, 68 King street, east
Robertson, Miss, confectioner, 69 Clyde street, east
Robertson, Miss, Ardmore, 71 Clyde street, west
Robertson, Miss, Annat Lodge, 35 John street
Robertson, Mrs, 24 Maitland street
Robertson, Mrs, Blairburn House, 6 Montrose street, west
Robertson, Mrs, dairy, 3 Sutherland street
Robertson, Mrs, Elm Park, 3 Lower Sutherland crescent
Robley, Harrington, Carleton, Millig street, west
Rodger, James, carter, 42 Princes street, west
Rodger, John, carter and dairyman, 7 Lomond street
Rodger, William, 32 Sinclair street—house, 34
Ronald, Mrs, Dover Cottage, 26 King street, west
Roper, Mary, 17 Maitland street
Ross, David, coachman, 9 Adelaide street
Ross, James, watchmaker, 16 Clyde street, west
Ross, John, mason, 65 Princes street, west
Ross, William, bill-poster, 53 Sinclair street
Ross, Miss, dressmaker, 53 Sinclair street

Ross, Misses, milliners and dressmakers, 43 Princes st., west
Rowson, Rev. S. B., R.C.C., 62 King street, east
Roy, Gabriel, watchmaker, 21 Clyde street, west—house, 2 James street
Rumgay, James, joiner, 79 Princes street, east
Russell, Wm., coal merchant, 35 Princes street, east—house, 36 Princes street, west
Russell, Mrs, 18 Clyde street, east
Russell, M. C., confectioner, 48 Clyde street, west
Ruthven, John, saddler, 10 Maitland street

S

Samuel, Miss, Dunbeg, 48 James street
Scott, Mrs James, 82 Clyde street, west
Scott, Mrs, 9 John street
Scoular, William, Leewood Villa, 112 Princes street, west
Sellers, Peter, gardener, 181 Clyde street, east
Sellers, Miss, 137 Princes street, east
Service, Neil, joiner, 59 Princes street, east
Service, H. & M., dressmakers, 18 Princes street, east
Service, Janet, 12 John street
Service, Mary, 4 Maitland street
Service, Mrs, 117 Princes street, east
Service, Mrs, refreshment rooms, 14 Clyde street, west
Service, Mrs, 153 Clyde street, east
Service, Mrs, 10 Clyde street, east
Shanks, Miss, Burnside House, 22 Campbell street
Shanks, Mrs, 39 Princes street, west
Sharp, James, Ardenclutha, 11 Adelaide street
Sharp, Thomas, butcher, 66 Princes street, east
Sharp, William, Glenfeulan, Millig street, east
Shaw, William, grocer and spirit merchant, 14 Sinclair st. —house, 18 Colquhoun square
Shaw, William, 59 King street, west
Shearer, James, 68 Princes street, east
Shearer, William, 72 King street, east
Shearer, Miss, 1 George street
Shields, William, joiner, 4 Glasgow street

Short, George, shoemaker, 4 John street
Shoemakers Workshop, 19 Princes st., east—R. Stevenson
Sinclair, Mrs, 68 King street, east
Skene, Mrs J., 1 Montrose street, west
Skimming, Alexander, cartwright, 79 Sinclair street
Sloan, Charles, Springfield Cottage, 61 James street
Sloan, Dr. S., M'Master's Cottage, 170 King street, east
Sloan, Miss, Craigie Lea, 4 Argyle street, west
Slorance, George, gardener, 23 Maitland street
Smellie, Miss, Ellangowan, 50 Colquhoun street
Smith, Alexander, gardener, 31 William street
Smith, Alexander, 14 Clyde street, west
Smith, Captain M. H., Beaulah Lodge, 39 Colquhoun street
Smith, David, plumber, 10 Argyle, street, east
Smith, David, mason, 23 Maitland street
Smith, James, Methill Field, 63 James street
Smith, John, Hermitage, 76 Sinclair street
Smith, Patrick, Westfield, 17 Glasgow street
Smith, Robert, gardener, 40 Clyde street, east
Smith, Robert, mason, 4 Maitland street
Smith, William, Fernbank, 21 Montrose street, east
Smith, Wm., baker, 30 Princes st., west—ho. 16 James st.
Smith, Miss, Payta Villa, Sutherland street, north
Smith, Miss, 1 George street
Smith, Miss, The Baths, 72 Clyde street, east
Smith, Mrs, grocer, 133 Clyde st., east—ho., 6 Charlotte st.
Smith, Mrs, 24 James street
Smith, Mrs, Rossdhu Villa, 28 King street, west
Smith, Mrs, 19 Lomond street
Smith, Mrs, 121 Princes street, east
Smith, Mrs, Giffnock House, 204 Princes street, east
Smith, Mrs, bootmaker, 13 Sinclair street
Smith, Mrs, mangle-keeper, 57 Sinclair street
Snell, Miss, Rossdhu Villa, 30 King street, west
Snodgrass, Andrew, boot and shoemaker, 2 Princes st., east
Snodgrass, James, Maitland street
Snodgrass, Matthew, farmer, East Millig Farm, Millig st., e
Somerville, James, Carron Bank, Millig street, west

Somerville, James, grocer, 82 King street, east
Somerville, Mrs, 128 Clyde street, east
Spalding James, writer and insurance agent, 44 Princes st., e.
Spence, James, gardener, Ardvuela, Queen street
Spence, William, Ardlui, 23 Charlotte street
Spence, Mrs, 32 Clyde street, west
Speirs, Wm., barber, 26 Maitland street—house, 14
Spratt, Miss, Springvale Cottage, 97 Princes street, east
Springfield Academy, 51 James st; Thomas Harker, master
Sproul, Matthew, book deliverer, 16 Princes street, west
Spy, Andrew, coal merchant, 19 Sinclair street, house, 12
Spy, Robert, letter carrier and coal mercht., 10 Princes st., w.
St Michael and All Angles Church, William street, Rev. J.
    S. Syme, Incumbent
Stables and Coachhouse, Argyle st., w.—D. Black, cab-hirer
Stamp and Tax Office, 44 Princes st., east—James Spalding
    distributor and collector
Stephen, Mrs, 40 Clyde street, east
Steven, Thomas, J.P., Ardlui House, 5 Montrose street, east
Stevenson, Charles, porter, 99 Clyde street, east
Stevenson, John, coachman, 82 Clyde street, east
Stevenson, Robert, plasterer, 110 King street, east
Stevenson, Robert, boot and shoemaker, 78 Princes st., e., and
    38 Clyde street, west—house, 76 Princes street, east
Stewart, Adam, labourer, 1 Adelaide street
Stewart, Alexander, Collinslee, 5 Havelock street
Stewart, Captain Wm., Seaview Place, 18 Argyle street, east
Stewart, Christopher, saddler, 16 Glenfinlas street
Stewart, Donald, carter, 4 Maitland street
Stewart, Edward, Westwood Villa, 20 Argyle street, west
Stewart, Peter, mason, 26 Sinclair street
Stewart, Walter, Glenan, Queen street
Stewart, William, photographer, 61 Princes street, east
Stewart, Miss, milliner, 80 Princes street, east
Stewart, Mrs, 62 Princes street, west
Stewart, Mrs, Greenoak, 33 Argyle street, west
Stewart, Mrs, East Thorn, 8 Adelaide street
Stirling, James, J.P., Rockend House, 76 Clyde street, east

Stirling, William, tailor, 14 Maitland street
Stirling, Mrs, Woodland Place, 124 King street, east
Stirling, Mrs, draper, 20 Maitland street—house, 14
Stirrat, Mrs, 152 King street, east
Stoker, Archibald, ploughman, Glenan Farm, Queen street
Storer, James, 35 William street
Strachan, Mrs, 14 Maitland street
Strath, David, saddler, 26 Sinclair street
Stuart, John, Thistle Bank, 22 Charlotte street
Sutherland, John, shoemaker, 16 Charlotte street
Suttie, Mrs A., 13 Clyde street, west
Swan, Mrs, Oakbank, 12 Argyle street, west
Swanson, William, boot and shoemaker, 63 Clyde street, east
Sword, John, Methven Villa, 34 Clyde street, east
Syme, Rev. J. Stuart, Parsonage, 16 William street

T

Tait William, Netherlee, 53 King street, west
Tait, Miss, 75 Princes street, east
Taylor Robert, surveyor, 24 William street
Taylor, William, joiner, 179 Clyde street, east
Taylor, William, joiner 53 Clyde street, east
Taylor, Wm., M. Rosebank Terrace, 10 Campbell street
Taylor, Miss, Sunnybrae, 29 Argyle street, west
Teacher, William, Rockfort House, 84 Clyde street, east
Telfer, James, florist and fruiterer, 30 Princes street, east—
    house, 9 Adelaide street
Temperance Hall, 5 Maitland street
Temperance Hotel, 4 Clyde street, west—Wm. Gatenby
Temperance Hotel, 60 Princes street, east—Mrs Sharp
Templeton, James, Drumgarve, 31 John street
Thomson, Alexander, plumber, 2 James street
Thomson, Alexander, Balmoral Cottage, 2 Bell street
Thomson, James, J.P., Fairfield, Luss Road
Thompson, James, Grange, 24 Suffolk street
Thomson, John, Woodneuck, 58 King street, west
Thomson, Peter, spirit merchant, 86 Princes st., e ; ho. 84
Thomson, Robert, boatbuilder, 59 Princes street, west

Thomson, R & J. drapers, 50 Clyde street, west
Thomson, William, joiner, 59 Princes street, west
Thomson, William, gardener, 19 Maitland street
Thomson, Miss, ladies' boarding and day school, Glenfruin
    House, 67 James street
Thomson, Misses, Union Villa, 46 King street, west
Thomson, Mrs, 3 King street, west
Thomson, Mrs, Glenorchy Villa, 20 Adelaide street
Todd, Peter S., boat-builder, 39 Colquhoun square
Todd, Mrs James, Woodlea, 24 Montrose street, west
Topping, William, Marion Villa, Alma Crescent
Torrance, Miss, 113 Clyde street, east
Tosh, Misses, 83 Princes street, east
Towers, Miss, 172 Princes street, east
Town Hall & Court House, 33 Princes street, east
Town Mission Reading Room, 95 King street, east
Trail, Anthony, mason, 10 Charlotte street
Trought, S. E., protrait and landscape painter, 39 Princes
    street, west
Troup, Rev. James, M.A., Seirra Cleare, John street
Turnbull, Duncan, Woodville, 16 Argyle street, west
Turnbull, Mrs, Rannoch Villa, 18 Glenfinlas street
Turner, Mrs, Woodland Place, 126 King street, east
Tweedlie, Robert, Parkend Cottage, 164 King street, east
Tyson, Mrs, 66 Clyde street, east

U

United Presbyterian Church, Sinclair street
Union Bank, 24 Colquhoun square,—Wm. Drysdale, agent
Ure, Miss, embroidary printer, 44 Princes street, east
Urie, Rev. Wm., Sefton Cottage, 71 James street
Urie, Miss, Sefton Cottage, 71 James street
Urie, Miss, 10 Sutherland street
Urie, Mrs, china warehouse, 21 Clyde street, west—ho. 20

V

Vallance,, Miss. Stewart Green, 30 Lomond street
Vannan, Robert, Blawlowan, 17 Granville street
Vair, Thomas, coach builder and hirer, 25 Colquhoun square

Veitch, John, senior, 5 Princes street, east
Veitch, John, junior, spirit dealer, 34 Princes street, east
Volunteer Artillery Drill Hall, 115 Princes street, east

W

Waddell, David, Eva Cottage, 38 King street, west
Waddell & Jack, spirit merchants, 39 Clyde street, east
Waldie, John, coach proprietor, 45 & 47 Sinclair street—
    house, 17 Clyde street, east
Walker, Robert, J.P., Eskville, 20 Glenfinlas street,
Walker, Robert, 7 Colquhoun square
Walker, R. D., Maple Bank, 217 Clyde street, east
Walker, Wm., 101 Clyde street, east
Walker, Miss L., Hilsrig, 46 James street
Walker, Mrs R., Elmtree Villa, 19 Suffolk street
Walker, Mrs R., Rockbank House, 80 Clyde street, east
Walker, Mrs, 157 Clyde street, east
Walker, Mrs, ladies' nurse, 7 Colquhoun square
Wallace, Matthew, Rosebank Terrace, 8 Campbell street
Wallace, Mrs, Westwood, 7 Glasgow street
Wallace, Mrs, 108 Princes street, west
Wallace, Mrs, 11 William street
Ward, C., coal merchant, 24 Princes street, west
Ward, John, tinsmith, 37 James street
Wardlaw, David, baker, 59 Clyde street, west.—house, 51
Warnock, John, flesher, 25 Clyde street, east—house, 31
Warren, Timothy, St. Clair Villa, 35 King street, west
Waters, Wm., upholsterer, 36 Clyde street, west—house, 70
    King street, east
Watt, Robert, draper, 1 Clyde street, west—house, 62 Princes
    street, west
Watt, J. A., china merchant, 51 Clyde street, west, and 12
    Princes street, east
Watt, Mrs, Taybank, Alma crescent
Watt, Miss, Hoptoun Park, 21 Campbell street
Watt, Mrs, 10 Sutherland street
Watson, James, mason, 15 Colquhoun street
Watson, John, baker, 55 Clyde street, west

Watson, John, 58 Princes street, west
Waugh, James B., 48 Clyde street, east
Webster, John, merchant, Clyde Cottage, 51 King street, w.
Webster, Robert, Ardenvahr, 22 Suffolk street
Weir, Duncan, gardener, 127 Clyde street, east
Weir, Mrs, 26 William street
Wemyss, Robert, J.P., Bennochy, Abercromby street
Wemyss, Miss, Abercromby street
West Established Church, William st.—Rev. J. Baird, B.D.
West Free Church, Colquhoun street—Rev. Alex Anderson
West Free Church School, Colquhoun street—Miss Mitchell,
Wheeler, Miss, 48 Clyde street, east
Wheldon, Daniel, carter, 17 Sinclair street
White Alex. butcher, 22 Maitland street
White, James, joiner, 34 Colquhoun street
White, John, plasterer, 58 Clyde street, east
White, John, dentist Woodbank, 25 Argyle street, west
White, Mrs, Wardfield, 2 Montrose street, west
Whitelaw, Mrs, Grenhaugh, 32 William street
Whittle, Miss, 8 Charlotte street
Wilkie, Robert, labourer, 39 Clyde street, west
Williams, Mrs, Stewart Green, 30 Lomond street
Williamson, Alex., sen., Queen's Hotel, 74 Clyde street, east
Williamson, Alex., junior, ærated water manufacturer, 61
    Clyde street, west—manufactory, 6
Williamson, John, upholsterer, 39 Clyde street, east
Williamson, William, tinsmith, 73 Princes street, east
Wilson, Andrew, Rockville, 78 Clyde street, east
Wilson, Gilbert, painter, 16 Charlotte street
Wilson, John, Holyrood place, Princes street, west
Wilson, John, flesher, 42 Clyde street, west—house, Devar
    Cottage, 16 King street, west
Wilson, Rev. John, Camden Villa, 9 Montrose street, east
Wilson, Robert, tobacconist, 7 Princes street, east—house, 34
    Clyde street, east
Wilson, William, mason, 13 Charlotte street
Wilson, Miss, Chapel Acre, Luss Road
Wilson, Mrs, 20 James street

Wotherspoon, Miss, teacher of music, Pomona Villa, 5 Granville street
Wotherspoon, Mrs, Rosebank Terrace, 80 Princes street, w.
Wright, Rev. T., Towerville, 2 King's Crescent
Wylie, George, seaman, 11 Maitland street
Wylie, Robert, Lochiel Cottage, 1 Suffolk street

Y

Yates, Mrs, 153 Clyde street, east
York, Miss, Fairthorn, 7 Havelock street
Young, Gavin, surgeon dentist, 67 Clyde street, west
Young, George, engineer, 175 Clyde street, east
Young, James, Rockmount, Luss Road
Young, William, Loch Sloy Cottage, 28 William street
Young Miss, fruiterer and confectioner, 23 Clyde street, w.
Yuille, Archibald B., J.P., Brownhill, 27 Colquhoun street
Yuile, Miss, Prospect Cottage, 40 James street

Z

Zenkeisen, Victor, Dhuhill, Luss Road

NAMES OF HOUSES AND PLACES.

A

Aberdale,	137 King street, east
Agnew Villa,	1 Montrose street, east
Airdbank,	25 Montrose street, east
Albert Cottage,	203 Clyde street, east
Albert Villa,	2 Stafford street
Albion Cottage,	8 Lomond street
Alder Lodge,	67 Clyde street, west
Allan Bank,	66 Clyde street, east
Alma Cottage,	24 Lomond street
Alma Place,	King street, east
Anchorage,	20 Suffolk street
Annat Lodge,	35 John street
Annandale,	125 King street, east
Annfield Villa,	17 Suffolk street
Annock Bank,	15 Montrose street, east
Annsfield,	10 Montrose street, west
Ardbeg Cottage,	50 Grant street
Ardenclutha,	11 Adelaide street
Ardenlade,	Abercromby street
Ardenlee,	John street
Ardenvahr,	22 Suffolk street
Ardgowan Cottage,	22 Suffolk street
Ardlui House,	5 Montrose street, east
Ardlui,	23 Charlotte street
Ardshiel,	Millig street, west
Ardvuela House,	Queen street
Argyle Cottage,	7 Sutherland crescent lower
Argyle Park,	42 James street
Argyle Place,	Clyde street, west
Ardmore House,	72 Clyde street, west

Ashburn House,	14 Montrose street, west
Ashens,	56 King street, west
Ashfield,	30 William street
Ashgrove Cottage,	142 King street, east
Ashmount,	Millig street
Auchentiel,	Suffolk street
Augusta Place,	Clyde street, west
Auld's Place,	Princes street, west
Ava Cottage,	14 Glasgow street

B

Ballimore Lodge,	20 Montrose street, west
Bank of Scotland,	10 Clyde street, west
Baranfrow,	Colquhoun street
Barwood,	7 Montrose street, east
Baths. The	72 Clyde street, east
Bath House,	137 Princes street, east
Beaulah Lodge,	39 Colquhoun street
Beauly Cottage,	9 Glasgow street
Beechwood,	13 Argyle steeet, west
Bellevue,	74 Clyde street, west
Bellevue Bank,	64 Clyde street, east
Bellview,	110 Princes street, west
Belmont,	Millig street, east
Benatine Lodge,	27 Argyle street, west
Bennochy,	Abercromby street
Birkfell,	20 Charlotte street
Birkhall,	1 Havelock street
Blairburn Villa,	104 Princes street, west
Blair Cottage,	61 Princes street, east
Blairkip,	17 Glenfinlas street
Blairlomond,	6 Stafford street
Blairnairn,	6 Montrose street, west
Blawlowan,	17 Granville street
Bloomfield,	33 Lomond street
Bythswood Terrace,	Clyde street, west
Bonnie Brae,	66 Sinclair street
Bonnyton,	1 Sutherland crescent, upper

Bowling Green,	. Luss Road
Brackenhill Cottage,	32 Lomond street
Braehead,	13 Montrose street, east
Braeside,	87 Sinclair street
Brandongrove Cottage,	91 Princes street, west
Brandongrove House,	83 Clyde street, west
Brooklyn Villa,	8 Granville street
Brooklee,	13 Granville street
Brownhill,	27 Colquhoun street
Brownhill,	Luss Road
Brucefield,	28 Lomond street
Burnbank,	23 John street
Burnbrae,	Campbell street
Burnshill,	15 Granville street
Burnside Cottage,	24 Campbell street
Burnside House,	22 Campbell street
Bute Cottage,	8 Sutherland crescent, lower
Byron Cottage,	96 Princes street, west

C

Canton Cottage,	5 Suffolk street
Camden Villa,	9 Montrose street, east
Carbrook,	29 Montrose street, east
Carden Bank,	9 Granville street
Carisbrooke,	50 King street, west
Carleton,	Millig street, west
Carrick House,	195 Clyde street, east
Carron Bank,	Millig street, west
Cawdor Lodge,	Sinclair street
Chapel Acre,	Luss Road
Chapel Acre Lodge,	Luss Road
Chapelfield House,	33 Argyle street, east
Charing Cross,	Sinclair street
Clarefoot,	7 Granville street
Claremount House,	15 Suffolk street
Claremont Villa,	78 Clyde street, west
Clarendon House,	James street
Clarkfield,	13 Campbell street

Claverton House,	121 Princes street, east
Clifton Cottage,	29 Argyle street, east
Clyde Cottage,	51 King street, west
Clyde View,	5 King's Crescent
Clydesdale Bank,	10 James street
Colquhoun Place,	27 Colquhoun square
Colquhoun Villa,	31 Colquhoun street
Colquhoun's Land	Maitland street
Collinslea,	5 Havelock street
Congregational Church,	19 Princes street, west
Cora House,	131 Princes street, east
Cornwall House,	62 John street
Craigendoran Farm,	Clyde street, east
Craigie Lea,	4 Argyle street, west
Cranley Lodge,	32 Charlotte street
Curling Pond,	Princes street, east

D

Dailnabruich Cottage,	8 Argyle street, east
Dahlbeg,	86 Clyde street, west
Dalblair,	10 Granville street
Dallglenan Cottage,	John street lane
Dallglenan Lodge,	44 James street
Dargeeling House,	7 William street
Devaar Lodge,	34 Charlotte street
Devar Cottage,	14 King street, west
Dhuhill,	Luss Road
Dhuhill House,	Luss Road
Dingwall's Land,	Princes street, west
Dougal's Place,	Princes street, east
Doune Cottage,	160 King street, east
Dovehill,	64 Sinclair street
Dover Cottage,	26 King street, west
Drumgarve,	31 John street
Duart Cottage,	14 Adelaide street
Dunbeg,	48 James street
Duncairn,	Sutherland street, north
Dunfillan,	31 Montrose street, east

E

East Bank Cottage, . .	205 Clyde street, east
East Bay Place, . .	169 Clyde street, east
East Burn Cottage, . .	37 King street, east
East Burn Chapel, . .	47 King street, east
East Burn House, . .	93 Clyde street, east
Eastburn Place, . .	King street, east
Easterton, . .	16 Glasgow street
Easterton House, . .	89 Clyde street, west
East Seaside, . .	70 Clyde street, east
East Thorn, . . .	129 Princes street east
Eastwood House, . .	211 Clyde street, east
Ebenezer Cottage, . .	33 William street
Edenbank, . .	Colquhoun street
Edenwood, . .	4 Lower Sutherland Crescent
Edgemount, . . .	3 Havelock street
Egremount House . .	36 Charlotte street
Elgin Villa, . .	34 Lomond street
Ellengowan, . .	50 Colquhoun street
Ellenbank Cottage, .	100 Princes street, west
Elmpark, . .	3 Lower Sutherland crescent
Elmtree Villa, . .	19 Suffolk street
Elmwood Cottage, . .	18 Montrose street west
Elmwood House, . .	18 Glasgow street
Endrick Cottage, . .	98 Princes street, west
Enmore, . . .	King street, east
Episcopalian Church, .	William street
Eskville, . . .	20 Glenfinlas street
Established Church, .	Clyde street, east
Ettrick Bank, . .	85 Sinclair street
Eva Cottage, . .	38 King street west

F

Fairbank, . .	24 Argyle street, west
Fairfield, . . .	Luss Road
Fairthorn . . .	7 Havelock street
Fairyknowe, . .	26 Lomond street
Farnie House, . .	84 Clyde street, west

Fern Bank,	21 Montrose street, east
Ferniegair,	Row Road
Findhorn,	Queen street
Flower Bank,	68 Clyde street, west
Fountain Bank,	69 Sinclair street
Fruinfield Villa	43 Lomond street

G

Galloway Cottage,	37 Colquhoun street
Garnet Bank,	19 Campbell street
Gas Work,	88 Princes street, east
Gay's Cottage,	20 Colquhoun street
Giffnock Cottage,	6 Adelaide street
Giffnock House,	202 Princes street, east
Glenan,	Queen street
Glenan Bank,	26 Campbell street
Glenan Cottage,	27 John street
Glenan House,	29 John street
Glenan Farm,	Queen street
Glenlea,	30 Argyle street, east
Glencairn,	4 Stafford street
Glendarroch House,	37 John street
Glenelg Villa,	33 Montrose street, east
Glenfeulan,	Millig street
Glenfinlas House,	119 Princes street, east
Glenfruin House, and School,	67 James street
Glenmore,	28 Campbell street
Glenorchy Villa,	20 Adelaide street
Govane Bank,	15 Glasgow street
Gowan Bank,	110 King street, east
Gowanlea,	Charlotte street
Grange, The	23 Suffolk street
Greenbank,	15 Campbell street
Greenbank Cottage,	87 Princes street, east
Greenburn Lodge,	24 Clyde street, east
Greenhaugh,	32 William street
Greenknowe,	27 Montrose street, east
Greenoak,	35 Argyle street, west

H

Hartfield, . . .	. John street lane
Hartree, . . .	. James street
Hawthorn Bank, . .	37 Argyle street, east
Hawthorn Hill, . .	. 52 Grant street
Hayfield, . . .	. Queen street.
Hayfield Cottage, ., .	63 King street, west
Hazelwood, . . .	. Alma Crescent
Heath Bank, . . .	87 Clyde street, west
Heath Bank Dairy, . .	3 Sutherland street
Heathfield, . . .	12 Montrose street, west
Heath Cottage, . .	. 4 Sutherland street
Heath Villa, - -	- 34 William street
Helensburgh Library, -	9 Princes street, east
Helenslee, - - -	- 21 Suffolk street
Hermitage, - - -	- 76 Sinclair street
Hermitage Cottage - .	- 82 Sinclair street
High Stuck Farm, - -	- Henry Bell street
Hillside Cottage, - -	4 Montrose street, west
Hilsrig, - - -	- 46 James street
Holly Villa, - - -	- 26 Suffolk street
Holmglen, - - .	- 28 George street
Holyrood Place, - -	- Princes street, west
Homeston House, - -	- 29 William street
Hopetoun Park, - -	- 21 Campbell street
Hopewell Cottage, - -	- 23 Lomond street
Huntly Villa, - -	- 3 Granville street

I

Industrial School, - -	- 11 Grant street
Iona Place, - - -	- Clyde street, east
Iona Terrace, - .	- George street
Ivy Cottage, - -	69 Princes street, east
Ivy House, . .	77 Clyde street, west

J

Janelee, - - -	- . 10 Adelaide street
Janeville Lodge, - . . .	- 21 Charlotte street

Jardine's Land,	-	-	- James street
Jordonhill Cottage,	-	-	- 6 Sutherland street

K

Kent Cottage,	-	-	36 King street, west
Killearn Lodge,	-	-	- 11 Granville street
Kilinn Cottage,	-	-	- 10 Lomond street
King Street Hall,	-	-	- 21 King street, east
Kintyre Villa,	-	-	- 25 Charlotte street
Kirkmichael Farm	-	-	- Cemetery Road

L

La Bella Villa	-	-	149 King street, east
Laigh Stuck Farm,	-	-	- Bell street
Lansdowne Park,	-	-	- Millig street, east
Larchfield Academy,	-	-	- 35 Colquhoun street
Larch Villa,	-	-	- 29 Colquhoun street
La Retraite,	-	-	- 4 Suffolk street
Larkhill,	-	-	- 45 Lomond street
Lauder Villa,	-	-	- 144 King street, east
Laurel Bank,	-	-	- 8 Argyle street, west
Laurel Cottage,	-	-	102 Princes street, west
Laurel Green,	-	-	- 60 John street
Laurel Villa,	-	-	22 Montrose street, west
Leewood Terrace,	-	-	- Princes street, west
Leewood Villa,	-	-	112 Princes street, west
Lenylea,	-	-	- 33 John street
Letrewel,	-	-	16 Montrose street, east
Leven Villa,	-	-	- 52 James street
Lilly Bank,	-	-	- 11 Argyle street, east
Lindens,	-	-	- Milligs street, east
Lochiel Cottage,	-	-	- 1 Suffolk street
Lochview,	-	-	- Princes street, west
Loch Sloy Cottage	-	-	- 28 William street
Lomond Cottage,	-	-	- 41 Lomond street
Lorne Cottage	-	-	- 166 King street, east
Lorn House,	-	-	- 79 Clyde street, west
Lorne Place	-	-	- Princes street, west

M.

Madgefield, - - -	46 Colquhoun street
Maitland Cottage, - - -	2 Maitland street
Maple Bank, - - -	217 Clyde street, east
Marian Lodge, - - -	- Queen street
Maryfield - - -	17 Campbell street
M'Farlane's Place, - -	Maitland street
M'Lachlan's Land, - -	Colquhoun street
M'Master's Cottage, - -	170 King street, east
Meadowbank, - - -	125 King street, east
Merlefield, - - -	48 Colquhoun street
Methilfield, - - -	63 James street
Methven Villa, - - -	34 Clyde street, east
Middledrift, - - -	69 James street
Millbrae, - - -	60 Sinclair street
Millerslee Villa, - - -	King street, east
Millglen, - - -	13 Argyle street, east
Millhill, - - -	75 Sinclair street
Millig Cottage, - - -	46 Argyle street, east
Millview, - - -	81 Sinclair street
Milton Cottage, - -	- 97 Princes street, west
Montrose Villa, - -	- 33 Colquhoun street
Moorlands, - - -	- Luss Road
Morrison's Land, - - -	- George street
Mossbank Cottage - -	40 King street, west
Mossbank House, - -	16 Suffolk street
Mossgrove Cottage, - -	43 King street, west
Moss Cottage, - - -	1 King street, west
Myrtlebank - - -	127 King street, east

N

Netherlee, - - -	53 King street, west
Newark Cottage, - - -	28 Clyde street, east
Newark Villa, - - -	28 Clyde street, east
Northwood, - - -	- Luss Road

O

Oakbank, - - -	12 Argyle street, west
Oakbank Cottage, - -	151 Clyde street, east

Oakfield,	1 Henry Bell street
Ochil Bank,	13 Montrose street, east
Oddfellows' Hall,	28 Colquhoun square
Omaha	Milligs street, east
Oriel Cottage,	7 Suffolk street
Osbourn Villa,	50 Grant street
Oxford Bank,	62 Sinclair street

P

Palestine Place,	James street
Park Cottage,	1 King's Crescent
Parkend Cottage,	164 King street, east
Park Free Church,	Charlotte street
Park Free Manse,	17 Charlotte street
Parkgrove,	185 King street, east
Parkhill,	1 Granville street
Park House,	144 King street, east
Parklee Cottage,	12 Adelaide street
Park View Cottage,	16 Adelaide street
Parsonage,	16 William street
Payta Villa,	5 Lower Sutherland Crescent
Pinelea,	11 Montrose street, east
Police Office,	31 Princes street, east
Pomona Villa,	5 Granville street
Portland Place,	John street
Porton Cottage,	11 Glasgow street
Post Office,	9 Princes street, east
Prison,	48 Sinclair street
Prospect Cottage,	40 James street

Q

Queen's Hotel,	74 Clyde street, east
Queensmount,	Queen street

R

Rachan,	Queen street
Rannoch Villa,	18 Glenfinlas street
Richmond Cottage	27 William street
Rifle Drill Hall,	5 Colquhoun street

Rockbank House,	82 Clyde street, east
Rockend House,	56 Clyde street, east
Rockfort House,	, 84 Clyde street, east
Rockfort Place	Clyde street, east
Rockland Cottage,	30 George street
Rocklee House,	207 Clyde street, east
Rockmount,	Luss Road
Rockville,	78 Clyde street, east
Roman Catholic Chapel,	Maitland street
Ronbank,	3 King's Crescent
Rosebank House,	84 Princes street, west
Rosebank Cottage,	12 Campbell street
Rosebank Terrace,	82 Princes street, west
Rosebank Villa,	77 Sinclair street
Roselea,	52 King street, west
Rosemount	44 Colquhoun street
Rosemount Cottage,	5 Argyle street, east
Rosevale Cottage,	14 Campbell street
Rossdhu Villa,	30 King street, west
Rowanbrae,	19 Charlotte street
Rossdhu Place,	Princes street. east
Ruhe.	Charlotte street

S

Saint Clare Villa,	33 King street, west
Seabank,	26 Clyde street, east
Seabank Place,	Clyde street, east
Seafield Place,	Clyde street, west
Seaview House,	Clyde street east
Seaview Place,	Argyle street, east
Sefton Cottage,	71 James street
Seirra Cleare,	John street, lane
Shaftsbury Place,	Sinclair street
Shawfield,	53 Suffolk street
Sherwood,	2 Lower Sutherland Crescent
Skerryvore,	Alma Crescent
Springfield Academy,	53 James street
Springfield House,	John street

Springfield Cottage, ... 61 James street
Springvale Cottage, . . 97 Princes street, east
Stewart Green, . . . 30 Lomond street
Stewart's Land, . . . Glenfinlas street
St. Leonards, . . . 17 Montrose street, east
Sunnybrae, . . . 11 Suffolk street
Sunnyside, . . . 16 King street, west
Sunnyside Cottage, . . 59 John street

T

Taybank, ... Alma Crescent
Tay Cottage, . . . 71 Princes street, east
Temperance Hall, . . 5 Maitland street
The Cemetery, ... Cemetery Road
The Manse, . . . 38 Charlotte street
Thistle Bank . . . 22 Charlotte street
Thornden . . . 52 Colquhoun street
Thornhill, . . . 27 George street
Thornton Lodge, . . . 89 Sinclair street
Thornybrae, . . . 54 Sinclair street
Torrwood Villa, . . . Colquhoun street
Town Hall, . . . 33 Princes street, east
Trees Bank, ... 3 William street

U

Underwood, . . 9 Lower Sutherland Crescent
Union Bank, . . . 24 Colquhoun square
Union Villa, . . . 46 King street, west
U. P. Church, ... Sinclair street
U. P. Manse, ... James street

V

Valleyfield, . . . 44 King street, east
Verreville, ... 50 James street
Violet Bank, ... 65 James street
Volunteer Artillery Drill Hall, . 113 Princes street, east

W

Walton Cottage, . . . 131 Princes street, east
Wardfield, . . . 2 Montrose street, west

Warriston Lodge,	Queen street
Wellcroft,	John street
Wellcroft House,	85 Princes street, east.
Wellfield House,	12 Stafford street
Wellington Lodge,.	19 Montrose street, east
West Bay Cottage,	80 Clyde street, west
Westburn House,	30 Campbell street
West Established Church,	William street
Westfield,	17 Glasgow street
West Free Church, and School,	Colquhoun street.
West Free Manse,.	2 King street, west
Westlea	24 Montrose street, west
Westwood Cottage,.	106 Princes street, west
Westwood Villa,	20 Argyle street, west
West Seaside,	68 Clyde street, east
Westwood,	7 Glasgow street
Whinbrae	66 King street, east
Willowburn Cottage,	10 Glasgow street
Windsor Cottage,	201 Clyde street, east
Woodbank,	25 Argyle street, west
Woodburn House,	39 John street
Woodcliff,	6 Lower Sutherland Crescent
Woodend Cottage,	14 Argyle street, west
Woodend Farm,.	Queen street
Woodend House,.	Millig street, west
Woodend Nursery,	9 Montrose street, west
Woodhill,	2 Upper Sutherland Crescent
Woodland Place,	King street, east
Woodlee,.	22 Argyle street, west
Woodneuck,	60 King street, west
Woodside Cottage,	7 Sutherland street
Woodside Place,	9 Sutherland street
Woodstock,	Upper Sutherland Crescent

Y

Yewbank,	19 Glasgow street
Young's Place,	Princes street, east

PROFESSIONS AND TRADES DIRECTORY.

Aerated-Water Manufacturer.

Williamson, Alexander, junr., 6 Clyde street, west

Architects.

Dingwall, John, Glenan House, 29 John street
Leiper, William, Tertesie, 12 Sutherland street, north
Spence, William, Ardlui, 36 Charlotte street
Thomson, Alex. G., I.A., 2 Bell street

Auctioneer.

Campbell, Peter, 40 Sinclair street

Bakers.

Dixon, Robert, 17 Clyde street, west
Gilchrist, William, 14 Princes street, east
Hunter, James, 36 Princes street, east
Wardlaw, James, 59 Clyde street, west
Morris, Mrs, 37 Clyde street, west
M'Lachlan, David S., 73 Clyde street, east
M'Lachlan, Lachlan, 3 Clyde street, east
M'Nicol, John, 131 Clyde street, east

Bankers.

Breingan, Alex., Bank of Scotland, 10 Clyde street, west
Drysdale, William, Union Bank, 24 Colquhoun square
Orr, R. D., Clydesdale Bank, 10 James street

Berlin Wool Repositories.

Dickson & Aitken, 20 Princes street east
M'Ewan, Miss, 9 and 11 Sinclair street

Blacksmiths.

Bain, James, 71 Sinclair street
M'Murrich, Daniel, 122 Clyde street, east
Murrie, John, 27 Colquhoun square
Rodger, William, 34 Sinclair street

Boat Builders.

Henderson, Joseph, 32 James street
Thompson, William, 57 Princes street, west
Todd, Peter, 29 Colquhoun square.

Booksellers and Stationers.

Allan, A. P., 27 Clyde street, west
Battrum, William, 50 Princes street, east
M'Kim, Adam, 48 Clyde street, west
Macneur, Alexander, 19 Clyde street, west
Millar, Mrs, 11 Princes street, east
Pettit, William, 6 Sinclair street
Provan, Andrew, 48 Princes street, east

Boot and Shoemakers.

Elliot, Robert, 41 Clyde street, east
Fisher Daniel, 4 Maitland street
Hall, Robert, 20 George street
M'Nicol, Alexander, 14 Clyde street, east
M'Kechnie, Angus, 48 Sinclair street
Paton, John, 8 Maitland street
Smith, Mrs, 13 Sinclair street
Snodgrass, Andrew, 2 Princes street, east,
Stevenson, Robert, 73 Princes street, east, and 38 Clyde
    street, west
Swanson, William, 63 Clyde street, east

Builders.

Barclay, Andrew, 21 Colquhoun square
Comrie, Alexandar, 152 King street, east
Galloway, George, 11 Sinclair street
Jack, John, 64 Clyde street, west
Millar, David, 159 Clyde street, east

Cab Proprietors.

Black, David, 12 Glasgow street
Vair, Thomas, 25 Colquhoun square
Waldie, John, 45 and 47 Sinclair street

Carriers to and from Glasgow.

Blackwood, John, 25 William street .
Gillies, William, 69 Princes street, east
M'Kinlay, Duncan, 28 Princes street, west

Carters.

Black, David, 12 Glasgow street
Hamilton, William, 68 Princes street, east
Lamont, Hugh, 14 James street
M'Kinlay, Duncan, 28 Princes street, east
M'Naughton, John, 35 James street
M'Neil, Hugh, 24 James street
Rodger, John, 7 Lomond street
Russell, William, 38 Princes street west
Waldie, John, 45 and 47 Sinclair street

Chemists and Druggists.

Campbell, L. J. M., 5 Sinclair street
Harvie, George, 38 Princes street, east
Reid, D. Stevenson, 28 Clyde street, west
Rennards, J. R., 55 Clyde street, east

China and Stoneware Merchants.

Murray, Mrs, 22 Clyde street, east

Pettit, Alfred, 13 Clyde street, east
Urie, Mrs, 21 Clyde street, west
Watt, Miss, 51 Clyde street, west, and 12 Princes street, east

Coal Merchants.

Campbell, Robert, 43 James street
Cornall, Francis, 17 Princes street, east
Dunlop, William, coal merchant, 31 Princes street, west
Eman, John, 19 Colquhoun street
Ewing, Peter, & Co., 37 Princes street, east
M'Cabe, John, 78 King street, east
Russell, William., 37 Princes street, east
Spy, Andrew, 19 Sinclair street
Ward, C., 24 Princes street, west

Confectioners.

Campbell, Miss, 81 Clyde street, east
Dickie, Robert W., 3 Sinclair street
Finlayson, Miss, 57 Clyde street, east
M'Crae, Kenneth, 82 Princes street, east
M'Donald, D. R. 58 Princes street, east
M'Kechenie, William, 24 Sinclair street
Reid, Mrs, 1 Clyde street, west
Young, Miss, 23 Clyde street, west

Contractors.

Hamilton, William, 68 Princes street
Kerr, William, 21 Colquhoun street
Lindsay, John, 53 King street, east
M'Kinlay, Duncan, 28 Princes street, west

Day and Boarding Schools.

Ashmount—Miss Murdoch, Millig street, west
Established Church School—John Fraser, Clyde street, east
Barwood,—Misses Peat, 7 Montrose street, east
Glenfruin House,—Miss Thomson, 67 James street
Industrial School—George Mair, 11 Grant street
Kintyre Villa—Miss Nicol, 25 Charlotte street

Larchfield Academy—Alex. Mackenzie, 73 Colquhoun street
Springfield Academy—Thomas Harker, 51 James street
West Free Church School—23 Colquhoun street

Dairies.

Buchanan, Mrs, 11 Colquhoun street
Gillies, Mrs, 85 Clyde street, east
Henderson, John, 32 James street
Lamont, Hugh, 14 James street
M'Arthur, Mrs, 17 Princes street, east
M'Menemy, Peter, 90 King street, east
M'Naughton, John, 35 James street
Russell, Mrs, 18 Clyde street, east
Robertson, Mrs, 3 Sutherland street
Russell, Mrs, 36 Princes street, west
Rodger, John, 7 Lomond street

Doctors of Medicine and Surgeons.

Finlay, Dr James, Millbrae, 60 Sinclair street
Gibb, Dr G., Lorn House, 79 Clyde street, west
Henderson, Dr Francis, Seabank, 26 Clyde street, east
Messer, Dr Fordyce, 9 William street
Reid, Dr Douglas, Easterton, 89 Clyde street, west

Drapers.

Anderson, Miss, 15 Sinclair street
Clark, John, 66 Clyde street, west
Hay, Mrs, 1 Princes street, east
Little, Mrs, 95 Clyde street, east
Muir, Robert, 54 and 56 Princes street, east
M'Callum & Son, 5 Clyde street, east
Stirling, Mrs, 20 Maitland street
Thomson, R. & J., 50 Clyde street, west
Watt, Robert, 1 Clyde street, west

Dressmakers.

Buchanan, Miss, 13 Colquhoun street

Campbell, Miss, 95 Princes street, east
Crawford, Miss, 81 Princes street, east
Davidson, Mrs, 1 George street
Drummond, Mrs, 5 Colquhoun street
Forbes, Mrs, 1 Sinclair street.
Forsyth, Miss, 19 Maitland street
Gardiner, Catherine, 64 Clyde street, west
Glover, Mrs, 25 Colquhoun square
Hillen, Miss, 21 Argyle street, west
Law, Mrs, 3 William street
Love, Miss, 84 Princes street, east
Martin, Miss, 172 Princes street, east
Millar, Miss, 26 Colquhoun street
M'Auslan, Miss, 66 Princes street, west
M'Ewan, M. and W., 3 Colquhoun street
M'Farlane, Miss, 42 Clyde street, east
M'Laren, Mrs, 32 Clyde street, west
M'Leod, Miss, 26 Sinclair street
M'Leod, Miss, 15 Maitland street
M'Lean, Miss, 24 Colquhoun street
M'Taggart, Miss, 30 John street
Ramsay, Miss, 9 Montrose street, west
Ross, Miss, 53 Sinclair street

Fishmongers.

Filleul, Charles, 68 Princes street, east
Moir, Mrs, 25 Clyde street, west

Fleshers.

Cuthill, James, 16 Princes street, east
Jamieson, Joseph, 60 Clyde street, east
Henderson, Miss, 30 Princes street, west
Sharp, Thomas, 66 Princes street, east
Warnock, John 25 Clyde street, east
Wilson, John, 42 Clyde street, west

Fruiterers.

Arroll, Walter, 33 Clyde street, west

Bryson, William, 9 Princes street, east
Frame, Miss, 46 Princes street, east
Paton, William, 8 Princes street, east
Peddie, William, 70 Princes street, east
Ramsay, James, 12 Princes street, west
Telfer, James, 30 Princes street, east
Young, Miss, 23 Clyde street, west

Gardeners.

Arroll, James, 7 John Street
Arroll, John, 32 Colquhoun street
Arroll, Robert, 40 John street
Begbie, Robert, 47 Clyde street, east
Bryson, William, 9 Princes street, east
Combs, George, Helensburgh Cemetery
Dewar, Donald, 1 James street
Paton, William, 8 Princes street, east
Ramsay, James, 12 Princes street, west
Robertson, David, 52 Princes street, east
Tait, James, 76 Princes street, west
Telfer, James, 30 Princes street, east

Grain and Seed Merchants.

Gardner & Lindsay, 43 Clyde street, east
M'Farlane, R. S., 2 Clyde street, east
M'Menemy, Peter, 26 Princes street, east

Grocers and Provision Merchants.

Allan, George, 84 King street, east
Buchanan, James, 49 Clyde street, west
Buchanan, Thomas, 11 Colquhoun street
Burgess, James, 40 Princes street, east
Cairns, Alexander, 2 Princes street, west
Cameron, Neil, 50 Clyde street, east
Campbell, Finlay, 24 Clyde street, west
Campbell, Robert, 42 James street
Dickson & Veitch, 18 Clyde street, west

Hill, Samuel, 13 John street
Lennox & Chapman, 8 Clyde street, west
M'Callum, Donald, 55 Clyde street, west
M'Nair, William, 9 Clyde street, west
M'Lean, Donald, 74 Princes street, east
Mitchell, John, 2 Sinclair street
Mitchell, A. R., 62 Princes street, east
Shaw, William, 14 Sinclair street
Smith, Mrs, 133 Clyde street, east
Somerville, James, 82 King street, east

Hairdressers.

Rankin, John, 49 Clyde street, east
Speirs, William, 26 Maitland street

Hotels.

Imperial Hotel, 19 Clyde street, east—James Fraser
Queen's Hotel, 74 Clyde street, east—Alexander Williamson
Temperance Hotels { 60 Princes street, east,—Mrs Sharp
                   { 4 Clyde street, west—Wm. Gatenby

House Agents.

Battrum, William, 50 Princes street, east
Campbell, Peter, 40 Sinclair street
Hunter, John, 12 Adelaide street
Pettit, William, 6 Sinclair street, east

Ironmongers.

M'Connell, Thomas, 10 Sinclair street
M'Lellan, Adam, 9 Clyde street, east

Joiners and Glaziers.

Buchanan, George, 104 Clyde street, east
Buchanan, William, 74 Princes street, west
Buchanan, Robert, 1 William street,
Buchanan, Thomas, 71 Clyde street, east
Dow, John, 26 Colquhoun square
Ferguson & Shields, 22 John street

Grant, J. & R., 8 Campbell, street
Kerr & Bishop, King street, east
Murray, D., 12 King street, west
Murray, P., 20 King street, east
M'Auslan, Archibald, 118 King street, east
M'Coll, Duncan, 33 Princes street, west
Service, Neil, 59 Princes street, east

Letter Carriers.

Black, Charles, 6 Clyde street, west
Ingles, John, 24 Princes street
Snodgrass, John, 1 Princes street, east
Spy, Robert, 10 Princes street, west
Yates, Alexander, 3 King street, West

Mangle Keepers.

Bain, Mrs, 6 Colquhoun square
Ferguson, Mrs, 61 Clyde street, east
Fisher, Miss, 53 Princes street, west
Hyndman, Mrs, 22 James street
M'Cafer, Miss, 17 Maitland street
Smith, Mrs, 57 Sinclair street
Rathbone, Mrs, 14 Glenfinlas street
Watson, Mrs, 15 Colquhoun street

Midwives.

Chapman, Mrs, 10 Glenfinlas street
M'Farlane, Mrs, 9 Maitland street
M'Pherson, Mrs, 24 Maitland street
Slorance, Mrs, 23 Maitland street
Walker, Mrs, 7 Colquhoun street

Milliners.

Campbell, Miss, 59 Princes street, east
Forbes, Mrs, 1 Sinclair street
Law, Mrs, 3 William street

M'Callum & Sons, 5 Clyde street, east
M'Callum, Miss, 7 Clyde street, west
M'Ewan, M. & W., 3 Colquhoun street
Porter, Miss, 26 Clyde street, west
Rankin, Mrs, 34 Clyde street, east
Ross, Miss, 44 Princes street, west
Stewart, Miss, 80 Princes street east
Thomson, R. & J., 50 Clyde street, west

Music, Pianoforte, and Harmonium Warehouse.

William Battrum, 7 Sinclair street

Nurserymen.

Arroll, John, Colquhoun street
Arroll, Robert, Colquhoun street
Bryson, William, King street, east
Fleming, Brothers, Millerslee Nursery, East King street
Ramsay, James, Montrose street, west
Robertson, David, Argyle street, east

Painters and Paperhangers.

Angus, George, 63 Clyde street, west
Dickson, Mrs, 16 Sinclair street
M'Culloch, J. W., & Son, 29 Princes street, east
M'Pherson & Carson, 18 Colquhoun street
Muirhead & Peddie, 24 Princes street, east

Photographers.

Bald, A. H., Richmond Cottage, 27 William street
Stuart, John, Thistle Bank, 22 Charlotte street

Plasterers and Slaters.

Armit, Allan, 23 William street
Dempster, Donald, 95 Clyde street, east
Forsyth, James, 48 Princes street, west
Stevenson, Robert, 110 King street, east

Plumbers and Gasfitters.

Crawford, Thomas, 20 Sinclair street

Grant, James, 18 Princes street, west
M'Kinlay, William, 51 Clyde street, east
Reid, William, 23 Princes street east

Police Superintendent.

Anderson, John, 33 Princes street, east

Printers.

Battrum, William, 52 Princes street, east
Campbell, William, 9 Colquhoun street
Pettit, William, 6 Sinclair street

Saddlers.

Ruthven, John, 10 Maitland street
Stewart, Alexander, 44 Clyde street, east

Surveyor.

Taylor, Robert, 24 William street

Tailors and Clothiers.

Brash, John, 2 Clyde street, west
Caldwell, William, 20 Clyde street, east
Davidson, John, 30 Sinclair street
Irvine, John, 6 Princes street, west
M'Leod, Donald, 78 Clyde street, east
Patterson, William, 35 Clyde street, west

Tobacconists.

Glen, Peter, 43 Clyde street, west
M'Menemy, Thomas, 42 Princes street, east
Robb, David, 5 Clyde street, west
Wilson, Robert, 7 Princes street, east

Umbrella Makers.

Parlane, Mrs, 39 Clyde street, west
Speirs, William, 26 Maitland street

Upholsterers and Cabinetmakers.

Paterson, John, 52 Clyde street, west

Porter, Clement, 14 Princes street, west
Waters, William, 36 Clyde street, west

Watchmakers and Jewellers.

Freebairn, Mrs, 40 Clyde street, west
Roy, Gabriel, 22 Clyde street, west
Ross, James, 16 Clyde street, west

Wine and Spirit Merchants.

Anderson, Miss, 109 Clyde street, east
Campbell, Finlay, 24 Clyde street, west
Fowler, James, 27 Clyde street, east
Lennox & Chapman, 8 Clyde street, west
Kyle, Andrew, 47 Clyde street, west
M'Auslan, Mrs, 89 Clyde street, east
M'Donald, D. R., 58 Princes street, east
M'Nair, William, 9 Clyde street, west
Mitchell, A. R., 64 Princes street, east
Mitchell, John, 2 Sinclair street
Ponds, James, 3 Clyde street, west
M'Millan, Hamilton, 32 Princes street, west
Shaw, William, 14 Sinclair street
Thomson, Peter, 86 Princes street, east
Veitch, John, jun., 31 Sinclair street
Waddell & Jack, 39 Clyde street, east

Writers.

M'Lachlan, George, 6 Princes street, east
Spalding, James, 44 Princes street, east

Veterinary Surgeons.

Gardner, Duncan, 43 Clyde street, east
M'Dougall, John, 122 Princes street, east

THE ROYAL FAMILY.

Her Most Excellent Majesty (Alexandrina-) Victoria, By the Grace of God, of the United Kingdom of Great Britain and Ireland, and of the Colonies and Dependencies thereof in Europe, Asia, Africa, America, and Australasia, Queen, Defender of the Faith. Her Majesty, the only child of his Royal Highness Edward, Duke of Kent (b. Nov. 2, 1767, d. Jan. 23, 1820, m. 1818 Victoria-Mary-Lousia, b. Aug, 17, 1786, d. March 16, 1861, daughter of Francis, Duke of Saxe-Coburg), fourth son of King George III., was born on the 24th May 1819, succeeded to the Crown on the demise of her uncle, his late Majesty William IV., on the 20th June, 1837, married Feb. 10, 1840, His Royal Highness Francis-Albert-Augustus-Charles-Emanuel, Duke of Saxe, Prince of Coburg and Gotha, who was born August 26, 1819 and died December 14, 1861 ; and has issue—

1. Victoria-Adelaide-Mary-Lousia, Princess Royal, b. Nov. 21, 1840, m. Jan. 25, 1858, Prince Frederick-William of Prussia.

2. Albert Edward, Prince of Wales, b. Nov. 9, 1841, m. March 10, 1863, Princess Alexandria-Caroline-Maria-Charlotte-Lousia-Julia, b. December 1, 1841, eldest daughter of Christian IX- King of Denmark, and has issue Prince Albert-Victor-Christian-Edward, b. Jan. 8, 1864 ; Prince George-Frederick-Ernest-Albert, b. June 3, 1865 ; Princess-Lousia-Victoria-Alexandria-Dagmar, b. Feb. 20, 1867, Princess Victoria-Alexandra-Olga-Mary, b. July 6, 1868 ; Princess Maud-Charlotte-Mary-Victoria, b. Nov. 26, 1869 ; Prince Alexander, John-Charles-Albert, b. April 6 1871, d. April 7, 1871.

3. Alice Maud-Mary, b. April 25, 1843, m. July 1, 1862, Prince-Fredrick-William-Louis of Hess ; his issue, Princess-Victoria-Albert-Elizabeth-Matilda-Mary, b.

April 5th, 1863 ; Princess-Elizabeth-Alexandrine-Louis-Alice, b. Nov. 1st, 1864 ; Princess-Irene-Marie-Lousie-Anna, b. July 11th, 1866; Prince-Ernest-Louis-Charles-Albert-William, b. Nov. 25th, 1868 ; Prince ——, b. Oct. 7th 1870.

4. ALFRED-ERNEST-ALBERT, Duke of Edinburgh, b. August 6, 1844, m. January, 23, 1874, H.I.H. the Grand Duchess Marie Alexandrovna, daughter of the Emperor of Russia, b. Oct. 17, 1853.

5. HELENA-AGUSTA-VICTORIA, b. May 25, 1846, m. July 5, 1866, Prince Frederick-Christian-Charles-Agustus of Schleswig-Holstein, and has issue, Prince Christian-Victor-Albert-Ludwig-Ernest-Anton, b. April 14, 1867 ; Prince Albert-John-Charles-Frederick-Alfred-George, b. Feb. 26, 1869 ; Princess Victor-Lousie-Sophie-Augusta-Amelia-Helena, b. May 3, 1870

6. LOUSIA-CAROLINE-ALBERTA, b. March 18, 1848, m. March 21, 1871, Marquis of Lorne, K,T,, John Douglas Sutherland Campbell.

7. ARTHUR-WILLIAM-PATRICK, b. May 1, 1850.

8. LEOPOLD-GEORGE DUNCAN-ALBERT, b. April 7, 1853.

9. BEATRICE-MARY-VICTORIA-FEODORE, b, April 14, 1857.

Cousins of the Queen.—George Duke of Cumberland (ex-King of Hanover) b. May 27, 1819.

George-William-Frederick-Charles, Duke of Cambridge, b. March 26, 1819, suc. 1850; Augusta, b. July 19, 1822, m. June 28, 1843, Frederick, Grand Duke of Mecklenburgh-Strelitz, and has issue; Mary b. No. 27, 1833, m. June 12, 1866, Francis-Paul-Charles-Louis-Alexander, Prince of Teck, and, has issue, Princess Victoria-Mary-Augusta-Lousia-Olga-Pauline-Claudine.Agnes, b. May 26, 1867 ; Adolphus.Charles b. August 13, 1868 ; Francis.Joseph.Leopold.Frederick, b. Jan. 9, 1870. Their father Adolphus.Frederick, who died July 8, 1850, was b. Feb. 24, 1774, m. May 7, 1818, Augusta, daughter of Frederick, Landgrave of Hesse.Cassel, b. July, 25, 1797.

Maternal Cousin of the Queen.—Leopold II., King of the Belgians.

PUBLIC BODIES, SOCIETIES, &c.

H. E. Crum Ewing, Esq., Lord Lieutenant of the County.
Archd. Orr Ewing, Esq., of Ballikinrain, M.P. for the County.

TOWN COUNCIL—1874-5.
Provost—Thomas Steven.

Bailies—William Bryson, and Archd. M'Auslan.

Treasurer—J. W. M'Culloch.

Councillors.

Andrew Provan,	Daniel M'Millan,
Alex. Breingan,	D. Murray,
John Dingwell,	John Stewart,
John Cramb,	F. Campbell,

Town-Clerk—G. Maclachlan, Deputy Treasurer,—R. D. Orr.

Assessor—John Hunter. Surveyor of Streets—R. Taylor.
Police Superintendent—John Anderson.
For New Council see commencement of Directory.

PORT & HARBOUR TRUSTEES—(Under 9 Vic. cap. 16)
The Provost, Magistrates, Treasurer, and Councillors.

Treasurer—R. D. Orr.   Clerk—George Maclachlan.
Harbour Master—James Ferguson.
Assistant Harbour Master—James Lennox

JUSTICES OF THE PEACE.

The Provost, Helensburgh.	Richard Kidston	James Alexander
William Kidston.	Robert D. Orr.	Thomas Falconer.
James Thomson.	Robert M'Nicol.	James Finlay.
Alexander Anderson.	Thomas Steven.	William Orr Ewing, Row.
Robert Walker.	Hugh Miller	A. H. Dennistoun, ,,
William M'Allister Donald	James Stirling	Peter Drew, ,,
Walter Buchanan.	Thomas M'Micking	John Gilmour, ,,
Alexander Breingan.	William Drysdale.	G. H. B. M'Leod, Shandon
John Ure.	Archibald B. Yuille.	William Jamieson, ,,
John Brown.	Andrew Oswald.	Walter M'Lellan ,,
Alexander Dick.	John Anderson	J. B. Cowan, ,,
H. E. Crum Ewing, jun.	W. A. Corbet.	£. B. Brown, Garelochhead
Robert Wemyss.	John M'Gregor.	Depute-Clk, G. M'Lachlan

PARISH OF ROW SCHOOL BOARD.

Rev. Dr. Duff, Chairman.	William Kidston.	Alexander Breingan.
John Macfarlane.	Thomas M'Micking.	Geo. Maclachlan, Clk. & Tr.
Robert D. Orr.	John Cramb.	

PAROCHIAL BOARD.
Chairman—John Cramb,
Inspector of Poor—Alexander Kinniburgh, Helensburgh.

CLERGY.

Church of Scotland, Row—J. Laurie Fogo.
Ch. of Scotland, Helensburgh, J. Lindsay.
Ch. of Scotland (west) Helensburgh—J. Baird, B.D.
West Free Ch.—A. Anderson.

Park Free Church—W. H. Carslaw, M.A.
U. P. Church— D. Duff, M.A. L.L.D.
Episcopal—J. Stuart, Syme.
Congregational—J. Troup M.A.
Roman Catholic-S. B. Rowson.

FAST DAYS FOR HELENSBURGH
The Thursday before the first Sunday of May and November.

FAIRS.
On the second Tuesday of February, on first June, 6th August, and 12th November; but should these days fall on Saturday, Sunday, or Monday, then on the Tuesday following.

Steamers to Dunoon, Garelochhead, Greenock, and Glasgow several times a-day, Railway communication with Glasgow several times a-day.   Omnibus to Row and Shandon in connection with the five p.m. train.

KING STREET HALL—James Lennox, keeper,

REGISTRAR FOR THE PARISH OF ROW.
Alexander Kinniburgh, Helensburgh.

PRISON,
Prison Keeper—Angus M'Kechnie, Surgeon—Gabriel Gibb.

BANKS.
Bank of Scotland—A. Breingan, agent; R. M'Cowan, acct.
Clydesdale Bank—R. D. Orr, agent ; S. Bryden, acct.
Union Bank— Wm. Drysdale, agent ; Wm. Bonthron, acct.

CEMETERY COMPANY.

Superintendent and Secretary—William Drysdale.

GAS LIGHT COMPANY.

Honorary Chairman—Sir Jas. Colquhoun, of Luss, Baronet.

Directors.

Peter Walker, Chairman.
William Swanson.
David Waddell.
L. M'Lachlan.

G. Gibb.
Alexander Breingan.
A. Lennox.
John Black.

Treasurer—Robert D. Orr.   Clerk—George Maclachlan.

Surveyor—Robert Taylor.   Manager—William Smith.

INSURANCE OFFICES AND AGENTS.

North British—J. O. Stewart.
Scottish National—R. D. Orr.
Phœnix Fire,   do.
Royal—Alexander Breingan.
English and Scottish Law—
    George Maclachlan.
Scottish Union-G. Maclachlan
Caledonian—Jas. Spalding.
Scottish Provident-J. Spalding

London and Lancashire Fire—
    Andrew Provan.
Scottish Amicable—J. Hunter.
Life Association of Scotland,
    William Drysdale.
Northern—William Bryson.
London and General Plate
    Glass—James Spalding
Scottish Provincial, S. Bryden

THE PUBLIC LIBRARY.

Post Office, 9 East Princes street.

President—Provost Steven.   Vice-President—A. Breingan.

Secretary, J. Spalding.   Treasurer, J. Mitchell.

SUBSCRIPTION READING ROOM.

William Battrum, 52 Princes Street.   (See advertisement.)

HELENSBURGH SUBSCRIPTION LIBRARY.

Established in 1860—William Battrum. (See advertisement.)

CURLING CLUB.

Patron—Sir James Calquhoun of Luss, Bart.:.
President—Robert Little.
Vice President—J. W. M'Culloch .
Representative Members—D. R. M'Donald and P. Campbell..
Chaplain—Rev. John Lindsay.
Treasurer—R. S. M'Farlane.. Secretary—William Bryson,

BOWLING CLUB.

Patron—Sir James Colquhoun of Luss, Bart. :
President William Smith. Vice President—James Sharp.
Secretary—M. C. Graham.. Treasurer—A. Breingan..
Honorary Secretary, George Maclachlan..

HELENSBURGH AND GARELOCH INVESTMENT AND BUILDING SOCIETY.

Donald M'Callum—Chairman.

Directors. .

John Stuart.	John Mitchell.
James Forsyth.	R. S. M'Farlane.
Alexander Breingan.	William Bryson.
William M'Nair..	D. R. M'Donald.

COLPORTEUR COMMITTEE.

President, William Kidston, Esq. Treasurer, R. D, Orr, Esq.
Secretary—James Spalding, Esq.
Colporteur—Angus M'Allister, Helensburgh..

HELENSBURGH TOWN MISSION. .

Treasurer, A. Breingan, Esq. Secretary, W. Kidston, Esq.;.
Missionary—Alexander Ralston..

HELENSBURGH SABBATH SCHOOL UNION.

President—G. M'Lachlan.　Vice-President—Wm. Leiper.

General Secretary—S. Bryden.　Treasurer—J. Alexander,

Directors.

M. Buchanan.

Robert Urie.

Duncan M'Intyre.

Robert Melville.

James Stewart.

Angus M'Allister.

Rev, John Baird.

Chairman of Sabbath Forenoon Meeting—James Spalding.

Penny Savings Bank open every Monday evening from 7 to 8 o'clock, in Mission Hall, Colquhoun Square.

HELENSBURGH AND GARELOCH AUXILIARY
TO THE NATIONAL BIBLE SOCIETY OF SCOTLAND.

President—Sir James Colquhoun, of Luss, Bart

Vice-Presidents.

C. Campbell, Esq. of Colgrain. John Gilmour,'Esq., Row.

W. Kidston, Esq. of Ferniegair W. Colquhoun, Esq. Rossdhu.

Provost Steven.

Directors.

Messrs Walter Buchanan, Alex. Breingan, John Anderson, Thomas M'Micking, Alex. Anderson, R. D. Orr, James Somervail, Andrew Oswald, A. B. Drysdale, J. Alexander, and John Cuthbertson, Helensburgh ; Forrest Frew, Lyleston ; Dr H. Miller, Broomfield ; Edward Caird, Finnart ; and the Ministers of the Gospel in the district, who are Subscribers, *ex-officio.*

Representative Director to Glasgow Board, Alex, Anderson,

.　Treasurer—Mr W.ᵉDrysdale.

Secretary—Mr J. Spalding.

Collectors.

Dists.	Dits.
1. Mrs M'Lachlan and Miss Graham.	6. Miss Neil.
2. Miss Bankier.	7. Miss M. Paterson.
3. Misses Leslie.	8. Miss E. Gilmour.
4. Miss Samuel.	9. Misses Kemp.
5. Miss Brown.	10. Row—Miss C. Watson.
	11. Shandon, Miss Jane Taylor

MASONIC LODGE 503 ST. GEORGE, HELENSBURGH.

Office Bearers.

James Marsland, R.W.M. | Duncan M'Kinlay, S.W.
James Ross, J.W. | William Smith, Treas.
John Thomson, Secretary.

HELENSBURGH LODGE OF THE LOYAL INDEPENDENT ORDER OF ODDFELLOWS, M.U.

Trustees.

Alexander Breingan, Robert Stevenson, Thos. Buchanan.
Treasurer—John Brash.

1st DUMBARTONSHIRE VOLUNTEER ARTILLERY

Rank.	Name.	Residence.
Captain	Dr F. Messer	Helensburgh.

Lieutenants—William Anderson, and John Proudfoot Dick.

1st DUMBARTONSHIRE VOLUNTEER RIFLES.

Rank.	Name.	Residence.
Captain	Alexander Breingan	Helensburgh.

Lieutenants—Robert Orr, and Henry Spence.

HELENSBURGH AND GARELOCH HORTICULU-RAL SOCIETY.

Patrons.

Sir James Colquhoun of Luss, Baronet
H. E. Crum Ewing, Ardencaple Castle, Lord-Lieutenant of Dumbartonshire
John Ure, Esq., Cairndhu.
William Colquhoun, Esq., Luss
Robert Napier, Esq., West Shandon
Colin Campbell, Esq., Colgrain
John White, Esq., Ardarroch
Thomas Watson, Esq., Inchalloch
John M'Donald, Esq., Belmore
Edward Caird, Esq, Finnart
Wm. Jamieson, Esq., Shandon House
Professor Swan, Ardchapel
A. B. Yuille, Esq., Darleith
William Drysdale, Esq., Union Bank
M. A. Muir, Esq., Ardenvoir
Professor Cowan, Greenhill
Walter Buchanan, Esq., Bathwing

Sir James Watson, Broomknowe
James Sharp, Esq., Ardenclutha
John Gilmour, Esq,, Mount Vernon
Thomas Crawford, Esq, Garelochhead
Robert Brown, Esq., Bendarroch
Major Dennistoun, D.V.R., Roselee
David Waddell, Esq., Eva Cottage
T. Steven, Esq., Provost of Helensburgh
Forrest Frew, Esq., Lyleston
William Kidston, Esq., Ferniegair
William Couper, Esq., Woodstone
J. M'Lellan, Esq., Craigmore
Seaton Thomson, Esq., Lagary
J. M. Martin, Esq., Auchenfroe
John Thomson, Esq., Linnburn
Charles Kidston, Esq., Glenoran
Victor Zinkeisen, Esq., Dbuhill House
James Young, Esq., Rockmount

President, A. Breingan, Esq.   Treasurer, R. D. Orr, Esq.
Vice-President, J. Sharp, Esq.   Secretary, Wm. Bryson, Esq.

HELENSBURGH POST OFFICE.

WILLIAM BRYSON, Post-master.

RECEIVING BOXES—West Corner of William Street and King Street; East Corner of Princes Street and George Street; Corner of Stafford Street and Luss Road.

DESPATCH OF MAILS—First, 8-50 a.m.—Box closes at 8-35. Second, 12-45 p.m.—Box closes at 12-30. Third, 3-45 p.m. direct bag to Edinburgh—Box closes at 3-25. Fourth, 5-40 p.m.—Box closes at 5-25. Fifth, 6-50 p.m.—Box closes at 6-35. The 3-25 p.m. Despatch meets the London Limited Mail for English and Foreign mails.

ARRIVALS.—First, Post-cart by Road 4 a.m.—Delivery at 7 a.m. Second, 10-40 a.m.—delivery immediately. Third, 4-55 p.m.—delivery immediately.

SUNDAY—Open from 8 till 10 a.m. ; Box closes at 2 p.m.

MONEY ORDER OFFICE.—Open from 9 a.m. to 6 p.m.; Saturdays from 9 a.m. to 8 p.m.

POST OFFICE SAVINGS' BANK.—Open from 9 a.m to 6 p.m.

POSTAL TELEGRAPH OFFICE.—Open from 7 a.m. to 8 p.m. Sundays from 8 to 10 a.m.

CAB FARES IN AND OUT OF THE BURGH,

FARES FOR ONE HORSE FOUR WHEELED CARRIAGE.

1. By DISTANCE.—A party not exceeding two grown up persons, and without any luggage, other than a carpet-bag or the like, hiring a carriage at a stance, or when driven along disengaged, to be driven to any place within the boundary of the burgh, One Shilling; and if they return another Shilling. This charge to include going from the nearest stance to the hirer's residence, and waiting ten minutes, but if the carriage be detained in starting more than the ten minutes, or kept waiting for the return of the passenger more than ten minutes, a charge of waiting at the rate of Sixpence for each quarter of an hour or part thereof, after the expiry of ten minutes shall be allowed.

When a carriage is called, but not used, Sixpence, if the place be under half-a-mile from the stance ; if more One Shilling.

FOR STOPPING OR CALLING WITHIN THE BURGH.

2. By TIME.—For the first quarter of an hour, One Shilling ; for every additional quarter of an hour, Sixpence.

For an airing into the country, within eight miles of the Townhouse of Helensburgh, and returning either by the same or a different road, One Shilling for the first quarter of an hour, and Sixpence for every subsequent quarter of an hour. Unless the hirer wishes a slow rate of driving, the pace shall at least be six miles an hour. This clause not to refer to parties on business, or who do not return by the cab.

Whether by distance or time, the hirer pays tolls.

No charge to be made for drivers.

If more than four growing up persons, Sixpence extra for each additional one, or for each two children above six and under twelve years of age. No additional for one child above six, or children under six.

Luggage under fifty-six (56) lbs. , free ; above 56 lbs., Sixpence.

From 11 at night till six in the morning, double fare.

POPULATION IN 1871.

	Males.	Females.	Total
Row Parish (Landward),	898	1186	2084
Helensburgh	2536	3428	5970
			8054

Parliamentary Constituency in Row Parish, about 550; Municipal, 750

ROW,

Two Miles from Helensburgh—west

Adams, Mrs, Beechwood Cottage
Allan, Walter, Gardener, Rowmore
Ardencaple Toll—J. Murrie
Armour, James, gardener
Blatherwick, Charles, M.D. Dunaivon Cottage
Broad, Richard, Cumberland Terrace.
Brown, James, High Laggary
Calderwood, J., coachman, Clifton Cottage
Caldwell, James, Auchengare
Campbell, J., gardener, Ardencaple
Campbell, John, church officer
Corbet, Robert, Arrol Cottage
Carroll, Mrs, Dunmore, Cumberland Terrace.
Clark, William, gardener
Cochran, Andrew, joiner, Beechwood Cottage
Cochran, Malcolm, Point Cottage
Cochrane, Mrs,
Collins, J. H., View Park
Colquhoun, Angus, collector of Pier dues
Couper, William, Woodstone
Cribbs, Matthew, coachman, Ferniegair
Dalglish, Miss, Dunrowan
Dennistoun, Richard, Rowmore Cottage
Dennistoun, A. H., Roselea, J.P.
Douglas, R. D., Cumberland Terrace
Drew, Peter, Ardencaple House, J.P.
Duke, Mr, Cumberland Terrace
Dundas, Miss Hamilton, Aldownick
Edye, Captain, R.N., Artarman
Elliot, Robert, gardener
Established Church—Rev. J. Laurie Fogo
Ewing, H. E. Crum, Ardencaple Castle, Lord Lieutenant of
    Dunbartonshire
Ewing, William Orr, Row Lodge

Bryden, John, gardener, Glenoran
Cameron, David, coachman, Ardencaple Castle
Carson, David, Ardencaple Lodge
Colquhoun, James, coachman, Dalmore
Fletcher, Mr, Cumberland Terrace
Fogo, Rev. J. Laurie
Fraser, William, teacher
Gay, Mrs
Gillies, Mrs, Old Torr
Gilmour, John, Mount Vernon, J.P.
Glen, James, farmer, Letterwell,
Gordon, John, Ardenconnal
Gourlay, James, Ardenconnal
Halliday, John, gardener
Hamilton, George W., Auchinlea
Hamilton, John, Woodcliff
Hamilton, Mrs, Armadale
Hamilton, Mrs, Laggary
Hannay, Mrs, Hazelwood Cottage
Hatherlay, Joseph, Cumberland Terrace
Hutchison, William, Old Torr
Jamieson, Captain, Hollylee
Johnston, Mrs, Old Torr
Kennedy, Donald, Old Torr,
Kidd, William, gardener, Woodstone
Kidston, Charles, Glenoran
Kidston, Richard, Ferniegair, J.P.
Kidston, William, Ferniegair, J.P.
Kidston, Miss, Ferniegair
Knox, Alexander, mason
Lang, J., gardener, Torrwood
Leadbetter, Mrs, Ardenmore
Liardet, Lieutenant, R.N., Ardenmore Cottage
Lindsay, John,
Liston, Harry, gardener, Inchalloch

Little, R., Dalmore

MacGeorge, Andrew, Glenarn

Macreadie, James, coachman, Ardenvhor

Macreadie, Misses, Dunrowan

Macreadie, John, Dalarne

Millar, Mr, High Laggary
Millar, Mr, gardener, Ardenconnal
Morrison, Duncan
Moultrie, William, Green Cottage
Muir, M. A., Ardenvhor
M'Auslan, Mrs, Row Hotel
M'Callum, Alexander, gardener, Cairndhu.
M'Dougall, Alexander
M'Dougall, Miss, Post Office
M'Farlane, Duncan, farmer, Torr
M'Farlane, Malcolm, blacksmith
M'Farquhar, Mrs, Dunmore
M'Geehan, Hugh, mason, Beechwood Cottage
M'Gregor, Peter, gardener, View Park
M'Quilkin, Walter, gardener
M'Ilvean, Walter, boot and shoemaker
M'Kellar, John, gardener, Lagarie
M'Kellar, Mrs,
M'Kenzie, Alexander, gardener, Dalmore
M'Kenzie, John, gardener, Armadale
M'Lachlan, Mrs, Kirk Park
M'Lennan, Martin, Glebeside
M'Lean, Donald, gardener, Armadale
M'Lellan, Archibald, gardener
M'Leod, Donald, gardener, Artarman
M'Leod, Duncan
Nisbet, Alexander, Clifton Cottage
Niven, William, gardener, Lagarie
Parry, Captain J. P. Jones, R.N., Beechwood Cottage
Parlane, William, Glebeside
Pettie, Misses, Kirk Park
Post Office, Miss M'Dougall

Reid, Miss, Ulston Grove
Rigby, Mrs, Dunard
Robertson, James, gardener. Ferniegair   ♣
Robertson, James, gardener, Glenoran
Robertson, Robert, coachman, Glenoran
Row Hotel, Mrs M'Auslan
Row, Public School, William Fraser
Shaw, William, gardener, Row Lodge
Sammells, William, Cumberland Terrace
Sellars, George, blacksmith
Smith, A., Artarman
Smith, Joseph, Cumberland Terrace
Smith, J., High Lagarie
Smith, William, butler, Kirk Park
Spearing, Henry, waiter, Kirk Park
Spy, Duncan, mason, Kirk Park
Spy, Isaac, Glebeside
Spy, Miss, Sewing Mistress
Stafford, James
Stewart, James, gamekeeper, Ardencaple
Stewart, Peter, mason, Old Torr
Stewart, Mrs, Ardencaple Farm
Studley, Mr, Cumberland Terrace
Taylor, John, gardener, Ardencaple Castle
Taylor, John, mason
Thomson, Andrew, Ardenvohr Lodge
Thompson, Seton, Lagarie
Ure, John, J.P., Carindhu
Wallis, Benjamin, Cumberland Terrace
Watson, Sir James, Broomknowe
Watson, Thomas, Inchalloch
Winter, James, gardener, Ardenvohr
White, John, Ardencaple Farm
Young, Mrs, Rowmore
Young, Miss, Glebeside

ROW WATER COMMITTEE.

John Gilmour, Esq, Convener | Andrew M'George, Esq.
Alex. Dennistoun, Esq. | Alex. Nisbet, Esq.
James Gourlay, Esq., Row. | Thomas Watson, Esq.
Matthew Muir, Esq.. | James Caldwell, Esq.
Duncan M'Farlane, Esq. | Alex. M'Dougall, Esq.
John Lindsay, Collector. | Wm. Murray Manager of Work.

SHANDON.

INCLUDING BLAIRVADDICK AND FASLANE ESTATES.

Five Miles from Helensburgh, west.

Omnibus leaves Helensburgh at 5 p.m. daily ; leaves Old Toll,
Shandon, at 7-50 a.m., in connection with the 9 a.m. train.

Archibald, George, gardener, Croy
Ballie, Mrs, John, Jamieson's Cottage
Ballie, Miss, dressmaker, Jamieson's Cottage
Barr, John, coachman, Garemount
Brechin, Rev. John, Free Church
Brodie, Andrew, keeper, Bolernick
Brown, Hugh, coachman Belmore
Bryce, James, gardener, Letrualt
Cameron, Donald, gardener, Summerhill
Cavana, Robert, coachman, Woodburn
Cochran, Archibald, Chapelburn,
Colquhoun, Angus, Ardenconnal Lodge
Cowan, Alexander, Glenfeulan
Cowan, John Black, M.D., J.P., Greenhill
Crichton, Charles, gardener, Blarvaddick
Cunningham, Miss, Woodburn
Cuthill, Lawrence, Bolernick Farm
Dick, John, Shandon Bank
Duncan, Walter, gardener, Garemount
Fisher, Andrew, coachman, Lagbouic

Free Church, Rev. John Brechin
M'Gee, Manus, gardener, Berriedale
Gillies, Malcolm, labourer, Shandon House
Glen, John, Letterwell
Glen, Robert, Stuckinduff Farm
Hamilton, James, M'Kinlay's Land
Hannighen, Mrs, West Shandon Lodge
Hartley, Mrs, Letrualt
Hoag, John, coachman, Blairvaddick
Hunter, George, gardener, Broomfield
Jamieson, William, J.P, Shandon House
Johnston, David, Croy
Keith, Duncan, church officer
Kerr, James, Ardgare,
Ley, John, butler, West Shandon
MacLellan, John Alexander, Craigmore
Macleod, Professor George, H.B., M.D,, F.R.C.S., Funnery
Mathieson, John, J.P. Ardgare
Marshall, William, gardener, Greenhill
Maxwell, James, gardener, West Shandon
Maxwell, Thomas, gardener, Ardgare
Miller, Dr. Hugh, J.P., Broomfield
Munroe, Alexander, grocer
M'Donald, John, Belmore
M'Donald, Mrs, Norman
M'Donald, Mrs, Belmore
M'Donald, Roderick, gardener, Shandon House
M'Farlane, Alexander, Bolernick Cottage
M'Farlane, John, Lennox Bank, Faslane
M'George, James, M'Kinlay's Land
M'Kellar, Hugh, M'Kinlay's Land
M'Phail, Donald, gardener, Funnery
M'Pherson, Alexander, Woodside Cottage
M'Kenzie, Donald, gardener, Broomknowe
M'Kinlay, Duncan, ferryman
M'Lellan, Mrs, Craigmore
M'Lellan, Walter, J.P., Blairvaddick

M'Lellan, Miss, Oakbank
M'Nicol, John, ploughman, West Shandon
Napier, Robert, West Shandon
Neil, James coachman, Glenfeulan
Omnibus Station, Old Toll
Reid, James, Berriedale
Robertson, Donald, gardener, Glenfeulan
Ross, Hugh, gardener, Ardchapel
Scoular, Andrew, coachman, Greenhill
Sinclair, Duncan Leigh, Bolernick Farm
Shaw, Archibald, shepherd, Bolernick Cottage
Swan, William, LL.D., Professor of Natural Philosophy,
    University, St. Andrews, Ardchapel, Shandon
Taylor, Mrs Henry, Stuckinduff
Taylor, Mr, gardener Linburn
Thomson, Mrs, Linburn
Thomson, Thomas, coachman, West Shandon
Turner, Duncan, Lagbouie
Vallance, Thomas, road surfaceman, Old Toll
Watson, Gavin, gardener, Letrualt
Walker, Mrs, G. Lyon, Garemount
Weild, Mrs, Summerhill
Weir, Archibald, ploughman, Hill Cottage

GARELOCH-HEAD.

Eight Miles from Helensburgh—west.

Aitken, Mrs, Woodbank
Berry, Captain Thomas, Smithfield
Berry, John, Dunivard
Borland, J. C., Dunivard House
Bowling Club, J. C. Borland
Brown, R. B., J.P., Bendarroch

Brown, Robert, slater
Buchanan, John, mason, Fernbreck
Caird, E., J.P., Finnart
Cameron, Angus, hotel and pier master
Campbell, Archibald, Ash Tree Cottage
Campell, Captain Duncan, Roseland
Campbell, Mrs, Allan
Campbell, Alexander, Woodlee
Campbell, Neil, Kilmalee
Campbell, Malcolm
Campbell, Mrs, Craigellan
Campbell, John, Lockhart, feuar, Bathurst
Campbell, P., feuar
Campbell, Mrs A., Roseland
Chisholm, J., Bloomfield
Clark, Peter,
Clement, Andrew, Mambeg
Colquhoun, Miss, Elderberry Cottage
Collector of Pier Dues, Angus Cameron
Connor, John, Schoolhouse
Craig, Mrs, Craigielea
Cruickshank, J, Glencairn House
Donaldson, James
Established Church, Rev. J, Paisley
Frazer, D.
Fraser, James, Spring Bank
Gailey, John, Restaurant
Gilmour, Alexander Smith, Oakfield
Grabowsky, Ernest Adolphus, Woodlea
Halket, Thomas, Glencairn Cottage
Hamilton, James, feuar
Hamilton, John, joiner
Hamilton, Robert, joiner
Hamilton, William, joiner
Hardley, John, engineer, Woodlea
Henderson, James, Rowmore
Kemp, D., Argyle Cottage

Kenney, Henry, Inkerman Cottage
Kennedy, Mrs W., grocer and baker
Kerr, Mr, Gowan Bank
Kilpatrick, Rev. David, Free Chnrch Manse
Kirkland, George, Aldavhu
Leitch, Archibald, New York Cottage,
Lemon, J., Woodland Cottage
Leslie, James, carter
Logan, William, Laurel Bank
Macdonald, Mrs, Belmore
Macfarlane, Mrs
Macfarlane, John, Faslane, and Lennox, Bank
Maclachlan, Miss, Lochview Villa
Mantague, John, Woodlee Place
Monroe, Duncan, shoemaker
Myers, D., Elm Grove
M'Allister, William, gardener, Ardarroch,
M'Aulay, Aulay, Fernicary House
M'Aulay, Daniel, Fernicary
M'Aulay, Robert, Dunchattan Cottage
M'Call, S. & W., Dalnadhui
M'Christie, J., Lochview House
M'Connell, John, High Rowmore House
M'Dougall, Daniel, Bathurst Cottage
M'Fadyen, Alexander, gardener
M'Farlane, Duncan, Strone
M'Farlane, Duncan, Greenfield
M'Glashan, D. & A., tailors,
M'Gillivray, Charles,
M'Intyre, D., forrester
M'Kechan, Finlay, grocer
M'Kinlay, Captain D., Heatherbank
M'Kinlay, Mrs Draught House
M'Lachlan, D. Baker
M'Lachlan, John, Boatman
M'Lean, A.
M'Lean, Wm., Constable
M'Lellan, John, Post Office

M'Millan, William, builder
M'Nab, F. & D., ferrymen, Portancaple
M'Pherson, Mrs, Lochside Cottage
M'Nab, D.. Roseland
M'Phee, J., Turner Villa.
M'Phun, David, grocer and flesher
M'Phun, Finlay, postman
M'Phun, John, Oaklea Cottage
M'Tague, John, Woodlea
M'Vicar, D., mason
Paisley, Rev. J., Glenald
Paterson, John, Bendarroch Lodge
Paterson, Joseph, feuar
Post Office—David M'Phun
Pow, John, gardener, Finnart
Provan, C., Fairyknowe
Rennie, William, Ash Pank Cottage
Robertson, Archibald, Rock House
Robertson, Mrs, Burnside
Roy, William, grocer and feuar
Scotland, James, Woodlea
Shaw, Mr, Ballernick. Cottage
Smith, Hugh, Raefield
Smith, D.
Smith, Mr, Glencairn, House
Spy, James
Stalker, Archibald, tailor, Fernbreck
Stark, Wm., Roseland
Stewart, Mr, Rowantree Cottage
Stewart, Miss, Rowmore Cottage
Stobo, William, Somerset House
Toll, Mrs, Cowan
Turner, C. J., Woodburn
Ure, Archibald, gardener
Watt, W. Rosebank
Watson, Alexandar, coachman, Ardarroch
Watson, Miss, Lily Bank Cottage
Whelden, Daniel, Roseland

White, J., Ardarroch
Wilson, Captain
Wink, Mrs, Roanmore Cottage
Wright, Mrs, Whistlefield
Young, Thomas, Lorn Villa
Young, Miss, Biblewoman

ROSENEATH.

Situated opposite Row—near access by Ferry, or by Steamer from Helensburgh.

Anderson, James, roadman, Hill of Campsail
Angus, Peter, Clandrag Cottage
Argyll, Duke of, Roseneath Castle
Armour, Mrs, Glen Avon
Austin, Mrs, Laurel Bank
Begg, Robert, Victoria Buildings, Clynder
Bell, Matthew, joiner
Blane, Mrs, grocer, Rahane
Brabender, John, smith, Clachan
Brodie, Mrs, Springbank, Clynder
Brown, Sir Wm., Roseneath Castle
Campbell, Duncan, agent for the Duke of Argyll, Willow-burn
Campbell, John D., J.P. (of Peaton), Gareloch House
Campbell, James, feuar, Stroul
Campbell, James, feuar, Crossowan,
Campbell, Malcolm, Stroul Farm
Campbell, William, Primrose Bank, Rahane
Campbell, Mrs, Achnashie
Campbell, Mrs, Campbell's Villas
Campbell, Mrs R., Stroul Cottage
Campbell, Miss, Female School
Campbell, Misses, Glengair
Cassels, Mr, Glenowan Cottage
Chalmers, Archibald, cab proprietor, Clynder
Chalmers, Robert, farmer, Little Rahane
Chalmers, William, gardener to the Duke of Argyll

Chalmers, William, piermaster, Clynder
Clark, John, gardener to Mr Renton, Maybank
Clement, Mr, Mamore & Mambeg Farms
Cree, Alexander, Woodneuck
Cumming, Thomas, gardener to Rev. Dr, Story
Cunningham, Matthew, Stroul
Dick, Mr, Glenowan
Ekhout, Mr, Rosebank Terrace
Established Church,—Rev. Dr. Story
Established Church School—William Stewart
Ferry—William Whyte, spirit dealer
Finlay, Mr, Auchnacloich
Fitzgerald, Mrs, Kenmuir Cottage
Forbes, Mr, Portkill Cottage
Fraser, Mr, Roseneath Farm
Free Church—Rev. John M'Ewan
Girdwood, Mrs, Laurel Bank
Gossling, Barker, Aitkenshaw
Gossling, G. J., surgeon, Aitkenshaw
Gray & Body, grocers, Clynder; house, Clandarg Cottage
Henderson, D., gardener, Glengair
Henry, Mrs, Annachmore House
Hill, Mrs, Frith Cottage
Howie, Matthew, Clachan Farm
Kerr, Miss, Springfield
Lennie, Mrs, Lorne Villa
Livingstone, John, fisherman, Rahane
Mair, Miss, Forrester's Cottage, Campsail
Maughan, W. C., C.A., Kilarden
Meal Mill—Robert M'Neilage
Monteith, Henry, Monteith Cottage
Monti, Mr de, Altmore House
Morgan, John, gardener
Morrison, Robert, grocer, Clynder
M'Arthur, John, Springfield House, Clynder
M'Arthur, Mrs, Woodend Cottage, Rahane
M'Aulay, John, Clachan Farm
M'Cunn, John Fernbank

M'Donald, John, farmer, Meikle Rahane
M'Dougal, Miss, grocer, Clachan
M'Ewan, Rev. John, Free Church
M'Farlane, Donald, carter, Clachan
M'Farlane, John, ploughman, Clachan
M'Farlane, John, Rahane Cottage
M'Farlane, John, 2 Clynder Terrace
M'Intyre, Walter, precentor, Clachan
M'Kellar, Donald, gravedigger, Hill of Campsail
M'Kellar, James, joiner, Clynder
M'Kenzie, John, gardener, Burntmill
M'Lean, John, joiner, Clachan
M'Lean, Mrs, Hill of Campsail
M'Lellan, Peter, Stroul Villa
M'Neil, John, gardener, Clynder
M'Neilage, Robert, miller
Parker Mrs, Armadale Villa
Pollock, Thomas, gardener, to Mr Reid
Post Office—John M'Lean
Rae, G., Oakbank Cottage, Rahane
Rae, Miss, Clynder House
Ravie, Duncan, joiner to the Duke of Argyll, Rosebank
    Cottage
Registrar—William Stewart, School House
Reid, Frank, Elmbank
Reid, Andrew Paterson, Tighnamara
Renton, John, Maybank Cottage
Robertson, George, Stroul Lodge
Robertson, Mr, Flower Bank
Robertson, Mrs, Ferndell
Smith, Donald, joiner, Clachan
Smith, Mrs, Woodside Cottage
Stewart, William, parish schoolmaster
Story, Rev. Dr., The Manse
Story, Mrs, Kenmuir Cottage
Sutherland, Mrs, Clynder View
Taylor, Malcolm, Letter Farm
Temperance Hotel, Clynder

Thom, Robert, of Barremman, J.P.
Thom, R. W. Barremman, J.P.
Turner, Neil, 1 Clynder Terrace
Turner, Robert, shoemaker, Clynder
Turner, Mrs, Stroul
Walker, Malcolm, Stroul Villa
Walker, John
White, William, ferryman & spirit dealer
Wilson, Misses, Whitelea
Wilson, Mr, Glenowan
Yuille, David, Flower Bank

COVE AND KILCREGGAN.

Six miles from Helensburgh by Row and Roseneath.

Abercromby, A. Ainsworth, Craigrownie Castle, Cove
Addie, Miss, Carradale, Kilcreggan
Alexander, Henry, Woodside Lodge, Cove
Anderson, David, Knockderry, J.P., Cove
Anderson, Mrs Dundas, Kilcreggan
Arthur, Mrs, Glenlea, Kilcreggan
Bain, George, South Ailey,   Cove
Bird, Gregory, Grafton Lodge,   ,,
Blackie, Robert, J.P., Ferndean,   ,,
Blackwood, Alexander, butcher,   ,,
Boyd, Miss, Aiden Burn, Kilcreggan
Boyd, Mrs, Greenhill, Kilcreggan
Brown, Miss, Primrose Bank, Kilcreggan
Burns, Miss, Cove Cottage
Campbell, Charles, Warrambien
Campbell, Donald, Little Aiden, Kilcreggan
Campbell, George, Fisherman's Cottage, Barbour Shore
Campbell, Miss, Seymour Lodge, Cove
Chalmers, John, Holly Bank, Kilcreggan
Christie, J. Fyffe, Clyde Home,   ,,
Clark, Robert, Ivy Hill,   ,,
Cochrane, Mr, North Ailey,   Cove
Cook, Charles, gas manager,   ,,
Corbet, Thomas, J.P., South Park,   ,,

Couper, Miss, Rocklea, Cove
Cove Pier—Donaldson Gray
Cruickshank, James, Primrose Bank, Kilcreggan
Cumming, Mrs, Cove Cottage, Cove
Currie, D., grocer,   „
Denham, William, Argyle Cottage
Donaldson, James, gardener, Ardenlea, Kilcreggan
Donaldson, Alexander, J.P., Heathfield,   „
Donaldson, Robert, Woodbine Cottage,   „
Douglas, James Brydon, Ellangowan
Duncan, J. Thomson. Lucerne Villa, Cove
Dymock, Mrs, Belmont, Kilcreggan
Fergus, Dr., Clairmount Cove
Ferguson, Mrs, Seaview, Kilcreggan
Finlay, Miss, Strathlea, Cove
Finlayson, Mrs, Craigievar, Kilcreggan
Fleming, Isaac, baker, Cove and Kilcreggan
Frame, William, Aiden Cottage   „
Fraser, John, Auchengower, Cove
Free Church School—William M'Cracken
Galbraith, Mr, Clyde Bank Villa, Kilcreggan
Gibb, Mrs, Argyle Buildings,   „
Gordon, Thomas, Park Place, Cove
Gray, Donaldson, piermaster and carriage hirer, Cove
Gow, Mrs, Auchendarroch,   Kilcreggan
Graham, James, Ardenclutha,   „
Groundwater, Mr Dundas   „
Harrow, Captain David, Woodend, „
Harrow, James, Aiden Grove   „
Harvey, Robert, grocer, Cove Post Office
Henderson, J., Inspector of Poor Board House, Kilcreggan
Hunter, William, carriage hirer, Seaview, Kilcreggan
Hunter, William, Maybank, Kilcreggan
Jackson, James, Ardmore,   „
Johnston, Mrs, Carlton,   „
Keith, Miss, milliner, Janefield   „
Kerr, A., shoemaker,   „
Kibble, John, Letter House, Loch Long

Kidd, Thomas, Mount Ailey, Cove
Kilcreggan Pier—James Irvine
Kinloch, Mr, Lethington
King, Mr, Argyle Buildings, Kilcreggan·
Laresche, Mr, Woodlands,   „
Lamont, Mrs, Lindowan,   „
Lang, George, Oaklea,   „
Lang, William, The Copse,   „·
Leckie, Alexander, Thornbank,   „
Learmonth, R., Viewfield Cottage ,,·
Letham, Miss, Janefield,   „·
Lyle, Mrs, Greengrocer   „
Marquis, Archibald, Ferryman, Coulport
Martin, Mr, Claremount, Cove
Martin, Mrs, Linn Villa,   „
Millar, John, Rosebank, Kilcreggan
Millar, Baillie, Knockderry Castle, Cove
Millar, Gavin, B. Belcairn, Cove
Mitchell, Mrs Alexander, Wintoun House, Kilcreggan·
Moncrieff, Mrs, Windsor, Kilcreggan·
Muirwood, J., Armadale
Murchy, John, J.P., Deepden
M'Adam, William, baker
M'Arthur, Donald, Shanton Cottage, Cove
M'Arthur, Mrs, Burncliff Cottage,   „
M'Clure, Robert, Kirklea,   „
M'Cracken, William, School House, Kilcreggan
M'Crone, Mr, Craigallan   ·   „
M'Culloch, Mr, Bloomfield, Cove
M'Ilroy, John, Craigrownie Cottage·
M'Farlane, Alexander, Oakbank, Kilcreggan
M'Farlane, John, Glendhu Cottage,   „
M'Farlane, Mrs James, Ferry House, „
M'Gaan, John, Elleray
M'Kellar, John, Greenbank, Kilcreggan
M'Kenzie, Dr., Rockburn   „
M'Kenzie, John, Duchlage
M'Killer, Mrs, Fish Shop   ,,·

M'Lachlan, J., plumber, Cove
M'Lean, Alexander, Glen Dhualt, Cove
M'Lean, Mrs, Seaview, Kilcreggan
M'Lellan, Adam, Albert Park, Kilcreggan
M'Lean, J., boatbuilder and grocer, Kilcreggan
M'Nair, Mr, Knockderry Farm, Cove
M'Neilage, Archibald, Clerk & Treasurer to school board
    Fernbank, Kilcreggan
Newman, Dr., Italian Villa, Cove
Ovenstone, Captain, Huddersfield, Kilcreggan
Orr, Robert, Meikle Aiden, Kilcreggan
Osborne, Alexander, Brookvale, Cove
Patterson, Miss, Lorn Villa, Kilcreggan
Patterson, John, Daisy Bank, Kilcreggan
Patterson, Mr, Belgrove, Cove
Post Office—Andrew Kerr
Post Office, Cove—Robert Harvey
Irvine, James, Kilcreggan Pier
Public Reading Room and Library—Cove
Ramsay, Miss M., Lindowan, Kilcreggan
Reid, John, Dunarden, Cove
Richardson, David, Hartfield, Cove
Robertson, Mr, Aiden Cottage, Kilcreggan
Robertson, Robert, W., J.P., Rockingham, Kilcreggan
Roy, James, Balgair, Kilcreggan
Scrimgeour, Charles, Benvue, Kilcreggan
Shanks, Rev, David, Established Church Manse, Cove
Sharp, Miss, Woodburn, Kilcreggan
Smith, James, Finnartmore, Kilcreggan
Sommerville, Mr, Lindowan,   ,,
Spy, Aaron, painter, Cove
Stewart, Mrs, Villa Marina, Kilcreggan
Steel, John, St. Kilda,   ,,
Stirling, John, Annfield,   ,,
Summerville, Mr, butcher, Argyle Buildings, Kilcreggan
Taylor, Mr, Milnaveulin, Coulport
Temperance Hotel, Argyle Buildings, Kilcreggan, Mrs King
Thompson, George, Baroncliff, J.P., Cove

Thompson, Mrs, Rockburn, Kilcreggan
Turner, Miss, Braeside Villa, Cove
Walls, John, Glenrowan,,   ,,
Walker, David, Aidenkyle, Kilcreggan
Warden, Mrs, Edenvale
Walker, J., Ardpeaton
Warden, Robert, Aiden Cottage, Kilcreggan
Watson, Mr, Hazelcliff, Cove
White, William, Lilly Bank Cottage
Young, Robert, plumber, Cove
Young, Rev. Forrest F., U.P. Manse, Kilcreggan
Yuille, Miss, Milliner, Argyll Buildings,   ,,

BURGH OF COVE AND KILCREGGAN.

John Murchie, Esq., Provost.

BALLIES.

Samuel Carson, Esq. | David Galbraith, Esq.

COMMISSIONERS.

Messrs Robert Clark.
 John Murchie.
 David Galbraith.
 C. Scrimgeour,
 George Thomson.

Messrs Samuel Carson.
 George Lang.
 Alexander Osborne.
 Robert Blackie.

Clerk---Mr W. M'Cracken.   Treasurer---Mr W. Graham. C.A.

GLEN FRUIN.
Between Helensburgh and Luss.

Battison, Walter, East Kilbride
Campbell, Peter, Daligan
Glen, John, Highfields
Grange, A., East Bannachra,
Jardine, Andrew, jun., Ballymenoch
M'Aslane, John, Inverlauren
M'Farlane, Duncan Strone
M'Farlane, John, Durling

M'Naught, Archibald, Drumfad
Niven, James, Blairnairn

LUSS.

Nine miles from Helensburgh

Arroquhar Hotel—John M'Nabb
Barclay, Henry, M.D., Arrochar
Begg, Robert, Blarnyle
Buchanan, Charles, Shegartan
Cairns, Mrs, Boiden
Campbell, Rev. Duncan, Luss Manse
Colquhoun, George, Shemore
Colquhoun, Sir James, Bart., J.P., Rossdhu
Colquhoun, William, J P., Rossdhu
Established Church—Rev. Duncan Campbell
Free Church—Rev. Neil Stewart
Galbraith, James, Edintaggart
Gray, R., Dumfin Mill
Granger, James, Tulloch, Arrochar
Hogg, William, Muirland School
Lang, George, Little Dumfin
Lennox, James, Doune
Lennox, Robert, Shantrone
Menzies, James, Auchengovin
Montgomery, W., Little Dumfin
M'Arthur, John, Glendoun
Munn, Nicol, Arnburn
M'Connochie, James, Nether Ross
M'Ewan, Archibald, Inchtavanock.
M'Farlane, Alexander, Hill House
M'Farlane, Duncan, of Camstradden
M'Farlane, —— Darroch Cottage
M'Indoe, James, Glenmolachan
M'Lean, Robert, Craggan, Arrochar
M'Lellan, James, wood merchant, Dumfin
M'Murrich, James, J.P., of Stuckgowan

M'Nab, Donald, Duchlage
M'Nab, Robert—Luss Inn
M'Pherson, Mrs, Tarbet Hotel
Ritchie, ——, Culag
Ross, David, gamekeepeer, Gallahill
Stewart, Rev., Neil, Free Church Manse
Templeton, ——, Camstradden Slate Quarries
Walker, Adam, Auchintullich Natra
Williamson, Robert, Auchintullich na Moan
Wylie, Andrew, J.P., Camstradden House
Wilson, Archibald, Rossarden

CARDROSS.

Three Miles from Helensburgh—east

Barr, Peter, boatman
Brand, David, grocer
Bryce, William, Blacksmith, Colgrain
Buchanan, Robert, teacher
Burns, J. W., J.P., Kilmahew
Calder, James, Colgrain
Calder, William, Braehead
Campbell, Colin, J.P., Camis-Eskan
Cardross Inn—John King
Clark, Peter, Burnbank House
Colquhoun, Walter, farmer Kilmahew
Crerar, Rev. Thomas, Free Church Manse
Cullen, William, High Milndovan
Cuthill, William, grieve to Colin Campbell, Camis-Eskan
Ferguson, Mr, Kipperoch
Davie, Alexander, boatman
Davie, James, Geilston
Davie, John, Walton
Donaldson, Mrs, Keppoch
Dunlop, Mrs, Albyn Villa
Dunn, Rev. William, The Manse
Established Church—Rev. William Dunn
Ferrier, Alexander, miller, Cardross Mill

Fleming, John, gardener to J. W. Burns, Kilmahew
Free Church—Rev. Thomas Crerar
Frew, Forrest, J.P., Lyleston House
Fletcher, Dr, Ardoch
Giles, Mrs, of Ardmore, Ardardan House
Gilmour, James, Geilston Tile Work
Glen, William, farmer, Wallacetown.
Govan, Mrs, Lea
Gourlay, Mrs, Auchenfroe
Graham, David, Auchensail
Harvie, William, Low Milndovan
Houston, Mrs John, farmer, Geilston
Kenneth, William, Lea Bank
King, John, Cardross Inn
Lennox, James, farmer, Wester Hill
Lennox, Peter, farmer Kirkton
Logan, James, slater
Martin, J. M., J.P.. Bloomhill
Meikle, Thomas, Barrs
Muir, John, Drumfork Farm
Montgomery, gardener, Glen Nursery
Morrison, Mrs, Hopewell Cottage
Murray, David, Moore Park
MacBryan, J. B., Cardross Park
M'Arthur, Peter, Hawthornhill
M'Dougall, Ronald, Clyde View Villa
M'Farlane, John, farmer, Murrays
M'Intyre, Daniel, Seafield
M'Intyre, Duncan, grocer
M'Intyre, James, farmer, Lyleston
M,Intyre, John, timber merchant, Geilston
M'Intyre, William, farmer, Ardoch
M'Kinlay, Captain John, Spring Villa
M'Kinlay, William, farmer, Ardoch
M'Leod, William, Cardross
M'Neil, James, Ardmore House
M'Ouat, James, farmer, Ardoch
Niven, John, Craigend

Paul, John, station master
Russell, A. C., Cardross Villa
Shields, Peter, grieve, Darleith
Service, John, Woodside
Snodgrass, Allan, farmer, Mollandhu
Stevenson, James, Asker
Taylor, Miss, Craigend Cottage
Traquair, James, Cairnedrouth
Traquair, John, Clyde Bank
Watson, James, Burntry Villa
Whitelaw, Alexander, Drumhead House
Wilson, Daniel, Flesher
Wilson, Mrs, Balleymenoch House
Wotherspoon, Robert, Brooks
Wylie, James, Ardoch Cottage
Yuille, Andrew, B., J.P., Darleith

BONUSES

Have been declared on Seven occasions, at intervals of Five Years. At the last investigation in 1871—

A Reversionary Bonus was allocated upon those Policies entitled to participate, in proportion to the Premiums paid during the five preceding years, varying from about One to upwards of One and a-half per cent. per annum on the sums Assured, according to age and duration of Policy.

The Reversionary Bonus may be applied, at the option of the Assured, in any of the following ways :—

    1. It may be added to the Sum Assured ; or
    2. Applied in Reduction of Future Premiums ; or
    3. Surrendered for its present value in cash.

The next division of Profits will take place in 1876

———o———

DISTRIBUTION OF PROFITS.

FIVE-SIXTHS of the PROFIT, arising from the whole Life Business, are divided every five years among Participating Policy-holders, in the Proportion each has contributed to the Fund.

All Policies taken out on the participating Scheme before 31st July in each year will rank for an additional year's Bonus over later Entrants, at next Investigation in 1876.

Copies of Prospectus, and all other Information, may be obtained at the Offices of the Company, or at any of the Agencies throughout the Kingdom.

By order of the Directors,

    GEORGE RAMSAY, *Manager.*
    JAMES BARLAS, *Secretary.*

AGENT IN HELENSBURGH,

    GEORGE MACLACHLAN, Writer.

COACH & OMNIBUS OFFICE,

73 & 75 SINCLAIR STREET,

JOHN WALDIE,

In returning thanks to his numerous Friends in Helensburgh and Neighbourhood for the liberal support he has
received in the past, begs respectfully to intimate that
at the above address

POSTING

IS CARRIED ON IN ALL ITS BRANCHES, WITH

OPEN AND CLOSED CARRIAGES,

Two and Four-Wheeled Dog-Carts, Waggonettes,

AND OMNIBUSES FOR EXCURSION PARTIES.

LORRIES, SPRING-VANS, CARTS, and WAGGONS.

Hearses and Mourning Coaches.

HORSES KEPT AT LIVERY.

CHARGES MODERATE.

BATTRUM'S
Pianoforte, Harmonium, and
MUSIC WAREHOUSE,
7 SINCLAIR STREET, HELENSBURGH.

Pianos and other Musical Instruments from various London Makers—J. Broadwood and Son, Collard and Collard, Cramer, Brinsmead and Sons, Ralph Allison, Metzler, &c., for Sale or Hire, and will continue to renew them as the demand increases. Hiring Prices from 10s to 25s per month, according to time of Hire. In all cases the hirers pay cost of removal, also a Fresh Stock of New and Standard Music of various publishers.

PIANOS & HARMONIUMS

Can be had on the Three Years system, as may be agreed, by being payed in advance per quarter, according to the instrument, on the same principal as some of the larger Houses in the Trade—Cramer and others—by Paying £2 10s, £3, £3 10s, £4, and upwards per Quarter—the instruments becoming the hirer's at expiration of the three years, provided the instalments have been duly paid as above stated. Other instruments that have been used, will be Let or Sold as may be bargained for.

www.ingramcontent.com/pod-product-compliance
Lightning Source LLC
Chambersburg PA
CBHW060605030726
47498CB00005B/1550